Mouth of the Lion

A Novel

Lily Richards

CASPERIAN BOOKS

The author would like to thank everyone who offered criticism and advice during the early writing stages; Jean and Ira for reviewing and commenting on the first draft of the manuscript; Shawn, Gill, and Sarah for their invaluable assistance in fine-tuning the final draft of the manuscript; and Mac for the proofreading.

This is a work of fiction. All the characters and events portrayed in this book are either fictitious or are used fictitiously.

MOUTH OF THE LION. Copyright © 2006 by Lily Richards. All rights reserved. Printed in the United States of America. No part of this book may be used or reproduced in any manner whatsoever without written permission except in the case of brief quotations embodied in critical articles or reviews. For information, address Casperian Books, PO Box 161026, Sacramento, CA 95816-1026.

www.casperianbooks.com

Cover illustration by Noel Sardalla

ISBN 1-934081-00-0

For Shawn

One: The End

This is not a nice story because I suspect I am not a very nice man.

It ends on a cool but sunny autumn morning with Luka walking into the kitchen smiling widely at me while opening the refrigerator. He pauses there for a moment before grinning and saying, "I've got to ask. What is that in the jar? Puréed alien?"

I look over his shoulder at where he is pointing on the top shelf and laugh. "It's basil preserved in olive oil," I reply. "The oil sets after a few months."

Luka rolls his eyes. "Just exactly when did you make the transition from microwaving pretzels for dinner to preserving basil?" he asks.

I shrug. "Probably around the time I cleaned up."

Luka pulls the orange juice out of the fridge and starts drinking straight from the carton despite the dirty look I'm giving him. "I didn't even know you remembered how to use an oven," he says lightly once he's swallowed. "I mean, a stove top, yeah. I think you helped me boil an egg once or twice to make tuna salad—"

"Don't remind me," I interrupt, groaning. "That tuna salad was sitting in the fridge for a month. Jon eventually had to come over and get rid of it for us because we both refused to touch it."

Luka laughs. "You have to agree that was excellent customer service." He pulls a few slices of cheese from the fridge and chews them thoughtfully for a moment before saying, "Thank Christ for microwaves. We'd have been in serious trouble without the ability to microwave pretzels."

I nod. "Yeah, we'd have died of starvation or ended up with fairly serious eating disorders instead."

Luka frowns and then pulls out a loaf of bread. "We probably did, you know. I mean, I know I microwaved those pretzels with every intention of eating, but I can't remember actually ever eating any of them. Want some toast?"

I nod, and he pops a few slices of bread into the toaster, then stands there tapping his fingers on the counter.

"That whole eating thing is still freaking you out, huh?" I finally ask to break the silence.

Luka grins brilliantly at me. "Not at all. Puréed alien is much less scary than the tuna salad. I knew what that started out as, but I have no idea what it evolved into."

The bread pops out of the toaster as if on cue, and Luka quickly slaps a slice of cheese onto each piece of bread before grabbing the phone from the counter and announcing, "I'm calling home."

I stand there dumbfounded as he dials the number because this is surreal, has been surreal since the moment he returned a few weeks ago, and I am still waiting for the other shoe to drop. Instead I hear the tones of the phone as he pushes fourteen buttons in quick succession and then, as he's pulling open the patio door, he says, "Mother? It's Luka. There's something I need to tell you."

I stand in the kitchen watching through the closed patio door as Luka sits down on the edge of the deck, talking urgently. I can't hear a word he's saying.

A little while later, Dee walks into the kitchen wrapped in a towel and nods at me before stepping out on the patio and sitting down next to Luka, who continues talking on the phone. Even from the kitchen I notice how he leans into Dee though, see Dee's hand settling on Luka's thigh reassuringly. When Luka finally hangs up a few minutes later, he buries his face in Dee's shoulder. I watch them for a few more minutes until I see Dee tentatively running a hand through Luka's hair and leave the kitchen to give them some privacy.

That's how the story ends. Anti-climactically and unexpectedly and utterly surreally.

How it begins is another question entirely, because I suspect that has always been a matter of perspective.

In one version of the story, it all began when a beautiful girl with black hair and blue eyes came down a mountain and went to a foreign land where she met a blond boy and in 1963 gave birth to a son, though she desperately wanted a daughter. That child was called Patrick. In the dead of winter of 1971, I followed, then Declan, who according to his driver's license is four months younger than I. In real life, with no such thing as a four-month pregnancy, he is five years my junior. Micky was fourth; a last-ditch effort to have the longed-for girl, he came into this world barely a year after Declan.

Mother blamed our father, one of five brothers himself, for her failure to have a daughter, and after Micky's birth we saw little of him. Rampant Catholicism prevented Mother from seeking a divorce, but for all intents and purposes our parent's marriage had been over for years, and with the birth of yet another son, Mother gave up the pretense altogether. In lieu of finding happiness in family life, she plunged herself into an academic career like only a daughter of socialism and barely literate peasants could.

Mother showed no interest in us boys, sometimes leaving us to the care of nannies and grandparents but more often than not trusting in our innate capability to raise ourselves, all the while dragging us across countries and continents in pursuit of dreams never quite realized. We grew, because boys grow, into men of many languages, men with no clear sense of identity or self, but men nonetheless.

Patrick and Micky, who, because of their age difference, are often mistaken for father and son, take after our mother's side of the family. They share the tall frame, the broad shoulders, and the raven hair of our myriad maternal uncles and cousins. Their tanned and weathered faces tell of centuries spent toiling on the terraced fields of unforgiving mountains; their angular features and aquiline noses whisper of ancestors descended from Diocletian himself, the last pagan emperor who built a glorious palace less than thirty miles from the land of our mother's fathers. Their rich tenors conjure up memories of sweet red wine and plum brandy, which permeated lazy Indian summers spent in the Dalmatian sun. Yet in temperament they are strangely like our father, quiet and reflective, almost brooding, with inner strength and faith beyond my comprehension.

Declan and I, closer in age, do look like brothers, twins even. We share our genes with granddaddy Sheahan, who left County Kerry to seek his fortune in the new world and married a Sicilian who gave birth to five sons as freckled and golden-haired as he was. Like our father, Declan and I are shorter than our brothers, with fair hair and even fairer skin. Our features are softer, reminders of Faerie, with chiseled cheekbones, full lips, and small, delicate noses. Our bodies are lean and all muscle; not the bulging peasant muscle of Patrick and Micky, but the battle-hardened, scarred and sinewy muscle of ancestors forged in battle. As much as we would deny it, in character we resemble our mother: mercurial, fickle, with fiery tempers and barely suppressed rage beneath a veneer of arrogance.

The one feature that designates the four of us brothers is our eyes: all of us have the same startlingly blue eyes, as indeed does every child born into the extended clan. Eyes that change from the sky-blue of happiness to an almost violet hue when we're angry. Eyes that bind us as brothers. As we found our anthem—"Born to Lose" or "Born to Run," I'm not sure which—we Sheahan boys changed our names, denied our ancestors, and refused our birthright, but look us in the eye and we are forever, undeniably, brothers.

But is that truly a beginning any more than the one I remember?

In my own recollection, Declan comes bursting into the world howling like a banshee in the early hours of Good Friday, a full month early. He is delivered by Baka and Tetka Jela out of necessity, because even at birth he is restless and urgent and entirely unstoppable. The midwife didn't make it up the mountain in time, though Dida went for her as soon as it became clear that it wasn't a false alarm.

When it starts, they order Patrick and me into the children's room and through the thin walls we listen to Mother moan. Soon, her moans turn to screams, which increase in pitch and intensity with every minute that passes, until we hear the piercing, high-pitched cry of a newborn infant as the sun rises over the mountain. Mother is panting harshly and yelling almost frantically for Baka to tell her the sex of the child. There's a moment of near-silence as Mother holds her breath and then Tetka Jela says, "Another boy, Mila," and Mother falls silent.

Patrick turns to me then, twelve years old and not quite past the snotty nose and banged-up knees stage, and says smugly, "You're not the baby anymore."

I give him a good kick to the shins under the blanket and scramble out of bed to peek out the door, trying to catch a glimpse of the new one. Through the crack in the door I see Mother collapsed lifeless on the bed with sweat still beading her face and her features distorted in agony. There's blood everywhere, and I start hating the bundle Baka is cradling instantly for killing my mother. I am too young to understand that she is neither dead nor hurt beyond the vagaries of delivering a child entirely without medical assistance.

Baka and Tetka Jela are fussing over the bundle that is still screaming loudly and relentlessly. I catch a glimpse of a beet-red, blood-smeared face when they twitch away the sheet the bundle is wrapped in for a second and think it is the most ugly thing I've seen in all of my five years. Then there are voices on the porch, the front door opens, and I withdraw hastily from my spying position before Dida or the midwife can see me.

Once the midwife is in my grandparent's room and Dida has left the house muttering something about feeding the chickens, I feel free to watch again and listen as the midwife proclaims both mother and son to be in excellent health and enquires whether a name has been chosen while cutting the cord and cleaning the babe. Mother only turns her head, while Baka mutters something underneath her breath, and the midwife shrugs and goes about her business.

The name for the baby arrives per urgent telegram fifteen kilometers down the mountain in Sinj a few days later, chosen, as were all our names, by granddaddy Sheahan, five thousand miles and an ocean away in America. Declan, it proclaims, Declan Kelly Sheahan.

And soon after, we're back in Trieste and Mother back at the university, doing whatever a tenure-track academic does. There's a girl called Elena that comes in the mornings as Mother leaves, who sends Patrick off to school and walks me to kindergarten, proudly pushing Declan ahead of her in the stroller. She comes to pick me up in the afternoon and then takes me home to feed us spaghetti carbonara and osso bucco and tells me to play and makes Patrick do his homework—no easy task—all the while carrying Declan fitted snuggly into the sling at her chest.

As spring turns to summer and Whit Sunday approaches, Declan starts looking less ugly and more like a doll, though a wailing one, and I still hate him. Baka endures the day-long bus ride from Sinj to Trieste several times and struggles her way through the city in broken Italian, pushing Declan ahead of her and chastising me to be a good brother while I wish him dead and yearn for the times when it was me that Baka cooed over. Then Nonna Sheahan arrives some time around Assumption Day and spends all her time bouncing the baby instead of me on her knees, and that makes me hate him even more.

An idea starts forming in my head soon after Nonna Sheahan departs. Around Michaelmas I beg to take Declan for a stroll on a Saturday morning. I march right down to the busiest intersection within easy ambling distance with the stroller and stand there on the street corner shouting, at the top of my lungs, a carefully rehearsed phrase in Italian. "Fratello piccolo da vendere!"

Little brother for sale.

I stand there an hour at least, amused driversby slowing and honking their horns, and still I shout until my voice is raw and tears are streaming down my face.

That's when Signora Bagliese on her way back from the market happens upon me and throws up her hands and mutters "Madonna mia" under her breath, before taking a firm hold of my shirt collar in one hand and the stroller in the other and starts steering us toward home.

Once there, she deposits me on the porch and walks straight into my mother's house, the baby in tow. I can't quite understand their conversation, though the words 'bambini' and 'responsabilità' and 'maternità' figure prominently in the shouting, and I listen to the cadence of Signora Bagliese's voice as it fires rapid volleys in Italian.

After a while, Patrick steps out on the porch and sits down next to me, nudging me with a foot that's grown to twice its length in the past few months. "You have to be nicer to Declan," he demands. "Promise me you'll take care of Declan from now on."

"Don't wanna," I whine, tears threatening to spill from my eyes. "I hate him."

"You have to love him," Patrick sighs. "Now more than ever."

"Why?" I ask petulantly.

Patrick fixes me with a stare and states empathically, "Because we're brothers and brothers should stick together and we'll need each other once the new baby arrives in the spring. Mother is certain she's having a girl this time."

But when the new baby finally makes an appearance during Lent, it is another boy, whom granddaddy Sheahan's telegram proclaims to be named Michael Ronan Sheahan and Elena carries home from the hospital.

That night, when both infants are wailing because one of them is hungry and the other is teething, I watch from the nursery doorway as Elena stands in the middle of the room torn between one crib and the other. After a moment's hesitation she goes for the new one. I watch fascinated for minutes as she settles in the rocking chair and starts feeding Micky while Declan continues to cry.

Then Patrick, going on fourteen and almost as tall as Elena, though most of that seems to be knees and elbows, pushes past me, muttering, "For God's sake, go find some ice."

He is about to lift Declan from the crib when I push him out of the way and say, "Let me."

His eyebrow almost hits his hairline, but then he shrugs and lifts Declan from the crib to settle him in my outstretched arms. "I'll go for the ice then," he says, and I nod. I sit there on the floor, cradling Declan and rubbing an ice cube over his gums while Elena in the rocking chair is smiling proudly at me. That night I vow never to let go again.

If you were to ask Patrick, I would wager he'd claim that the story began years later during a heavy snowstorm in 1981. Micky would settle for a few more years after that, the summer of 1987, and Declan? If there were any way to get an answer from Declan, chances are he would claim that the story really began on a rainy November night in 1993.

After watching Luka on the porch this morning, I am given to thinking that the story proper began on a Holy Saturday a millennium celebration later, and everything else was just an elaborate setup.

And if I were a rich man, I'd be spending the next year and ten thousand dollars on therapy, but I am not a rich man. I never have been. So words will have to do.

2

Splice: Filmmaking under the Influence

Wide-angle pan. Zoom.

It's 5 a.m. on Easter Sunday, and I'm noisily throwing up into the big salad bowl. The bowl wasn't exactly my first choice, but some random street kid Luka dragged in a while ago has been locked in the bathroom for the past ten minutes. We're not entirely sure what he's doing, but occasional muffled shouts indicate that he might be watching fluff spin in the toilet, with particular reference to the direction it's spinning in. Jon, who unadvisedly left his stash marinating in there, is banging on the door and shouting at the kid to either get a move on and throw up or unlock the bloody door.

I'm dimly aware of Luka walking past me, singing, "Happy birthday to me, happy birthday to me, happy birthday, dear Luka, happy birthday to me."

I stop choking long enough to protest, "It's not your birthday until tomorrow!" which causes Luka to enter my field of vision—even if I'm having trouble focusing—and shrugging dramatically before exclaiming, "Just pretend we're in Australia then," before walking off while my stomach starts spasming once again.

In between dry heaves, I vaguely wonder what Luka would do should he feel the need to chuck up his lungs. I suppose there is the kitchen sink, but a week's worth of dirty dishes makes it a less than desirable location for vomit. On the whole, I fear that life may be spontaneously evolving in the tepid water without the help of the quart of tuna salad Luka ingested a few hours ago. For once I thank my lucky stars that Luka has always been resilient in the face of nausea.

"Welcome to my life!" I gasp, seconds before I lose consciousness.

The vomit bowl tumbles to the floor.

Fade to gray.

Vignette.

Patrick has promised to take us all to McDonald's to celebrate Declan's fifth birthday. We haven't seen him since he left home three months ago. Patrick refuses to come to the house to pick us up, fearful of another confrontation with Mother, so I get Declan and Micky ready to go and then lead them down the street to the crossroads where Patrick is meeting us.

He's standing on the corner, his arm wrapped around the shoulder of a girl with purple hair; his girlfriend, I suppose. Micky and Declan start running as soon as they're sure it's really their brother. A few seconds later, Patrick is holding one boy in each strong arm, taking turns kissing and hugging them.

Patrick has changed a lot in those three months. I notice the tight black jeans, the Doc Martens boots, the green hair, and the safety pin stuck in one of his ears. There is something else too, something I can't quite put my finger on. Somehow Patrick looks older than his seventeen years; his jaw line is harder, and the baby fat is gone from his cheeks. Then I see his eyes sparkling like sapphires, and the realization hits me like the proverbial ton of bricks: Patrick is completely and utterly content for the first time in his life.

"Boys," he says after he disentangles himself from Declan and Micky's embraces, "this is my friend Annie; she's the drummer of a band. She'll come with us to McDonald's."

Declan and Micky politely say hello, but really they couldn't care less. They would go to McDonald's with a skunk if Patrick were carrying them there. And he does. He's got one boy in each arm, and his knees must be close to buckling under the strain, but he carries them, because he's carried them both since the day they were born and he stopped carrying me.

An hour later we're sitting in the restaurant flicking leftover French fries at each other. Declan is sitting on Patrick's lap, one arm wrapped around Patrick's waist, while Micky has settled on Annie's knees.

Up close Annie is quite pretty. She could be called beautiful if it weren't for the black lipstick, way too much eyeliner, and the purple hair. She has large gray eyes, a heart-shaped mouth, and the clearest Tinkerbell laugh I have ever heard. I begin to understand why Patrick left us for her.

Declan is prattling on about the train set he got for his birthday, and it's clear he expects Patrick to come home and play with him, but when he asks, Patrick just smiles sadly and says, "I can't come over today, mate, I have to take Annie home."

"Oh Annie can come and play with us too," Declan says brightly.

Patrick shakes his head, and quietly says, "No, Declan, Annie can't come to the house."

Declan's face begins to distort, as the tears are fighting their way to the surface, and then he's wailing just as loudly as he wailed the night Patrick left and for two nights after that. Patrick wraps his arms around him and starts talking soothingly into Declan's ear, but Declan just cries louder, and it's starting to look like Micky will join him soon. Patrick picks up Declan, motions to Annie to pick up Micky, and we walk out of the restaurant and start heading for home.

Declan doesn't stop crying. At the corner of our street, Patrick squeezes my shoulder because I'm getting too old for kisses. The boys aren't though, and I'm envious of my brothers. He holds them for a moment in his strong embrace and kisses Micky before pressing a final kiss on Declan's forehead and placing him in my arms. Then he takes Annie's hand in his and starts walking away.

Holding a sobbing Declan to my chest, I realize with absolute certainty

13

that Patrick has left for good. Until today, I thought he would return. Now I know he will never live with us again. As I start herding Micky and Declan toward the house, I fight the lump in my throat and the tears that are trying to fill up my eyes, because starting today I am the big brother.

Fade to gray.

Pause. Rewind. Rotate. Zoom.

It's just after five in the morning on an Easter Sunday in a godless age, and when I claw myself back to consciousness, Luka, in a rare display of brotherly affection, is wiping up the last of the vomit. Luka grins at me and points to the den. "Your paints are all set up in there, whenever you're ready."

I nod, still lightheaded. Coming to with my head pounding and my eyes throbbing, face-down in a puddle of my own spew at five on a Sunday morning isn't what I'd consider an auspicious start to the day. I can't be one hundred percent sure, but I think it all started with Marin County.

Tomorrow is Luka's birthday. His twenty-fifth in familial memory, his thirtieth as far as the rest of the world is concerned. Jon had been expected to arrive sometime in the early evening on Saturday, bearing Luka's birthday gift. Luka and his friend—I suppose I'd better call him the Kid to save myself the bother of having to ask his name for the fifth time—started getting antsy around seven. By nine, Luka was busy making a gallon of tuna salad, while the Kid was whining loudly about not wanting to go to sleep. At midnight, I decided that Jon wouldn't make it and I might as well settle for a little nap instead. The Kid was already nodding off and Luka was trying to set a new record on his video game.

I was jolted out of bed by the phone at 4 o'clock in the morning. Unable to locate the cordless on my nightstand, I staggered into the living room, where the Kid was passed out on the couch and Luka was curled up in a sleeping bag on the floor. Neither of them had stirred. I picked up the phone just as the machine kicked in.

"You're eight hours late, Jon," I said without waiting for the caller to identify himself. There are only three people I know who call at four o'clock in the morning; one of them was passed out on the floor next to me, and Mother has an unerring instinct for catching me in compromising situations. That left Jon.

"Man, I went up to Marin with this guy last Sunday, and the fan-belt broke, and we couldn't find a Volvo mechanic—anyway, it's a long story. I just got dropped off in Richmond, so I'll be there in half an hour. Get ready."

"Luka, get up. Jon's on his way," I said while hanging up the phone.

"Oh yeah? Has he crossed the county line yet, or is he still in Marin?" Luka asked groggily.

"He's over the bridge and should be here in half an hour," I replied.

Luka got out of the sleeping bag, briefly shook the Kid awake, and headed into my bedroom to get the bag of supplies from the closet.

The half-hour passed quickly as we frantically got everything set up and ready for Jon's arrival. By the time the doorbell rang punctually at 4:40 a.m., my paints were set up in the den, Luka's stuff was set up on the dining room table, and the mixing equipment was set up in the bathroom.

Jon strode straight past the Kid and waited just long enough for him to close the door again before pulling a small Altoids container out of one of his pockets. "Happy Birthday, man," he said to Luka, opening the metal box.

Luka gaped. I stepped up closer to see what all the fuss was about and couldn't believe my eyes. "You're sure that's meth?" I asked Jon, eyeing the three dime-sized rocks suspiciously.

Jon rolled his eyes. "Course it's meth, you idiot. What else would I bring here?" he muttered.

I swallowed hard. In all my years of tweeking I had never seen crystal shards that large. Hell, I hadn't even seen shards half that size.

"This is the best there is," Jon explained impatiently. "Took a lot of footwork to get that quality, and I only did it because it's a special occasion, so don't go expecting this every week."

I nodded and swallowed again. "Well, Luka, it's your birthday. You wanna do the honors?" I asked.

Luka just shrugged, taking the container and quickly walking off in the direction of the bathroom.

All junkies, even weekend warriors such as Luka and myself, have a highly developed routine because it takes a staggering amount of obsessive-compulsive behavior to use intravenous drugs on a regular basis.

That is the part that doctors and policy-makers and preachers don't get when they're trying to sell lies for truth. It's never just been about the rush or the high, not completely. The part that qualifies as the addiction is the routine, the desperate need for rituals, the need for an established sequence of events, a chain-reaction that is repeated over and over and over and never gets boring but grows more thrilling with each intricately staged performance.

I enjoy the rush just as much as the next man, but the one thing that makes me come running every time the word meth is whispered is the thought of drawing blood, of feeling the drug pulse to my brain. The throwing up, the tunnel vision, the occasional loss of consciousness, those are all just side effects of the ultimate adrenaline high that occurs at the moment I pierce the skin.

There are a million reasons for shooting up, from being led astray by wicked friends to running from the past, but in the final analysis, most all of them are no more than pithy excuses. The truth is, I can just as easily inject water and still get that mind-blowing burst of adrenaline; just the thought of sticking the needle into my veins sends shivers down my spine and makes my dick go hard. The rush and the high have only ever been the icing on the cake.

Neither Luka nor I are particularly suited to physical dependency. I swear I have never been addicted, and Luka only came within a breath of it once; to us the addiction is all in the mind. I don't care much for anything besides methamphetamines and the occasional line of cocaine. Pot just makes me sleepy, heroin has long been a sore point, and I don't do hallucinogens because I value my sanity, such as it is. Luka, on the other hand, doesn't discriminate amongst different substances; as long as they are injectable, he will consume them. Luka injects LSD, cocaine and heroin when they are offered to him; he buys only meth.

Luka and I dissolved the crystals in distilled water and prepped three syringes. A quarter gram each for Luka and myself, and an eighth of a gram for the Kid, who can't handle all that much. Luka went first. He prefers doing it standing up, and he doesn't care much for tourniquets; he usually asks one of us to apply pressure to his arm. We waited a few minutes for him to tell us the strength of the batch, and then I went to sit down and tie myself off while Luka got ready to inject the Kid.

The Kid never tries to inject himself. He says that as long as he doesn't know how to do it, he will never be in danger of becoming a regular user, because he will always be dependent upon others to help him. I haven't the heart to tell him that I've heard that old excuse a thousand times already, and it's never proved true in the long run. Sure, a man may insist that he can just go back to snorting lines, but years down the road, after sneezing half his brains out one night, being able to inject himself becomes a highly desirable skill for even the most stoic of users.

I sat down where I had set up my usual supplies. Besides the tourniquet and the syringe, I had an ashtray and cigarettes handy, as well as a bowl, just in case. Luka never vomits from speed and hardly ever from heroin. Me, I puke almost every time, unless I just get the dry heaves; it's reflex.

I wiped my arm with an alcohol pad and tied off the blood flow loosely with a tourniquet. When I felt and saw the vein pulsing through the skin like an obscene, subcutaneous parasite, I slowly slid in the needle and waited a few seconds before drawing back. My veins collapse easily. A tight tourniquet or too much impatience after inserting the needle often means that I have to start all over again.

I drew back slowly, and thick, red blood started trickling into the syringe. The blood was denser than the liquid speed; they didn't mix easily. My blood clots fast, even though I routinely take an aspirin the night before to thin my blood flow. I had a relatively short window before the blood clotted in the needle, and I've always hated deviating from the script. I quickly started pressing the plunger of the syringe and pushed the drug into my vein.

Perfectly executed.

Relief washed over me. There's always that fear at the back of your mind that the next shot is the one you'll screw up, the one where you accidentally pop the vein or miss and waste a syringe full of ambrosia. Instead, I had accomplished another mission flawlessly and elegantly in exactly the right way. Almost giddy with relief and excitement, I loosened the tourniquet without pulling out the syringe.

A couple of seconds, and I could feel the tainted blood traveling up my arm and to my heart. A single moment of thinking, 'oh shit, that stuff is strong,' before thinking about anything except the euphoria became entirely impossible. Then it hit me full force. I got dizzy and started hyperventilating, and Luka, who had finished with the Kid and had stepped up behind me, slowly pulled the syringe out of my arm and pressed a balled-up piece of tissue against it. He lit me a cigarette even before snapping the needle off the syringe.

My head still spinning, I bent my arm to press the wad of tissue tightly in the crook of my elbow. Even only marginally in control of my body,

I knew better than to let any of the precious blood seep from the wound.

Luka stuck the lit cigarette between my parted lips, and I took a drag mostly by reflex. That was when my stomach started rolling. I grabbed blindly for the bowl, which Luka was already holding out toward me, and started heaving. I hadn't eaten since the day before, so what I threw up was mostly water and some bile. Then I dry-heaved a little longer until the lights of the room started flickering and my concept of up and down and time was temporarily lost.

Through my blurred vision, I thought I saw Luka grinning, purple blotches dancing across his face. I opened my mouth to say something witty, the cigarette falling from my lips, but I'm not certain that it was my voice that sounded strangled and breathless, gasping, "Welcome to my life!" before the lights went out.

Fade to gray.

Vignette.
I wake up because Declan is bouncing up and down on the king-size bed, the only piece of furniture I have ever purchased, and chanting, "Get up! Get up! Get up! It's my birthday."

I let a non-committal grunt escape from my lips and slowly open one eye to glance at the alarm clock on the floor: six o'clock in the morning.

"Get back to bed before you wake the missus and come back at a more sociable hour," I growl. It's too late though. I'm already awake, and today is indeed Declan's birthday, his thirteenth, and his first birthday since he and Micky came to live with me.

"Don't want to," Declan whines.

I sigh and lift up the blanket. "Fine, birthday boy," I groan, "get under the covers and be quiet."

He happily dives underneath the blanket. Minutes later his regular breathing tells me he has gone back to sleep. I sigh again and roll over on my side hoping that I can go back to sleep myself.

Declan is really getting too old to be in our bed, as is Micky, who still ends up there almost every night, but they both have several years of neglect to make up for, and I have several years of guilt to redeem.

I look at the sleeping figure of my wife—God, it still feels strange to use that title—who's lying just a few feet away from me, her arm wrapped around Declan's shoulder. She's even more beautiful when she's sleeping. It has been nearly four years since I saw her for the first time and knew instantly that Patrick was right and there is such a thing as true love. It has been three years since I left the brothers I love so much to be with her. It has been four months since she said, "I do."

Of course, I never imagined our honeymoon quite like this, wearing flannel pajamas and sharing our bed with two boys edging precariously toward puberty. The week after I married her—made an honest woman of her to satisfy the Catholic schoolboy in me or perhaps prove something to Patrick and his heavily pregnant drummer—Declan turned up on our doorstep grinning sheepishly. He wouldn't tell me what had happened, only that he would rather run away altogether than go back home. So I sighed and called Patrick to intercede with Mother on Declan's behalf.

A week after Declan had moved from the couch to the spare room, Micky followed, turning up just like Declan had. When I swallowed my pride and called Mother to let her know Micky was safe, she seemed mostly relieved to have gotten shot of the boys at last. She told me I could keep them, and I didn't argue the point. Early in February, Patrick and I picked up a set of bunk beds and put them together in the boys' room. Now I just wish they would actually sleep in them.

I must have fallen asleep again, because when I wake up Micky is sprawled at the foot of the bed and Declan is pulling my arm. "Get up! We have to go see West Ham! Come on, you promised."

I groan. Declan wants to go to a football game for his birthday. That's fine as far as I'm concerned, but he could have had the decency to worship a team that wins at least occasionally, and it has been an exceedingly dry season for the Hammers. They are points away from the second division. Yet I'm strangely content. This will be the first birthday in eight years with all us Sheahan boys together again and a fifth Sheahan boy, Patrick's three-month-old son, to join the party.

I push Declan off the bed and give Micky a friendly jab in the ribs. "Go and put the kettle on," I say. "I'm not going anywhere without having a cuppa first."

Fade to gray.

Tilt. Pan. Zoom.

I remain seated on the couch a little longer to gather my strength. It's always a bad idea to get up too quickly after a period of unconsciousness or while the initial head rush is still going on. Luka lights me another cigarette and hands me a glass of water, then goes to check on the Kid. I eye the water suspiciously. I know that I should drink it, I've always had a problem with dehydration while spun, but that doesn't make the idea any more appetizing.

I have, I think, always had a troubled relationship with plain water. It tastes foul, and unimaginable things may happen to it before it comes out of the tap. There are countries I've visited, and even lived in on a few occasions, where nobody in their right mind would think of drinking the water without boiling it first. Of course, boiling it should kill off all the nasty microbes hanging about in the water, but just because they're dead doesn't mean that they aren't there.

Oh, bollocks, paranoia loop. The worst thing you can do while in an altered state of consciousness is getting stuck in a loop of seemingly irreconcilable dilemmas. I know that logically I should drink the water, but I also know that I can't drink it without consuming all the nasty things that may be lurking in the water. The Kid, who is still stuck in the bathroom, knows that he really should throw up, but he can't throw up without disturbing the spinning patterns of the bits of fluff in the toilet. So we are both temporarily stuck in a loop. The more we think about the problem, the more reasons we will come up with to make both positions equally strong in our internal arguments. There are only two ways to escape the loop: our bodily functions may go on autopilot and act independent of our will, or we can get distracted by something else and tangentially remove ourselves from the problem.

I try to put down the glass without thinking about what I'm doing and stagger off in the direction of the den. The sounds from the bathroom indicate that the Kid's body took matters into its own hands, figuratively speaking, so Jon may soon get to his stash.

Fade to black.

3

Spin: The Day After the Night Before

When I look up from my painting, the sun is already high in the sky, and my tongue feels like a dirty carpet. Suddenly, water doesn't sound as disgusting anymore. I walk back into the living room where Luka and the Kid are sitting at the dining room table. Luka is drawing and the Kid is writing while the Rolling Stones are quietly playing in the background. Jon must have wandered off some time during the past six hours.

"Hey," Luka says, "that was some good shit. I haven't rushed like that in months."

"Yeah, and it's got plenty of legs too," I reply.

The Kid doesn't even look up to acknowledge my presence. He probably won't stop until he crashes.

"What're you drawing?" I ask Luka.

He wordlessly pushes the paper toward me. It is a tweeker-drawing, done entirely with an extra-fine black ink pen, portraying a figure shooting up in a tangle of random patterns. I laugh when I see the words that are intricately hidden amongst the geometric shapes. "Adventures in mind expansion," I chuckle. "Is that what we call it now?"

"You better believe it," Luka smirks. "Starting today we are recreational life enjoyers."

Luka is still sweating profusely. His pupils are as large as half-dollar coins, and he's chewed his lower lip to a pulp. Yet he looks as happy as a lark, much happier than he ever appears while sober. I start to think that in Luka's case, all drugs should be considered medicinal; he only ever functions like a normal human being while high as a kite. I guess the drugs suppress the voices in his head.

I'm pacing up and down a waiting room, painted that particular shade of bile green the National Health Service patented for use in its hospitals, while the nurse is asking irritating questions. She's losing patience with me. "Mr. Sheahan," she says in what must be her most reasonable tone, "we really need to get the history in order to treat your brother with the proper medication. Now, when was he diagnosed?"

I try to remember amidst the chaos that's raging in my head. "Some time last year," I narrow it down. "They diagnosed him as bi-polar at first, then changed their minds and said it was probably paranoid schizophrenia."

The nurse is making notes on her clipboard. "What medication is he taking?"

I'm suddenly tired of pacing, and I sink into a chair, burying my face in my hands. It has been a roller coaster of a year, and I am so very tired. I am twenty-one, and I have spent the last three years dealing with Declan, the most fragile of the four of us, falling apart. High-strung and overemotional throughout his childhood, he is growing progressively more alienated and broken as the years go by.

Then there is Micky, who appears to be a statue carved out of stone, who has built walls of ice around himself. I briefly try to remember the last time he talked to any of us, and I fail. He certainly hasn't acknowledged my existence since we argued five months ago, yet he still lives under the same roof. I wonder for the umpteenth time how he can do it, how he can pretend none of us even exist.

In the midst of coping with the mental health crises of these polar opposites that are my brothers, I start to doubt my own sanity somehow. I'm beginning to think I'm trapped in a nightmare beyond comprehension. I'm dimly aware that my own life is unraveling at unprecedented speed. The woman I love is slipping further from my grasp each and every day I spend consumed by caring for children I never asked for, children I never wanted, children who were thrust upon me nonetheless. I want my life back, I want my youth back, I want what is rightfully mine; instead crisis after crisis demands my undivided attention, and I am so very, very tired.

"Mr. Sheahan," the nurse reminds me, and I can hear her fingers tapping on the clipboard.

"Sorry," I apologize, "it's been a long day. He's not taking any medication right now. He was doing fine until today."

The nurse looks puzzled for a moment. "What precipitated this incident?" she finally asks.

I look up at her and laugh almost hysterically. "It's his sixteenth birthday."

As I sit in the waiting room that night, waiting for the doctors to patch Declan back up and release him to my care, I have an epiphany: whatever else happens, whether I survive the next few years or not, my life will never be my own again because Declan is mine to keep.

Around three o'clock in the afternoon we start crashing, and we crash badly. It always seems that the better the rush, the longer the legs, the worse the crash at the end turns out to be. I drink several glasses of water in quick succession and try to eat a little bread, but after the first few bites I have to suppress the choking waves of nausea and give up on the concept of food. Luka doesn't even try. "Eating and sleeping cause cancer," he shrugs and wanders into the bathroom to mix up the next round of shots.

This time I'm greedy, and I go first. Luka is shaking so badly I know it'll take him longer than I care to wait to hit a vein. At any rate, we now know the strength of this week's batch, so there's no need to wait for Luka to test it. I slam the dose and soon feel much better. Since I'm only replenishing the amphetamines already cruising through my system, my stomach doesn't start spasming at the sudden shock. To be on the safe side, I remain seated on the couch for a few minutes until the last of the rush wears off and I'm absolutely certain I won't throw up.

When I walk back into the bathroom, Luka's still standing there desperately trying to find a vein. He's tied off his arm this time, always a measure of desperation, and he's frantically slapping his skin, holding the syringe clasped in his teeth. "I think I waited too long," he mutters through clenched teeth. "Every time I think I've found the vein it seems to move before I can get to it."

I step closer to have a look and I can see at least three blue veins pulsating through the skin. "Hand me the rig and don't move," I say. He wordlessly hands over the syringe. I take it and push it into the vein, then I tell him to finish up by himself. He curses but complies, and the shaking slowly diminishes as the drug travels through his system.

I wander back into the living room ignoring the Kid's pleas for help. If he wants to get his second shot, he'll either have to do it himself or get Luka to do it for him. I have never injected anyone else in my life and don't plan on starting now.

Luka emerges a few minutes later. "That's really fucked," he says. "You know that I can't do him right now, not until I stop shaking and the veins stop moving in front of my eyes."

I shrug. "He'll have to learn quickly then, won't he?" I say. "I don't use people for pincushions, Luka. Their body, their life. Live and let live."

Luka nods and sits down. There is little he respects, but he does respect the rules of the game. The fact that I do not sell drugs to others and I do not assist them in their consumption is what makes me different from dealers. Luka accepts that.

I'm not sure whether the Kid managed to inject himself. I don't care that much either. He may have given up and done the sensible thing and snorted the contents of his syringe. However he did it, he emerges from the bathroom a half hour later looking much better and again sits down to write.

I head into the bathroom for a shower and a change of clothes. Sally is coming over this evening, and while she'll probably figure out what I've been up to, I hope she doesn't until after we're at it like rabbits. Not that I care too much whether she notices or not, but if she does before I get into her panties, it might complicate things, and I'm not up for the drama.

Sally is my current research subject, or my latest whore, as Luka likes to call her. In the no-expenses-spared Hollywood production of my life, Sally is the extra without the speaking part—except when she gets loud. She is the woman who acts as real-life inspiration for the five romances I'm contracted to crank out to cover the bills.

I turned my back on Rome, and Babylon rose from the ashes mightier than any angel and said unto me, "Write, blessed are they, failed lovers and failed hacks, which are called unto the marriage supper of misogyny and romance." And I write, truer words than I could ever find in scripture, though they border on pornography, at least for the next three months or so. Not that I set out to become a writer of mediocre romances when the idea of writing first infested my impressionable schoolboy mind; these books are just one of my many sidelines. A few years ago, there simply came a point at which I wasn't going to spend another night serving food to uneducated louts, so I settled for writing anything anyone would pay me for, prostituting myself to the highest bidder.

As I climb into the shower I mull over how fortunate I am that the only way people can tell I'm tweaking after the first day is the smell. The speed leaks out of my pores and runs down my body, permeating my sweat and my piss. But smells can easily be disguised. All it takes is an abundance of talcum powder and some aftershave. Thankfully, like most fair-skinned people, I have naturally large pupils.

After I finish my shower, I carefully attempt to shave without scraping off half my face. Then I apply liberal amounts of powder and aftershave and put on fresh clothes. I'm finished just as I hear Sally's car pull up in the driveway.

She walks in as I'm coming out of the bathroom and surveys the scene. The Kid, enlivened by his last shot, is busy unscrewing the door of the refrigerator. Apparently he has taken offense at the direction in which it opens. She nods at Luka, who is frantically writing in his notebook now and barely acknowledging her. In a way, that probably reassures her. Luka has such complex and volatile relationships with most women that being completely ignored by him must feel almost therapeutic. I know for a fact that Luka's last sexual encounter was eighteen months ago and the only reasons he endured it were large quantities of cocaine, beer, a swimming pool, and a sunrise. He would happily have taken the drugs, the pool, and the sunrise without the girl.

With the obligatory greetings over and done with, Sally strides straight into my bedroom. I follow her, mentally preparing myself for the verbal assault that is sure to follow. I close the door behind me, and Sally swirls around like fury personified. "You're spun," she growls in a voice cold as ice.

"Aw, come on, Sal, do I look like I'm spun?" I reply, trying to sound offended. "I told you I wouldn't. Why do you always assume the worst just because the kids are out there high as kites?"

"Because I know that the only thing you cannot resist is a syringe," Sally says quietly, and I can hear the betrayal in her voice. She is so sexy when she's angry; I think for a fleeting moment that she's right, that I could quit forever, take her and marry her and never look back. Then I remember at whose altar I worship and how for the past eight years I've only ever had sex while I was spun and the fact that I don't believe in love anymore.

I believe in sex though, quite fervently at that, and right now I want nothing more than to fuck Sally raw. Of course, if I set this up right, I won't have to do any of the fucking myself. If I get her angry enough she'll pound me into the mattress like there's no tomorrow. That's what I want, Sally; show me who's boss, make me hurt so I can hate you just a little bit more. If I do this right, you know you'll want to, Sally, so let's quit pretending we're nice people and just get on slinging the dirt.

"Sally, I assure you I'm sober," I whisper as I start nuzzling her neck and caressing her back. Rigid at first, she reluctantly returns my kiss and starts melting into my arms. By the time my shirt finally comes off and she sees the needle marks that confirm her suspicions, we're too far down the road to orgasm for her to stop.

I can see she's furious, and Sally is best when she's fuming. She pushes me down on the bed and pins my arms down with one hand while ripping a condom wrapper open with her teeth. I issue the token protests, but she's already on top of me, her left hand still holding down my arms above my head. Her knees pin down my thighs as she slides herself onto my dick. She is so extraordinarily strong when she's angry.

"Don't you ever lie to me again," she hisses, spewing out each word to the beat of her contracting muscles. "I will tolerate weakness, but I cannot abide lies. Are. We. Clear?"

I nod eagerly. I have never wanted her more than now.

Her long, dark hair is unraveling, falling past her shoulders in a deluge of curls, the tips of which are barely brushing across my chest on each thrust down. Her green eyes, still shooting daggers at me, are open wide, her pupils dilated almost as much as my own, and her lips are slightly parted revealing a perfectly straight set of teeth. She's quite beautiful when she's fucking.

I still can't move, but why would I want to move when Sally is riding me, all her fury concentrated between her legs? As she is screwing me rougher and faster I wonder whether she unconsciously wants me to lie to her. She has never been as excited and as sexy as she is right now. I thank my lucky stars that speed delays orgasm. If I were sober, I would have come during those first few angry plunges. If I were sober, Sally wouldn't be here.

Sally lets go of my arms and arches her back, but I daren't move, as I can feel her muscles contracting rapidly around my dick and I know she is about to come. Her mouth opens further and she lets out a short, sharp scream as her muscles contract for a final glorious time, and her warm, wet fluids trickle down one of my balls. She lets herself fall onto my chest, panting heavily. Her hair is all over my face, and I can smell the strawberry shampoo, the scent of the French perfume she favors, and the sweat of her body, and I don't think I have ever been so excited before.

When she recovers, instead of letting me finish, she lifts herself from me and slowly starts getting dressed. She won't even look at me when I take off the condom, and I start finishing the job she began with my hand. Maybe, just maybe, I think, she's leaving me here like this, craving her body worse than any drug, so I'll want her even more next time. I'm certain she thinks that if she makes me want her enough without giving in, I'll choose her over the needle. I don't have the gumption to tell her it's been tried before.

I don't notice her leaving, but I hear the front door slamming as the blood rushes to my head, stars burst in front of my eyes, and my body shakes itself to ejaculation. "Geronimo!"

I hear the engine of her car revving as I reach for the box of Kleenex and start wiping up my jism and her cum, which have mingled and formed a sticky union on my belly.

I am alone on my twenty-third birthday. Technically, that's not entirely correct. I am alone sitting at the bar of a pub in Stepney, a pub that is absolutely packed. I'm smashed and looking for a fight, which is why I'm in Stepney. Over the past two months I have been barred from every pub in Bethnal Green.

I feel a hand on my shoulder as I down another shot of vodka, and I know without looking around that it's Patrick. You would think that with a wife and two young kids he would have something better to do than follow me around London, yet that's what he has been doing for nine weeks. The only saving grace is that he has been barred from just as many pubs as I have.

"Sod off," I shout above the din.

"Shan't!" Patrick shouts back. "We're going to get this over and done with, so either you get a move on and come outside with me, or I'll drag you outside by the scruff of your neck."

I turn around and take a swing, vaguely aiming at Patrick's face. Patrick doesn't flinch. He catches my fist in one of his enormous hands and twists my wrist painfully behind me, then he leans closer to my ear and shouts, "The way I see it, you've got two choices, lad. Either you come outside quietly or I break your frigging wrist. It's all the same to me."

I grudgingly slide off the barstool and do my best to stay vertical, while Patrick leads me out of the pub into the pouring rain without relaxing his grip on my wrist. In the alley behind the pub he lets go of my arm and throws me hard against the wall. "Right, lad, we are going to have this out today," he shouts, his face inches away from mine. "I have a wife and two kids under five with another one on the way, and I have absolutely no desire to spend the next few years following you around seedy pubs while you try to drink yourself to death and pick a fight with every bloke in East London. If pain is what you want, I'll give you all the pain you need."

I laugh and I think this may be the first time I have laughed since I've been on this binge, "Go for it, Patrick," I smirk. "Throw me your best punch."

I never actually expected him to deck me. In twenty-three years he hasn't laid a hand on me once, even when I've been a prat and deserved it, but I guess even Patrick has his breaking point. The first punch hits me square in the gut and knocks the wind out of me, and maybe it's because I've drank most of that fine establishment's vodka over the past five hours, but I feel my knees give out from under me.

I lie in the street panting, but Patrick isn't walking away this time. I came here looking for a fight, and he's going to give me the fight of a life-

time. He picks me up by my shirt and starts pummeling my face. He's pulling his punches too, at least a little bit. He wants to hurt me all right, wants to knock the anger and desperation out of me, but he doesn't want to cause permanent damage, and that makes me even angrier.

I start throwing a few punches his way, not that they'll do any harm since I see three different Patricks in front of me and don't know which one to aim at. I guess I decide that if this fight is going to get real, if I'm going to get Patrick to really hurt me, I'd better provoke him a little bit, so I aim a knee at his groin. I'm too drunk to aim properly, but I manage to come close enough to make Patrick furious. This is no longer therapy for the sad vodka-sodden parody of a man I've become; this is Patrick looking to kill me. We start laying into each other, fist for fist. Patrick may be bigger than me, but I fight dirty, and I give him the best I can.

I grab the first thing I can get my hands on, a beer crate by the looks of it, and aim it at Patrick's head. He's sober though, with much better reflexes, and pulls back just in time. Still, it hits him in the shoulder with a satisfying thump. Then there are fists raining onto my face. I'm laughing hysterically now, meeting Patrick's punches blow by blow with my own. I haven't felt so alive in months.

After a few minutes there's a break in the action. We're both panting from the exertion of the fight. I think I may have split Patrick's lip, and one of my eyes is starting to swell up alarmingly. Truth be told, I feel about ready to pass out, and if it weren't for the overwhelming desire to kick the shit out of my brother, I'd just curl up there in the alley. Patrick probably senses how tired I'm getting because he aims his final punch, not holding back this time. His fist, with all his weight behind it, connects with my nose, and the only reason my nose doesn't end up in my brains and I'm still alive after is that Patrick lets go of my shirt as he is throwing the punch. Even so I hear the sound of breaking bone and seconds later I can taste the blood that's running down the back of my throat.

I lie there in the street while Patrick is leaning against the wall breathing heavily. I lift my hand to my face, and there's blood running down my chin. "You son-of-a-bitch!" I howl. "You broke my fucking nose!"

"Yeah, and your nose may have broken my knuckle," Patrick responds nonchalantly. "Besides, you'll probably be better off not being able to get any candy up your nostrils for a few weeks. It's bad enough having you marinated in cheap liquor."

He picks up his jacket, which somehow ended up on the ground during the fight, and gingerly slips his right arm into the sleeve. "Now do yourself a favor and get cleaned up," he says calmly. "You have to start looking for Declan before he manages to kill himself."

"Why?" I shout. "Why does Declan get to be the drama queen?"

He looks at me with those bright, blue Sheahan eyes and says, "Because I didn't keep you out of trouble so that you could drink your life away and wallow in self-pity."

"She was my wife!" I yell, suppressing the urge to get up again and assault Patrick with my aching fists.

Patrick sighs. "When has that ever mattered?" he asks, avoiding my gaze. "Declan loved her just as much as you did, and right now he's hurting more."

He turns around and starts walking off into the rain that is turning to sleet, holding his broken hand close to his chest, while I remain there lying in the street, closing my eyes for just a moment, savoring the loneliness.

When I return to the living room, Luka looks up from his notebook and grins at me. "She thought she'd finally made you see the light and didn't check for tracks until after it was too late for her to stop. Congratulations!"

The Kid looks up too and gives me the thumbs-up before frowning slightly and saying, "You know it is customary for ladies to stay until both parties are sufficiently satisfied, right?"

I give him a look, but I'm feeling much too good-natured to pick a fight right now. Sally did her job beautifully, as always, leaving me with plenty of material to write come Monday morning.

"I dunno," Luka says looking at the Kid but talking to me. "If she actually stayed for the whole show there might be a danger of cuddling."

"I suppose you're right," the Kid sighs, looking straight back at Luka, "once you start to cuddle, you're only a few short baby steps away from foreplay, and that would be a very unmanly thing indeed."

"Couldn't have that," Luka responds casually, "after all, my brother is well known for his utter lack of interest in foreplay. Likes to get straight to the point, he does. Especially if it will hurt a little. Kind of runs in the family, that does. We like our women to hurt us."

They are still studiously avoiding me, like actors up on the stage pretending the audience doesn't exist. It's all a show though, orchestrated solely for my benefit and Luka's amusement. I'm looking straight at him when he finally turns to face me, not saying anything. I don't have to say anything at any rate, Luka and I have always been quite capable of communicating without the annoyance of words.

Don't turn this into a pissing contest, lad, my eyes are saying. You know you can't win, same way I never could beat Patrick at this game. You might have a tongue sharp as a fresh razor blade, but I'm still able to break every bone in your body, and don't think for a moment that I've grown softer with advancing age. Yeah, Luka, I've been noticing the hair thinning a little around the temples as I approach middle age. There are lines around my eyes that weren't there only five years ago, but underneath I am still cold as ice, hard as steel, and as hell-bent on destruction as ever.

Still, his gaze is defying me; he's holding out much longer than he used to, has grown much harder himself. That what it takes to make you feel like a man, brother? His eyes are mocking me.

I'm matching his look effortlessly, smirking a little, giving him the cocky smile that will irk him even more. Foolish boy, my eyes are screaming at him, didn't you learn never to challenge the master? I devised this sport. Everything you think you've done, everything you think you are, Patrick and I invented. You will never beat us at our own game.

The tension in the air between us is almost tangible now, crackling under the strain of the silent battle of wills we are engaged in. The Kid notices too; he's getting nervous, starting to fidget.

Luka cracks first and turns his eyes away with a shrug, conceding defeat. "Just having a bit of a laugh," he mumbles.

"All right, you've had your joke at my expense, now fuck off!" I say, and then I chuckle, partly because I won the staring contest and partly to defuse the situation.

They both grin and turn back to whatever they were doing. "One more thing," the Kid says, "the whole shouting 'Geronimo' thing? Kind of funny the first time, but it's definitely wearing off."

I resist the urge to deck him; he's obviously never learned when to drop a subject. Instead, I occupy my mind trying to figure out where that nagging feeling of wrongness I'm suddenly experiencing is coming from. Something was different this time, but I can't quite decide what that difference was. I'm sitting there mulling over every little detail of Sally's brief visit, trying to figure out if anything happened that was out of the ordinary.

Suddenly it hits me. Sally not only left me high and dry—she does that frequently enough—but she also left without a word. She didn't shout abuse, she didn't hit me, she didn't even kick the bed, nor do any of the other things she does when she's angry, and maybe that means she's not coming back.

"Oh shit," I mutter, "I may have pushed her too far this time."

"Never mind," the Kid says brightly, "we'll just go bar-hopping next week and find you a new toy. There must be plenty where that one came from."

Luka shakes his head. "No, she'll be back."

"How come?" I ask, genuinely wanting to know.

"You're in over your head," Luka explains, disgust echoing in his voice. "That girl is more than the usual eye-candy; she's clever. She also thinks she loves you. I could see it in her face."

"We all want what we can't have," I say. "If she's really clever, she knows I'll never love, not for all the opium in China."

Christ, Luka's doing it again, not saying anything because his eyes are already speaking volumes. Liar! they are screaming. You love madly, passionately, painfully.

Loved. Get your tenses right, lad, my eyes are replying coolly. That was London, nearly a lifetime ago. London undid us both, eviscerated us, took your mind and took my... Still, I suppose I've loved, which is more than you can say for yourself, brother.

If you are what love turns a man into, I am exceedingly grateful I have never felt its sting, Luka's eyes shout at me.

The unthinkable is about to happen. I have two choices right now: blink in order to redistribute the wetness that is collecting underneath my lower lids, or actually let the tears slide down my face. I choose the lesser of two evils and let Luka win the staring contest.

I suppose he must feel elated. He's probably sitting there smugly, reveling in the knowledge that he won a silent argument. I keep my eyes closed, giving them time to absorb the fluid. When I finally open my eyes, Luka is still looking at me, but he isn't gloating, much to my surprise.

"Having one very messed-up wench rip your heart out and trample it into the ground doesn't give you license to take it out on every woman you meet," Luka says quietly.

I can't believe he had the gall to say it. I know he's been thinking it for a fair number of years now, but I never, ever thought he would have the audacity to say it. Even Patrick hasn't mustered the courage to say that to my face. Worse, I'm not sure whether I should beat him for his impertinence or congratulate him for growing a pair of balls.

I'm still reeling because it's the closest he's come to mentioning Her in years, the only acknowledgement that he remembers. I'm not ready—I will never be ready—to hear Her name again.

I'm trying to hide the shock I feel at the memories Luka's comment has awakened inside my head and abruptly get up and stride into the kitchen. Once there, I frantically try to open the door of the refrigerator, but the door is stuck and won't give however much I struggle with it. Luka quietly steps up behind me and reaches for the other side of the door before I remember that the Kid changed the direction in which it opens. He sees the tears in my eyes and a brief look of surprise flickers across his face. Luka has not seen me cry in so long, perhaps he has forgotten I'm capable of tears.

"I didn't mean to upset you," he says and quickly changes the subject. "By the way, after Wonder Boy finished changing the door around, he had some screws left over, so we taped them to the side of the fridge."

I nod, because if I tried to talk now my voice would crack. Staring blindly at the bare refrigerator I try to collect myself. Remember, you're hard as steel, tougher than any man has a right to be, I chide myself silently. Pull yourself together. Don't acknowledge weakness, especially not in front of the lad. I reach for the milk carton. The treacherous voice continues its whispers in my mind. I've grown into a parody of myself. I poured the molten ice in libation and thrust the tempered steel into the sacrificial fires of the goddess that proved to be the devil incarnate as she emasculated me time and time again.

I was a man once, but that was London, where life was ruled by Sunday closing time, football matches at Upton Park and shopping at Whitechapel Market. The city of unrelenting rain and muggy summers that turned canals into cesspits reeking of decay. London, with its wafers of bread, the body of Christ, and Sunday Mass in Kilburn. God is dead, if ever he truly existed—London taught me that for all my sins. London, where on a stormy English night the stars went nova, tearing my world apart. The city where angels fell and I ceased being whatever I thought I was. But that was London; this is a continent away.

I'm still holding the milk carton. How long have I been standing here? How long has Luka been observing my internal dialogue? I force my mind out of its tailspin and raise the milk carton to my mouth. After a few long sips I return it to the refrigerator and walk off toward the bathroom. I need another shot now, anything to make me forget that which takes years of forgetting. I need to stay awake by any means necessary, because at night there are dreams, and my dreams are always nightmares, nightmares I have been running from as long as I can remember.

Luka, visibly shaken by my reaction to his accurate, if unkind, words, follows me into the bathroom and quickly mixes up another quarter gram while I throw up in the toilet. Because I'm shaking too much, he injects me, then cradles my head in his arms until the drug makes me forget. For a few precious moments we switch roles and he becomes the caregiver who tries to lick my bleeding wounds, and for that I love him more than I could ever express in words.

# 4

Overamp: A Tale of Masochism and Withdrawal

We're rapidly moving toward summer, and Luka is getting edgy. He has been with me almost three months, and that's longer than he has stayed in years.

A few days after Luka's birthday, I return home to find him and the Kid sprawled on the back porch with a couple of space bags. "Isn't it a bit early in the day to start drinking?" I ask, glancing at my watch.

"It's after noon," Luka replies nonchalantly.

"Yes, about five minutes past noon actually," I agree. "What's the occasion?"

The Kid grins around the aluminum bag of wine raised halfway to his mouth. "Chip is having a birthday bash at his place later."

"And you decided you were going to drink preemptively?" I ask.

"Well, he's invited everyone he knows, so there's probably not going to be enough alcohol to get us smashed unless we go there delightfully drunk already," Luka shrugs.

I nod. "Good point. Pass the bag."

He hands it to me, and I take a step forward, looking at him. He nods. I splash a generous measure to the ground, and Luka intones, "Free the souls of all the faithful departed from infernal punishment and the deep pit. Free them from the mouth of the lion; do not let Tartarus swallow them, nor let them fall into darkness."

The Kid is looking at us with his mouth hanging open while I raise the bag to my lips. "What the hell was that?" he asks Luka.

"A libation," Luka replies before snatching the wine out of my hand. "It's from the requiem mass."

"But you're not Christian!" the Kid protests, looking back and forth between Luka and me accusingly.

"Damn right, I'm not," Luka says, "but I was Catholic once, and that's a whole lot harder to shake than Christianity."

"But—"

I sigh and shove the bag of wine at the Kid. "Drink. You'll never understand because you weren't born to it," I say, and that ends the conversation.

It takes me three attempts to open the gate to Chip's backyard two hours later. The handle keeps on moving out of the way. We walk along the path to the shed, which has been the party room for years. There are five or six others already lounging around in lawn chairs, passing a couple of half-gallons of Old Crow around.

I half-turn to Luka and hiss, "I thought you said there wasn't going to be enough alcohol!"

"There's never enough alcohol," Luka replies with the kind of conviction only the severely drunk can muster. "Hey, Chip, happy birthday!"

"Hey, Luka, have a drink!"

Luka picks up the bottle offered to him and takes a few gulps before passing it to the Kid, who drinks and passes it on to me.

An hour later, while everybody is talking shit, I'm almost ready to nod off in my lawn chair when I see Myron stagger up to where Luka is leaning heavily on the Kid and slur, "You have a smoke?"

"No, I'm all out," Luka replies.

Myron is about to walk off, already turning, when his head snaps around again and he shouts, "Liar! You just had a cigarette."

"My last one, you stupid fuck," Luka replies.

I'm halfway to my feet when Myron's fist connects with Luka's jaw. Luka momentarily looks puzzled before picking himself up off the ground and launching himself at Myron while I'm staggering to attention.

Myron's back is blocking my view, but I can hear him gasping in agony a second later while I'm still stumbling across the yard. Meanwhile, Chip, who's closer, launches himself at Luka and pulls him off Myron, pushing Luka's face up with his palm. Myron spins around, holding his bleeding nose and cursing under his breath, but nobody's paying attention to him because a second later, Chip starts yowling and lets go of Luka's face to cradle his hand close to his body. Luka stares back at the assembled party with a self-satisfied grin on his face and a trickle of blood running from his mouth.

"You fucker, you bit me!" Chip yells enraged, tackling Luka to the ground and closing his hands around Luka's throat.

Definitely time to intervene. I finally reach the battlefield and spend a second contemplating which side to take. I haven't been insane enough to get into a fight with Luka since he hit puberty, and judging by the way Myron is holding his face and whimpering, Chip's finger wasn't the first body part to inadvertently get trapped between Luka's teeth. Besides, we're brothers, and blood's supposedly thicker than whiskey.

I sigh deeply and start kicking at Chip's hands with my steel-capped boots. At least I try to. Luka's enraged scream a second later convinces me that his head might have gotten in the way of my foot. "Sorry, sorry!" I shout, trying to sound suitably apologetic, and start kicking at Chip's chest with renewed vigor. "Fucking bastard! Get off my brother!"

That seems to do the trick. Chip falls back groaning, and I'm congratulating myself for a job well done when Luka, wheezing ever so slightly, launches himself at me, yelling, "You're supposed to take my side, you dimwit, not kick me in the head."

I try to say I'm sorry, I really do, but Luka's head hits me square in the belly and knocks me over breathless. Through the veil of agony that even the whiskey doesn't numb completely, I see the Kid struggling up to his feet and trying to grab Luka's arms to keep him from instigating further mayhem.

It's probably the stupidest idea the Kid's ever come up with, because Luka's about twice his size across the chest and grabs the Kid around the waist without so much as batting an eyelid, hauling him over his shoulder. He strides to the edge of the yard, with the Kid yelling abuse and banging his fists into Luka's kidneys, and heaves the Kid over the fence. Then he makes a show of wiping his shirt off, before glaring at the dumbstruck party and asking, "That it? Anyone else wanna play? 'Cause I'm just warming up."

"I think," a girl in the back says hesitantly after a few moments of silence, "I think the party's over. We need to take Chip to the hospital."

"Fine," Luka says. "It was a pretty boring party anyway." He picks up one of the half-empty whiskey bottles and walks over to me. "You coming or what?" he asks, holding his hand out.

I'm still too winded to talk, but I allow him to haul me up.

Once we leave the yard, Luka insists on climbing the neighbor's fence to collect the Kid, but the Kid is gone. After about half an hour of fruitlessly searching the neighborhood, I manage to drag Luka home, where he crawls underneath the dining room table without a word.

I'm ten years old, sitting in the stairwell with Declan, three months shy of his fifth birthday, on my lap. Through the crack in the door I can see Patrick's bulging duffel bag sitting in the hallway a few short steps from the front door. Mother is shouting at Patrick in the kitchen in a surreal moment of acknowledging his existence. She's using expressions I have only ever heard when old Father Mulroney had to fill in for Father O'Neill saying Mass, such as "harlot" and "whore of Babylon," and I make a mental note to look them up in the dictionary later on. Occasionally, when her English fails her, the curses and shouts continue in other languages. Very occasionally, Patrick shouts back.

Soon the thuds and crashes of broken crockery start resonating from the kitchen. They aren't aiming at each other, I suppose, but the throwing of china has always been a popular way of venting frustration in my family. Then there is a break in the fighting, followed by one final, earth-shattering crash, and I realize, even as I pull Declan closer to me, that Patrick, all 6'2" and bulging muscle, has toppled the china cabinet.

Seconds later Patrick emerges from the kitchen, picks up his duffel bag and opens the front door. I have never seen him so angry, and I can tell just how furious he is by the pallor of his face. I pick up Declan and push open the hallway door, and with Declan's hand firmly gripped in my own, I rush out after Patrick into the snow.

We catch up with him a few houses down the road. He is leaning on his duffel bag under a streetlight in the dusk, lighting a cigarette. "You shouldn't be out here; you'll catch your deaths," he says.

Declan is wailing. His little almost-five-year-old mind, which hasn't yet learned the difference between going away and dying, is jumping to conclusions. Last winter granddaddy Sheahan went away and never came back. He bolts from my hand and wraps himself around Patrick's leg, locking his arms and legs around it and showing no signs of ever letting go again.

I want to wail just as loudly as Declan is wailing, but if Patrick really goes I will be the oldest by default, and big brothers don't cry. Instead, I look at Patrick, lifting my hands slightly in supplication, and beg, "Please don't leave us, Patrick!"

Patrick takes a few steps, slightly dragging the leg that Declan is wrapped around, and puts his arm around my shoulder. "I can't stay, bro," he says. "You probably won't understand this now, but in a few years, you will meet a girl who's really special, special like Annie is, and you'll know why I had to leave."

I look at the boy, the man, who spent last August teaching Micky to swim, the man who took the training wheels off Declan's bicycle in June and spent two long weeks running after him, the man who got me the longed-for Sex Pistols record for my birthday three weeks ago, the man whose shoes I'll have to fill if he leaves. Maybe Patrick can see the terror in my eyes, because he pulls me closer to himself and says, "You'll do just fine, mate. Promise me you'll take good care of your brothers."

All I can do is nod as he points to the house, where Micky is peeking out from behind the curtains of the nursery window. Then Patrick gently lifts up Declan, who is still clinging to his leg sobbing loudly, and places him in my arms. Declan wraps his little arms around my neck, his legs around my waist, and continues crying into my shirt. Patrick kisses his head, tousles my hair, and picks up his duffel bag. He turns around and start walking toward the train station, and he never once looks back.

I stand there, Declan firmly wrapped around me, until Patrick turns the corner at the end of the street. When I finally turn around to carry Declan *back to the house, I see Micky still quietly peeking out from behind the nursery curtains.*

Years later, I will wonder whether I rocked the wrong brother to sleep that night.

For three days I watch Luka lying underneath the table, withdrawing from my world, only rising occasionally to relieve himself. The weekend approaches, and I am determined to follow the usual routine, hoping that the temptation of the drug is enough to draw Luka out from underneath the table. He doesn't take the bait and remains there, almost catatonic, while I, for the first time in months, go off to shoot up by myself.

I dissolve the crystals like usual, prepping two syringes in the hope that Luka will change his mind, even if I know already that it is a hopeless cause. Five minutes turn to ten as I wait for him to make his way into the bathroom, and when it is quite apparent that he won't, I empty one of the syringes back into the cooker and place the tip of the other in the filter to draw up. I've never been one to waste perfectly good drugs.

I tie myself off, hit a vein first try, though my hands are shaking at the newness of doing this by myself, and start depressing the plunger. I'm only halfway through the contents of the syringe before I realize this is too much, too fast, but I can't stop myself. My finger keeps on pushing the plunger as I start hyperventilating, already light-headed with the rush. I always knew that one of the capital sins would kill me one day. I just never thought it would be avarice.

I collapse in a messy heap on the bathroom floor, or maybe I pass out, it's hard to tell which. Then I start dry heaving as the pangs of pain start reverberating in my skull. The tunnel vision takes over, and I'm unable to move, suffer complete loss of motor control. All I can feel are the drum rolls in my head, my heart, which is beating much too fast, and the throbbing behind my eyes. When I start thinking I can move again, I don't dare to, don't dare to even pull the needle out of my arm, because I feel there's a considerable chance my heart will explode with the slightest movement.

Luka doesn't stir from beneath the table.

Later, much later, it feels like hours but it is probably only minutes, Sally lets herself into the house. She finds me there on the floor, the needle still stuck in my arm. She curses and yells for Luka, but he doesn't come. In between bursts of cymbals behind my eardrums, I hear her rummaging through the shelf behind me. Then her gloved hands enter my field of vision and carefully loosen the tourniquet and pull the needle out of my arm. A small trickle of blood oozes out of the puncture and runs down my arm, mingling with what I suppose must be vomit. There isn't enough blood though, and I start to think that I may have collapsed one of my best veins today.

Still cursing underneath her breath, Sally half-drags half-kicks me into the shower and turns on the water. I lie there, as catatonic as Luka underneath the table, with the ice-cold water washing over me.

An eternity later, Sally returns and starts stripping the freezing, wet clothes from my body. By now I'm able to cooperate a little, lifting my heavy arms and lolling head as she takes off the sodden shirt. Somehow it registers that Sally is standing there only in her jeans and bra while she is undressing me, and she's angry and sexier than ever before.

I still can't get up from the cold shower-floor, or even move much, but I can feel the excitement growing as Sally's nipples, hard from the cold water, peek through the lace. I suppose she notices the bulge in my pants as she pulls off my boots and socks, because she doesn't take off my jeans. Instead she leaves me lying there like a dog in the street, thinking about fucking her, as the throbbing gradually moves from behind my eyes to my groin.

I don't notice I'm keening until Sally rushes back into the bathroom fully dressed. She finally turns off the water and unsnaps my jeans, dragging me out of the shower. With her anger still burning brightly and the superhuman strength that is born out of her fury, she grabs me around the waist and somehow maneuvers me down the hallway and into my bedroom. As she is hoisting me onto the bed, I wrap my arms around her waist with all the strength I can muster and pull her down with me. Her entire body tenses, but she doesn't struggle as I press my dry lips to her clenched mouth.

She slaps me, hard, and shouts, "Fuck you, James, you almost died tonight!"

If I could, if I were capable of speech again, I would tell her that nobody ever dies from overamping on speed. It may be uncomfortable as hell, and it may leave you high and drained for days, but it doesn't kill you, which is why I like it so much better than heroin. The words are in my head, begging to get out, but my vocal chords are not cooperating, and all I can feel is that desperate need between my legs.

I press my lips to her mouth again and try to force my tongue between her teeth. I slip my hand underneath her shirt and start fondling her breasts, still only marginally in control of my own limbs. To Sally my caresses probably feel like the bumbling and inarticulate attentions of an inexperienced teenage boy feeling his way up a girl's shirt for the very first time. I move my clumsy hand down to her jeans and undo the buttons; Sally doesn't slap it away. She still isn't kissing me back, but she isn't fighting me either. As I move my hand slowly up and down her thigh, she relents and unlocks her jaw, letting my tongue into her mouth.

I'm kissing her for the longest time, which is strange, because I'm not a kisser. Of course, I'm usually not all that interested in foreplay either. But all my senses are in overdrive right now, fueled by adrenaline and too much amphetamine, and each sensation feels completely new and exhilarating. I vaguely wonder if this is what the world feels like to a newborn child before plunging my tongue back into the depths of her mouth. Her lips are unbelievably soft, and her mouth tastes kind of sweet, like hot apple cider or caramel, and I could spend hours doing this, trying to catalogue each new sensation in my mind.

At some point we must have rolled onto the remote for the stereo, because music comes on, but it hardly registers as I'm consumed by my absolute need to have her and to hold her and to make love to her. I try to force my mouth to form words again. "Sally... want..." is all I manage in a guttural groan.

She smiles, which is glorious; she hardly ever smiles around me these days, and I suppose I am to blame for that. When did I become so cruel I wiped the smile from her face? Probably around the time she worked out exactly why I wanted her to hurt me. I wonder what she thought before that. Did she really think it was a matter of preference, being dominated by some chit of a woman? Or did she think it was all in aid of curing me of my other, less wholesome, habits? Either of those reasons would have hurt less than the truth.

No such luck. I want her to hurt me so I can hate her kind a little more. I want her to tie me to the cast-iron bedposts and pound her fists into my face and chest and kidneys. I want her to bite and scratch and dribble hot wax on my skin. I want her to ride me rough and hard and leave without allowing me release. I want her to hurt me in order to prove that mere physical pain can never rival the exquisite mental tortures She devised.

I want her to hurt me so I can know that I'm still alive.

Except today. Today I don't want her to hurt me. I want her to love me instead, and that scares me more than she'll ever know. Right now, barely in control of my body, I'm as vulnerable and open as I'll ever be, ready and willing to give her as much as I can, more than I ever could give if I were in control of myself. As I caress her and kiss her and hold her to me tightly, I don't think about getting my rocks off like I usually do. I think about how I want to hold her close to me to recapture a little bit of what I lost long ago.

I look at Sally, and there are silent tears running down her face. This is the closest she'll ever get to that declaration of love she so desperately wants, and she knows it too.

A long time later, in my warped sense of time, I slowly ease myself into her, bare and honest for the first time in the months I've known her. There is no pain this time, no anger and no defenses, no walls I built around myself, and no need for any fast and furious fucking. She probably thinks we've reached a turning point in our entanglement, because she lets me lead, is happy to lie back and let me take control. I just lie there for a few minutes kissing her. An eternity later, I start thrusting slowly and gently. Just this once Sally will know what it feels like when I make love to a woman. This could be my greatest act of cruelty yet.

Eventually, after she's purred and growled her way to orgasm, I fall asleep for a few minutes my dick still inside her. I wake up with her head resting against my chest, and I'm spun, high as a kite; I won't go back to sleep for several days.

I pull her closer to me, "Thank you for taking care of me," I say, noting that my ability to form coherent sentences has returned. "Is Luka still under the table?"

Sally nods and snuggles up closer to me, pulling the sheets up to her chin. I'm too hot but strangely content, and I suppose just for a while I can let her stay close to me, let her be happy.

"It's been almost four days," I murmur as I stroke her back. "I was hoping he'd come out of it for the speed..."

Sally tenses. "You know what I think," she says. "As far as I'm concerned, your brother is holding you back. You—we—could be great if only you'd rid yourself of him and his drug problem once and for all."

This is when I realize that Sally will never be the one; I refuse to become what she wants, and besides, Luka and I are a package deal. I dislodge my arm from underneath Sally's shoulders and start getting dressed.

In the dining room Luka remains catatonic underneath the table.

Our sun goes nova on All Souls' Day. Declan disappears that same night, and when I finally pull myself together enough to go after him a few months later, he is long gone. I have been caring for Declan long enough to understand how his mind works, though—understand him probably better than he himself does—and he hasn't yet learned to cover his tracks like he will in the coming years. I spend a few days looking, calling in favors and banging on relatives' doors in the wee hours of the morning, Patrick growing more exasperated with every day that passes, before I pick up the trail. There isn't much left for me in London at any rate, so I leave Patrick to clear out the flat and get on the first transatlantic flight to Los Angeles. With Declan's picture and a list of names he is likely to use in my pocket, I start working my way up the west coast methodically.

After three weeks I track him down to a bridge in Portland. He's barely coherent and doesn't recognize me at first. He looks emaciated, like he has lost thirty pounds, with dark circles underneath his eyes, eyes that are much duller than any Sheahan boy's eyes have a right to be. It may be my mind playing tricks on me, but I can smell the heroin on him. I unobtrusively glance at his bare arms and see the tracks. No bruises, just needle-marks; there's an art to finding veins and somehow he's mastered it already.

"Time to go home Declan," I say, knowing that we can never go back to London again. "Time to get cleaned up and start over."

Declan, struggling to stay conscious, looks up at me, and without the slightest trace of emotion in his voice he says, "I'm Luka. Declan's dead. He slit his wrists in a bathtub in Barstow three months ago. When they found him he had already bled to death. Very sad."

I nod. I know I deserve that. I should have started looking for him the day he disappeared, but I was too wrapped up in my own grief and despair to care where he went. "OK, Luka, get your stuff together because we're blowing this state and heading down to the Bay Area. I've got the keys to Dad's house."

I end up packing all of Declan's things—there aren't that many—because he simply isn't sentient enough to do it himself. While I'm doing the packing, Declan goes off to slam one last shot. There is something else I need to do before we leave though, to keep a promise I made him a long time ago, and it's probably a good thing he's just shot himself up again, because this is going to hurt like a bitch.

I walk over to where Declan is leaning against one of the support pillars of the bridge. "Remember that night you walked in on me and—me?" I ask. "Remember what I promised you I would do if I ever caught you shooting up?"

Declan just nods; he's incapable of speech right now. I lean in closer and whisper in his ear, "I want you to understand that I'm doing this for your own good. I want you to understand that I never wanted to do this. I want you to understand that you left me no choice."

Declan nods again. He knows I have kept every promise ever made save one, and I will regret my one indiscretion for the rest of my life. He knows I will never fail again, and when they shove me in the ground, the epitaph will read, "He kept his promises." He knows what must be done and reaches out. Cold and calculating Sheahan eyes lock with dull and doped-up Sheahan eyes, and without losing eye contact I reach down and break his wrist.

We leave Portland shortly after sunset and he spends the first half of the drive south nodding off in the backseat. After we cross the state line into California he wakes up a little bit and moves up to the front seat. There are questions I need to ask now, in loco parentis, and I don't know quite how to begin, as they never covered those in the parenting guides.

"Shared any needles?" I ask, opting for to the point.

"A few," Declan drawls.

"Did you use bleach?" I ask.

"Yes," he replies, and I let out a sigh of relief. He's probably HIV-negative.

"You'll still need to get tested for hepatitis in a few months," I say quietly, but my heart is doing cartwheels. People can live for thirty years with hepatitis, and that's a long time when you are seventeen.

Declan just nods, cradling the broken wrist that I tied to his body in a makeshift sling.

"I'll take you to the hospital for that," I say pointing at his arm, "but first I'm going to lock you in the closet until you're clean."

"If you think it's necessary," Declan grudgingly agrees. "I'm not strung out though."

I laugh, but there is no humor in it. Whatever Declan may claim, I've seen my fair share of junkies over the past few years and I know what I'm looking at. Declan never believes for a moment that he has become hooked, though. Years from now he will insist that although he came precariously close to the abyss of addiction, he never went off the deep end. It's an essential aspect of Declan's drive for self-preservation to believe that addiction is a state of mind rather than a physical state, because Declan has never been held responsible for his state of mind.

The real withdrawal, what Declan dismissively refers to as "that bad case of food-poisoning," doesn't set in until quite a while after I deposit Declan in our father's empty house in Oakland. The first day or so he mostly sleeps and occasionally skulks around the house he has never been in before, while I settle down for what is to come.

I anticipate doing penance for Her in the process of getting my kid brother off heroin. I know what I'm doing this time. I am prepared to lock Declan in that closet and keep him there no matter how much he begs and pleads and shouts. I am prepared to wordlessly clean up after he vomits or shits himself, and I suppose I do some of that, but not nearly enough to lick my wounds. I am looking for redemption and forgiveness, and I haven't yet learned that the person who will never forgive me is myself.

Make no mistake, the withdrawal does come the second day, yet compared with what I've seen before and since, it is one big letdown. Oh, he sweats and shakes and vomits and even dirties himself once or twice, but it is all rather low-key and strangely disappointing. I would learn later that Declan comes off all drugs much better than most of us; even stepping back from the brink of heroin addiction he suffered less than I suffer each Sunday afternoon. Declan's resilience to withdrawal symptoms robs me of the redemption I am seeking.

The whole episode lasts just over thirty-six hours. On day four, Declan is heroin-free with no physical side effects and a smirk on his face that speaks volumes. How I hate him that day, when he, with a flick of his wrist and a minimum of discomfort, shakes the death sentence passed unto others so dear to me. As much as I love him, I want him to suffer, to feel the pain and desperation, but Declan just laughs it all off and kicks the dope without a single look back.

It is the first and only time Declan ever gets strung out.

He is changed forever though. When he left London, heroin wasn't the only thing he found. In the months before I tracked him down, he had cre-

ated a new reality for himself: a new name, a new birthday, a new identity. The Declan I knew was gone and would never come back. Declan carefully locked up all memories of the person he once was and decided to become a different person entirely. Maybe that horrible night in London, one of the souls Declan carries in his head permanently took over his body to protect his fragile mind. I don't think I'll ever know what happened. All I know is that I lost my brother and then found a person with my brother's DNA, never again the boy I'd known.

I have now been awake for four days, except for that half-hour nap on Sally's chest in the small hours of Friday morning, with no signs of tiring. It's the most annoying side effect of overamping. Last time it happened, a few years back, I was up for a week.

Luka has started coming out from underneath the table once a day to eat, but there is no real improvement. He still isn't talking to me, barely acknowledging my existence.

This evening though, things are different. When I come home Luka is sitting at the dining room table, calmly slicing up his arms with a blunt razor blade. I survey the scene, taking in the half-empty bottle of tequila on the counter, the empty 40s in the sink, and the piece of writing paper in front of Luka which has blood splattered all over it. Luka is pissed as a newt, as we say back in England, and alcohol has a tendency to give Luka ideas.

"I wish you wouldn't cut yourself in the living room," I say nonchalantly. "You're going to ruin the carpet one of these days."

Luka doesn't respond, but he gets up and staggers off down the hallway to my bedroom. He returns a few minutes later with the paper bag we keep the sharps in lodged underneath his arm.

"You're a bloody drama queen," I say as I walk into the kitchen to get a drink.

Luka doesn't respond. He sits down again, fishes a syringe out of the bag, and after a few seconds of contemplation, pushes it into one of his veins. He fills the syringe with his own blood and then starts to use it as a fountain pen on the paper in front of him.

"Great, now I live with the fucking Marquis de Sade," I shout and bugger off to bed, chasing dreams that won't come.

By morning, Luka is back underneath the table.

It's summer, and Luka is staggering up Telegraph Avenue toward the Free Clinic. He knows he has had too much to drink, and he's pretty certain he has just done something incredibly stupid. His t-shirt and left trouser-leg are drenched in blood, his own, and he's starting to feel lightheaded. Instinctively, he tries to keep his left arm above the level of his heart to slow the blood flow. Things are turning out very, very wrong; he hadn't intended to cut that deep.

He makes it to the clinic and goes up to the reception desk with the usual drunk-Luka-swagger. "Can I get a Band-Aid, please?" he asks, while blood drips onto the floor.

The volunteer medic looks at Luka and at the puddle of blood that is slowly forming on the floor next to him. "Can I see the injury?" he asks.

Luka smirks and slowly extends his arm, noting in a fairly detached way how the blood is dripping onto the papers strewn on the reception desk.

The medic winces when he sees the deep cut running diagonally across Luka's arm. This is no suicidal cut; there are no veins that are sliced open. This is a cut inflicted entirely for the purpose of causing pain, and it is much too deep; the bone is exposed. He shakes his head, "A Band-Aid won't do any good," he says matter-of-factly. "You need stitches, and you need them before you lose much more blood."

Luka nods and walks out of the clinic, setting off for Alta Bates Medical Center down the road. By the time he arrives there, the bleeding has diminished somewhat. There is still a small trickle of blood oozing out of the cut, but the big fat drops of blood stopped falling somewhere around Dwight Way. Luka walks into the emergency room and mutters, "Home, sweet home," under his breath before making his way to the triage station.

As always the old rule holds, even for people like him who are clearly without medical insurance: if you are acting psychotic or bleeding heavily from an open wound, you get seen first. Luka is very good at doing both. The nurse looks up and takes in the blood all over him. "Name?" she asks.

Luka frantically tries to recall what he told them last time. Oh well, here it goes. "Johnnie Walker," he says.

The nurse clearly doesn't have a sense of humor, because she just looks at him and raises an eyebrow. "How did you hurt yourself?" she asks.

"Umm, some crackhead attacked me with a broken bottle?" Luka ventures.

She obviously doesn't believe that one either. "I see," she says, "I'll be right back."

This isn't going well, Luka decides. The silly cow has gone to get security and they are bound to 51-50 him and cart him over to Herrick, and he really isn't up for that today. He gets up and bolts from the hospital before they can commit him, and then he's walking up Telegraph Avenue again, trying to figure out which bathroom he can use to bandage his arm. He's been permanently barred from Cody's, although he can't remember why except that there was a lot of alcohol involved. Eventually, he settles for Michael's Vegetarian Diner.

The waiters are a little too disturbed by the look of him with all the blood on his clothes to deny him the request to use the bathroom. He goes in and wraps a stack of paper towels around his arm as a makeshift bandage held in place by congealing blood and the sleeve of his sweater. Then he gets on a bus to go home.

I wake up at four o'clock in the morning because I'm bursting for a piss and stagger into the bathroom in the dark. I notice something is wrong even without turning on the light. There are bloodied paper towels all over the bathroom floor. I curse under my breath, thinking Luka has finally managed to accidentally kill himself, and head into the living room. He is lying in his sleeping bag underneath the dining room table, and his arm is bleeding.

I shake him awake, which takes far too long for my liking. Even when he sits up, he seems strangely distant and deathly pale, and all I can think is, fuck, he's lost too much blood this time. "Why didn't you go to the hospital?" I ask.

"I tried, but they wanted to 51-50 me and I'm not going to Herrick today!" he replies petulantly.

So I bundle him into the car and start driving toward Highland Hospital. It's a county hospital, and unlike Alta Bates, they're good at sticking their heads in the sand.

When the triage nurse asks how he got the cut, Luka meets her eyes full on and replies, "I was trying to give myself tiger stripe tattoos."

The nurse raises an eyebrow, clearly not believing a word of what Luka is telling her, before nodding slowly and saying, "Next time make sure you have black ink," before ushering him off to a cubicle. An hour later, Luka's cut is superglued together, and he is released to my care without further questions.

It's Wednesday evening when I finally run out of patience. I've been up for six days, and I'm no longer certain whether it's Friday's speed or the worrying about Luka that's keeping me awake. I'd like to believe that it's the sleep-deprivation that motivates me to do what I do, but in my gut I know differently.

I pick up the telephone and dial the number of a pager I rarely call. An hour later I'm driving across the Bay Bridge to a seedy neighborhood in the City to pick up a very expensive bag of China White for Luka. At this point, Mexican Black Tar heroin would be a waste of money; the only thing I know that will bring Luka out of even the most desperate catatonic state is a dream brought on by the finest China White heroin, and east-coast-quality China White can be gotten for the right amount of money, even in California, if you know where to look.

Every drug exacts its price: the price Luka paid for those months in Portland more than seven years ago is the knowledge that for him true peace, true happiness, is only ever achieved half-way between life and death in heroin dreams. Yet even heroin is nothing more than a quick-fix medication, and the effects wear off after a while.

5

Fragments: Through the Kaleidoscope of Truth

*I*t's very late when I'm shaken out of post-coital fatigue by loud knocking on the front door. Sally is up and moving to get dressed before I've shed the last of the sleepiness and stagger to my feet. "What time is it?" I mumble, trying to keep my balance while stepping into a pair of boxers.

"Just after two in the morning," Sally responds. "Who would knock at this time?"

I barely suppress a catty comment and reply, "Take a wild guess," before making my way to the front door without waiting for an answer.

When I unbolt the door and pull it open, Luka is lounging there, bracing himself against the frame. He's barely upright. "What happened to your keys?" I ask.

He looks at me uncomprehendingly for a moment and then staggers forward, whispering, "Ciaran?"

I catch him just before he falls and shake my head. He makes a sound halfway between a whimper and a sigh, his body heavily draped across my own, and mumbles, "Ba mhaith liom dul abhaile, a Chiaráin."

"It's James, Luka," I correct gently, walking him toward the sofa.

Once he settles into the cushions, Luka starts a chant, a litany of sorts, a recitation of names that are almost forgotten, left behind in the Old World long ago, almost all of them a verbal slap in the face.

I bend down to pull up one of Luka's half-closed lids and look at his pupil. It's reactive; only a matter of time then, and we have plenty of that.

Behind me somebody stirs, and when I look around, Sally is standing in the doorway. "Shouldn't we call an ambulance?" she asks.

"He's fine."

"For God's sake, James, he's incoherent!" Sally exclaims.

I shake my head. "He's perfectly coherent, but not necessarily in English."

Sally raises an eyebrow and looks back and forth between the two of us questioningly. "I don't recognize the language."

"Irish. He's speaking Irish."

"Oh. I didn't know—" Sally says before lapsing into silence as Luka's voice grows more urgent, unmistakably calling out names I have no desire to hear or explain. As if on cue, Sally asks, "Who's Ciaran?"

I wince. "I am."

Sally rallies beautifully. "Reality check," she says, "your names is James."

"That too," I agree.

"I see," she says curtly, "and I suppose Luka isn't really called Luka either?"

"He is now."

"And who is he really?" she asks.

"Exactly who he says he is," I reply.

"Oh for God's sake, James, if that is really your name," she's quite exasperated now, "are you completely incapable of giving me a straight answer?"

"Of course I'm not," I reply.

She nods slowly, looking at Luka who is beginning to stir on the sofa still muttering to himself. "Who is Catriona?"

I can't suppress the shudder, and my throat feels raw. "No one."

The door opens, and dull black hair and green silk twirls into the room on three-inch heels, plunging it into momentary silence. She lifts her arms like Christ welcoming his apostles to the last supper, and the silk slides back to reveal her stigmata. She smiles crookedly, some of the spark returning to her eyes, and the assembled party sighs. Their eyes follow her every movement; their rapt attention is focused on her face, bearing the mark of thorns.

They would follow her to heaven and hell and purgatory, all save one.

In this crowd, I have been cast, not Judas yet—never Judas—but Thomas. I know her power, but I doubt her deity.

I cannot rightly tell how long I stand there, my mind wandering, revisiting the past. I'm pulled back to the present by Luka's harsh, loud laugh. "And that is why you never deserved Her, James," he spits out, opening his eyes, alert again.

I fall back against the wall and allow my back to slide down pressed to the plaster, before burying my face in my hands, wondering whether Luka truly takes pleasure in pouring oil onto smoldering coals. I'm occasionally given to thinking that Luka conducts scientific experiments into the finer points of the human psyche, not out of viciousness, but to amuse himself. For most of his adult life, he has displayed an innate talent for sticking his fingers into festering wounds. Wounds that had best be left alone.

"Who is Catriona, Luka?" Sally asks, her tone edged with hysteria. It makes me wonder just how often she asked the question before I came back to myself.

Through the mists of pain that are settling in my mind, I can hear Luka answering, "Catriona is the one we go to extreme pains never to mention in front of James; She'll be dead eight years come All Souls' Day."

Luka has always been a shrewd observer of the human condition, and I really should not be surprised that when asked, he chooses to answer questions as bluntly and honestly as only he could. Yet the pain still coils tightly inside my gut at his words.

And I suppose if I had any sense at all, I would be walking out of room right now, but there is something to Luka's tone of voice, something raw and sharp and barely contained, that makes me want to conduct an experiment of my own. Except for family, Luka hardly interacts with the female of the species, and I admit, I harbor some perverse curiosities as far as his interactions with women are concerned.

"Just a girl then," Sally says, quietly moving around me into the room. "She was just some girl."

Luka's laughter this time is braying. "She was one in a million," he says, the smile in his voice evident even though I can't bring myself to look at him. "Of course I'm biased, I was so in love with the Bitch, still am for all my troubles. It's a bittersweet feeling now for the most part, a pain remembered in moments of contemplation and then locked far away again at the back of the might-have-been compartment of my heart where even those damned angels the priests would have us believe in fear to tread. You've got to understand though, She never threw me a bone, never messed with my head as royally as She fucked with my brother's."

Luka sighs almost blissfully. Long-forgotten memories are swirling in my mind, and bile is rising in my throat. Curled up in an almost fetal position, I start retching and throw up on the floor.

There is movement at the edge of my vision, and then Luka's hand settles between my shoulder blades, rubbing slow circles. I wish I could move away, but it's too late for escape now; I'm paralyzed with some unnamed emotion and Luka knows it.

"I'm sorry, James," he murmurs.

I force myself to nod, though I know he isn't really sorry. He's been waiting for years to say his piece.

Sally's voice, shriller than I have ever heard it before, interrupts the momentary silence. "Why exactly is it you don't like me, Luka?"

If I weren't feeling so thoroughly rotten right now, I would smile. It takes a special kind of arrogance and desperation to twist attention back to oneself like that. I raise my head just enough to see a look of genuine bafflement on Luka's face before he smiles faintly and replies, "I don't dislike you. You're just one in a long line of my brother's playmates I've seen come through that door, and you won't be the last."

Sally's expression changes from one of disbelief to anger. Luka has never been disrespectful to her face. Oh, he has ignored her at times and answered her in mocking tones at others, but he has never been palpably rude until now. "That's really all you see me as? A—a whore?" she asks incredulously.

Next to me, Luka is grinning wolfishly. "That's all you are, Sally. Don't fool yourself into believing you could possibly become more than that," he says. "Then again, you're quite aware of your status in this house already, so why not ask the questions you really mean to ask?"

"What answers do you think I'm looking for?" Sally snaps back.

"Answers?" Luka smiles. "Very well, the answers to your questions are: no, no, no, and yes. In that order."

Sally sighs. "What are the questions, Luka?"

"No, he doesn't love you. No, you'll never change him. No, I can't tell you anything that would make it possible for you to change him, but yes, I could tell you why, although I'm not sure that you'd be satisfied with my explanation."

"Well?" Sally asks, just as I pull myself together enough to manage a strangled, "No!"

Luka's fingers fasten around my biceps. His voice is low and steady when he says, "I'm sorry, James," again, just as insincerely, before continuing evenly. "A few years back, Micky referred to Catriona in a less than flattering context, probably to see what would happen, mostly to piss James off, I think. It ended in a most unpleasant scene with plenty of broken furniture, some broken bones, and quite a few other incidental injuries. James hasn't talked to Micky since. Of course, that might be because Micky isn't talking to James either.

"My point is that James—" he half turns to look at me, "you have never been forced to deal with the reality of what happened." He turns back to Sally, ignoring my erratic breathing wholesale except for the ever-tightening grip on my arm while he continues talking, not to Sally, but to me. "From where I've been standing, you've been doing very little except relive the most disastrous relationship in the history of the Sheahan clan, and I don't need to tell you that us Sheahans have turned dysfunctional relationships into an art form."

I try to shake my head in denial, but I'm still frozen, all my concentration focused on continuing to breathe. He suddenly lets go of my arm, letting the blood flow back to my hand, and darts across the room to rummage through his backpack, muttering, "I know it's in here somewhere."

"What is?" Sally asks, attempting to sound bored even through the slight hitch in her voice.

Luka pulls a notebook from his pack and flips through it for a second before pulling out a sheet and saying, "This. This is Her."

Sally gasps and my stomach starts churning again. This is impossible. I wiped every trace of Her existence from our lives years ago.

"Interesting, isn't it?" Luka says lightly. "Every woman that has walked through that door has looked like a cheap, second-rate copy of Her. You included. I don't think James has ever realized it, but I have. Look at the picture and then take a good, hard look at yourself in the mirror. He's fucking you because he can't fuck a corpse that has been dead and buried eight years."

My eyes shut tightly against the world, She comes to me softly in the night. Over the howling of the wind outside, I can hear whispers of sweet old country lilt. On my lips I can taste familiar flavors: the bitterness of stale tobacco, the caramel of Irish whiskey, and the sickly sweetness of a mouth that hasn't seen sustenance in the better part of a couple of days.

The fire within builds, and there is a jarring moment of truth brought by a faint moan in the wrong key. The familiar taste on my tongue turns to alien flavors, bubble gum and cherry cola and thousands of other vulgar American seasonings. My eyes fly open, and in the half-light from the lamp outside I can almost make-believe that it is really She, risen from the dead like Christ himself. Then my vision adjusts, and there is nothing but ash on my lips and the wrong woman bearing down on my cock, face caught in a grimace of ecstasy.

I turn away swiftly, once again failing to recapture a dream lost long ago.

"We don't fuck, Luka. We're having a relationship," Sally hisses.

I raise my head, fight the waves of nausea, and force out the words. "We fuck. Nothing more."

Luka smirks and walks to where Sally is rising out of the cushions of the sofa like Venus enraged. His hands close around her shoulders and push her back down, gently but firmly. With his mouth inches from Sally's ear, he quietly says, "Oh, he fucks you all right, honey. He takes you and gets what he wants while he's up there in the stratosphere, and then he has you dressed and out of the door before he hits solid ground. Ever wonder why he provokes you into leaving just as soon as the stars stop dancing in front of your eyes? It's so he doesn't have to see your face come morning and sobriety. It's so he doesn't have to face the truth: you are not Her."

Still almost immobile, I can feel my head nodding erratically in agreement.

Luka grins, absentmindedly playing with a strand of Sally's hair. "My brother has always had good taste in women though, so maybe, once you've stopped deluding yourself, and if you get me enough cocaine, I'll fuck you too."

Sally turns her head and shoves Luka away, "No."

"Your loss," he leers at her, "because I can be so much nicer than he'll ever be. I can do slow and gentle when you want it. I can even whisper sweet nothings and kiss you just like you've always wanted him to. I can give you a pretty good approximation of his body without the attitude or the baggage."

"So you're thinking you're God's gift to women now?" Sally spits out. Her arms, wrapped around her chest protectively, betray her fear despite the bravado of her tone.

Luka leans in closer again, tracing lips along Sally's neck, as he whispers, "No, Sally, I am God's reward to you for putting up with my brother."

For a fleeting moment it looks as if Sally is about to give in, but then her entire body tenses, her spine straightens, and she slaps Luka's face away. Luka laughs as he stumbles backwards and settles on the floor a few feet from me. "Little girl, do you think you'll be the only one of my brother's castoffs that I wouldn't fuck? I've always settled for the scraps he throws me, and eventually, he'll throw you my way too."

"I don't believe you," Sally says. There is doubt in her voice.

This time it's me who starts braying with laughter. My fingers scrabbling against the wall, trying to find handholds, I pull myself up to my feet. "Luka doesn't lie, Sally," I choke out. "For all his faults, he never lies."

Tears start running down Sally's face and Luka sighs. "Look, for what it's worth, you've lasted a hell of a lot longer than any of the others," he says, bending the truth rather than lying. He doesn't tell her that in my warped mind that translated as my hating her much more than I hated the others, who were blessed with indifference, if blessed is the right word.

That only makes her cry harder. "How can he—" she shudders and turns to me. "How can you let your life be dictated by a woman who has been dead for eight years?"

Luka looks at me pleadingly. "James, tell her." I suspect he wasn't bargaining for this.

"I—" I start, my voice scratchy and alien to my own ears.

"Tell her, or I will," Luka insists. He pauses just long enough to realize I won't—can't—speak, before continuing. "Once upon a time in London, James lost his faith, and like the good Catholic boy he was, he lost more than just that."

I sink down to my knees before the prone body of my goddess and cease to believe. Years of worship and dedication to everything that gave meaning to my life and this is what remains: an empty husk. If my obsession was not great enough for Her to cling to life, then no obsession will do.

My eyes start scanning the room, desperately searching for something— anything—I can believe in. In the dim light they settle upon the syringe on the floor a few feet away, still half-drawn and bloody, mocking me much like the image of a savior I no longer believe in nailed to the wall above.

I draw in a breath, my eyes still fixed on the floor, and I know with absolute certainty that there is only one altar I will worship at now, and at its center, my new altarpiece: a hollow plastic cross.

I look at Luka and for a moment our eyes do battle. "You don't know shit," I finally say, my voice shaking.

"She betrayed us both," Luka replies quietly.

I shake my head. "No. She never betrayed me."

"Jesus fucking Christ, James," Luka yells. "She died! That was her ultimate treachery."

"She—" I can't bring myself to finish the sentence.

"Our gods are supposed to be immortal, James. That is their only duty," Luka shouts. "And She was too much of a Bitch to give us even that."

"You are wrong," I mumble, even as my knees give out underneath me again and I'm doubling over with a new onslaught of sickness.

Through the tunnel vision, I can hear Sally far away, "She was human."

Luka's voice carries through the confusion reigning in my mind. "The line between humanity and divinity can be a little blurred at times," he says calmly. "Have you ever read old Irish fairytales? That's what She reminded me of, the tales my granddaddy used to spin when I was a little boy. I don't remember much of them, he died when I was four, but what I do remember is linked indelibly to my image of Her. Old tales of the Sidhe and their thrall.

"That was Her power, more than anything else. She mesmerized everyone She met and inspired undying loyalty in Her court. She was the kind of woman that poets write about. Don't get me wrong, She was never Juliet, never innocence and sweetness, never easy to love. She was fickle and dark and dangerous. She was Helen of Troy and Ovid's Corinna. That was the legend.

"She also spent most of her adult life strung out on heroin. She was a faithless whore who fucked everything with a dick and quite a few women, not always for money, and often in full view of my brother. He took every single blow and turned the other cheek, worshiping the ground She walked on. That was the reality.

"I suspect the truth as he sees it lies somewhere between the two."

I struggle to rise, my hands trying to find purchase amid the vomit on the carpet and shout, "You have no right to talk of Her!"

Luka laughs. "I have more right than you," he replies.

Sally's next question is inevitable, but I have been dreading it nonetheless. "Why?"

It's three in the morning and colder than I thought possible. It's snowing here for the first time in years.

She stands on the balcony dressed in her bartending clothes, a skimpy skirt and sleeveless shirt, and the snowflakes are swirling around her shivering body like tears.

I try to block out the sobbing in the far corner and open the door to step through into winter.

My throat is opening and closing with the effort to speak, but words fail me. What could I possibly say that would repair the damage I have done?

Through the fog in my mind I can hear Luka talking softly. "You are asking the wrong brother," he says. "They ran off together; disappeared for a while. By the time they got back and I came into the picture, it had all gone to hell in a handcart already. James has never explained that to me, and I can't really ask, what with the entire not-mentioning-the-Bitch rule. I think Patrick knows what happened, but he's never let on."

I say a silent prayer of thanks, because Luka just confirmed that nobody knows. Nobody knows just how badly, how irrevocably, I fucked up. My hopes that nobody has guessed are shattered with his next sentence though. "I'm guessing," he continues, "that James was the one who fucked up big, because guilt is just about the only thing that keeps us failed Catholics going." He shrugs. "Or maybe it's all just in James' head. God knows neither of the both of them ever did anything half-arsed. Doesn't matter either way, does it? It still went to hell."

"Look, far be it from me to dish out advice, but you seem like a nice girl, even if you have a few issues," Luka says. "You're not entirely stupid, and you look decent enough. You should go and find yourself a nice bloke who will make you happy, because James will never do that; he'll never be a worthwhile project for you. The Bitch ruined him for other women, just as She ruined me. It's the price we paid for loving Her."

Sally is still sniffling, but she is smiling more or less bravely through her tears. "Luka, the whole insanity thing is just an act, isn't it?"

Luka laughs. "I assure you I am still stark-raving mad," he chuckles. "But the fact that I realize I'm bonkers probably makes me much saner than any of my brothers. There's a certain peace of mind to be found in knowing exactly how unhinged you really are."

"And he doesn't, does he?" Sally murmurs sadly, more to herself than to Luka.

"He is living a nightmare of his own devising," Luka says quietly. "He created his own monsters. We all do, but he has never been forced to face his. If Patrick had had any sense at all he would have forced James to deal with his issues years ago."

"Why haven't you—" Sally begins.

"Because James owes Patrick more than he's ever owed anyone else, and no one but Patrick can change that. But Patrick won't, because there's nothing quite as effective for keeping James in check as dangling Damocles' sword over his head," Luka laughs almost bitterly.

This is where I act, where I have to move, mostly because I cannot bear listening to another word. I pull myself together and get up onto my own two feet, taking a few hesitant steps toward the sofa. Sally's eyes meet mine, and all I can see in her eyes is pity.

Rage, stronger than I've felt in years, overwhelms me. My hands clench into fists at my sides as I think about the things I will do to the deceitful, double-crossing rat who calls himself my brother. I expected this from Micky, who goes out of his way to gall me, show his disdain for all that I am. I expected this from Patrick even, because Patrick, self-righteous as he is, would rationalize that it was for my own good. I never expected it from Luka, whom I've raised like a son, whom I've coddled and humored and supported for all these years. Luka has finally crossed a line, broken one taboo too many, and he will pay for it, in blood and sweat and tears. I bring my fists up level with my chest in anticipation. The fury engulfs me.

Then I see the photograph lying on the coffee table. I thought I had locked up every single picture of Her, removed every trace of Her face from our lives. Reeling with shock, I look away and turn to Sally for distraction. Sally of the green eyes and the raven hair, Sally who looks just like—I'm panicking now. No, James, don't go there. Think different thoughts. Deny everything. Nothing is real.

By now Luka has noticed my balled fists. "I am sorry, James," he says again, "but there are truths you can't keep at bay with a mean right hook."

I nod, because his words are a needle and thread sewing my throat shut and tying my vocal chords into a knot. At the same time the traitor in my mind is screaming at me, shouting no, he's not sorry at all, James, he is forcing you to do what Patrick never accomplished, no matter how many times he beat you to bloody pulp. He's trying to force you to confront your demons, James, because one day soon you'll have to face the past.

I try to drown out the voice by repeating a litany of my own. This isn't real. This never happened. This is all just make-believe. Reality itself is what has gone off-kilter. If I refuse to acknowledge what is happening, if I refuse to believe in the existence of the scene in front of me, then it cannot be true.

You keep on trying to tell yourself that Ciaran James Sheahan, the voice in my head cackles maniacally. You try the escapism route again, see if it works any better now than it did the last few hundred times you tried. By the end of the night you'll still be running for the safety net of drug-induced torpor.

I join the cacophony of laughter inside my head with laughter of my own. Manic, hysterical laughter, because I'm not the crazy one. Luka is the madman, so how come I can hear those perfidious voices inside my own mind? I decide then that it must be a nightmare of sorts. No sane man would ever have an internal argument with disenfranchised voices, voices he could not claim as his own.

Luka is looking decidedly worried now.

As the laughter dies in my throat, I try to focus on Sally, but I have to avert my eyes because she looks so much like Her, I cannot bear to see her face while a heart is beating in my chest. Sally sees and understands. Today is the end of the line for us. She isn't even angry anymore. She just picks up her car keys and walks out the door without a single word or a single look back. Still the voices are heckling me, trying desperately to recapture my attention. I ignore them as best I can; they aren't real.

My eyes travel back to the photograph still lying on the floor. I don't know how long I stand there staring at a face I have done my best to forget. I drink in the raven hair, the fair and freckled skin, the bright red lipstick that was always slightly smudged, and I lose myself in the green oceans that were Her eyes.

I close my eyes to imprint the memory of Her face, and when I open them again, Luka is snatching up the picture and returning it to the safety of his notebook.

Finally, an eternity later, when my throat finally unties itself enough to strive for actual speech, with my voice still shaking, I ask Luka, "Have they all looked like Her?"

Luka never answers my question. I stand there, forlorn and hurting, unable to move for what seems like hours, frantically trying to hold in my mind the image of Her that is already fading fast. It hurts more than the overdose a few weeks ago, more than dying could possibly hurt me. There is a weight on my chest and it's getting harder to breathe and amid the ever-expanding hysteria I ask myself whether this is what drowning feels like.

Truth be told, I want to drown, I'd give anything to drown in those eyes. Instead I am still standing there, unable to move because my chest yet again feels like it's about to explode, standing there like a stone, unable even to cry, because I am cold as ice and hard as steel.

Stock-still, standing in the middle of the room, I become acutely aware of my heartbeat, of the blood pulsing through the arteries in my neck, of the ragged breaths that give way to hyperventilation, of the life that persists in animating my broken body.

In my mind I curse myself, because if I had the guts, I could have ended it all years ago. Oh, I'm not self-destructive in the way Luka is, his arms sliced from wrist to elbow, but in my darker moments I have contemplated death. I have mapped it out in my head countless times: a bottle of vodka, a steaming bathtub, and a cut-throat razor, or maybe a syringe of heroin, if I could get over my aversion to heroin, or maybe an overdose of those sleeping pills I eat like candy on the nights I need to sleep. In the end though, the little Catholic boy always wins out, and I don't follow through. I just continue the torture of living every day without Her. I continue the charade and stick needles into my arms, half-hoping that one day a needle will get me, half-knowing that I will never be Luka and harm myself beyond the catharsis of the needle.

That's why I keep on standing here, letting the pain wash over me in waves, reliving memories I thought banished forever.

Eventually, Luka comes over and forces a couple of pills into my mouth, probably Valium. Thank Christ for synthetic opiates. Then he raises a glass of water to my lips and prompts me to swallow. He grabs me around the waist and starts leading me into the bedroom, holding me as he maneuvers me onto the bed and lies down next to me. I wrap my arms around him and hold on tight, and for the first time since he was a little boy, he doesn't fight my embrace.

The tears start flowing and I don't much care whether Luka will think me a pansy for my wanton display of weakness. I sob into Luka's chest and don't stop again until all the pent-up anger and aggression has flown out of my eyes. Then, in the world between waking and sleeping, I whisper in his ear all I failed to tell Her in my foolishness, thinking I had a lifetime to speak. Luka just holds me, even tighter than before, his arms wrapped around my chest, and listens with tears running down his face.

6

Apotheosis: Finding My Religion

There is a brief period of respite lasting until just after Ascension Day, and then Luka storms into the house one afternoon, moments away from descending into hysteria. He strides straight past me to the back porch and nervously lights up a cigarette, repeating his new mantra with a shaky voice, "Deny everything. Deny everything. It isn't real. It is only in my head. Deny everything!"

I sit down next to him as he starts to sob frantically. "Luka, what happened?" I ask, although I already know the answer. I can smell her on him. That particular mixture of strawberry shampoo, French perfume and feminine musk I have come to associate with Sally. It certainly explains where he has been for a whole night and the better part of a day. This is one of the few Luka crises I cannot handle.

I look at my watch; it's 3 o'clock in the morning in England. Well,

Patrick hasn't had to deal with Luka for a while.

I walk into the kitchen, pick up the cordless, and hit speed dial number one. He answers on the fourth ring. "Morning, James," he says sleepily.

"Hi, Patrick. How are Annie and the kids?" I ask, thinking how ridiculous it is that all our early-morning calls start with pleasantries.

Patrick chuckles into the phone. "Annie is well," he says. "As for the kids, Liam discovered Annie's old drum set and is driving us all bonkers, Shane is falling off skateboards a lot, Siobhan is asking for a pony, and the twins are toddling. I was going to call you later this week anyway to tell you Annie's expecting again. We're hoping for another girl."

I fake a disgusted grunt and tease, "You know, Patrick, when the revolution comes you'll be the first against the wall on account of single-handedly overpopulating England with your brood. I mean, it's nice to know that an old fart like you has a hobby, but I would have thought five was more than enough."

Patrick sounds nonplussed. "You're just jealous I get some," he says. "Anyway, this will probably be the last one, what with Annie turning forty next year. Seriously though, I'm sure you didn't call at this unholy hour in order to inquire after the health of my children and my sex life."

I glance out the kitchen window to make sure Luka is still out of earshot before I quietly say, "I'm having a bit of a situation with Luka. He's been having a rough time of late, and I guess he went out and got some from one of my exes last night—"

Patrick whistles down the line. This isn't the first time that particular ugly monster has reared its head. "Does he know you know?" he asks.

"I don't think so," I reply. "But he's hysterical anyway and it's not as if I can talk him out of this one without letting him know I know."

Patrick sighs. "All right," he says, "give me a minute to fetch the Scotch and then let me talk to him."

I walk back out on the porch where Luka is still hysterically repeating his mantra and hand him the phone. "It's for you," I say, "Patrick."

"Tell him I don't want to talk to him," Luka shouts between sobs.

"Tell him yourself," I respond, firmly pressing the phone into Luka's hand. Then I go back inside the house and close the door. I don't latch it though, because I'm planning to listen to Luka's end of the conversation.

Luka is repeatedly saying, "Nothing is wrong. It didn't happen. It isn't real. Deny everything."

Patrick must be telling him that he doesn't sound all right, because Luka starts to get snotty. "News flash, Patrick. I'm not exactly known for my happy disposition," he yells. "I would've thought you figured that one out when I tried to slit my wrist in your basement, but you just had to do the noble thing and up and save me. Overzealous bastard!"

A short silence follows and then Luka shouts, "Fine! You want to know what's wrong, let me tell you what's wrong: I fucked James' whore, and this time it wasn't because I was drunk or out of my brains. I was stone-cold sober, and I did it because I wanted to and she wanted me."

Now there's a new one, I think. Hitherto Luka has not been known for any sexual acts performed without chemical aid. I don't really mind because Sally and I are definitely no longer together in any sense of the word and she wouldn't be the first former lover to invite Luka into her bed. Truth be told, most times I encourage this sort of thing because it ensures that Luka gets laid and I get the broads off my back, but I can see how Luka could be disturbed by the thought of taking one of my discards while completely sober; he has his pride after all.

Luka has started sobbing uncontrollably. "No, it's not all right, Patrick," he says between gasps for air. "I crossed a line today. She was James' and it don't matter that they broke up, she was still his. He never told me I could have her, but I took her anyway because I wanted to and I enjoyed it. I don't enjoy sex. I don't have sex. I don't even like girls."

Behind the door I cringe. I never informed Patrick of that little turn of events, never let it slip that in my expert opinion, Luka has never been overly interested in the fairer sex; Patrick tends to follow the Catholic party line a bit too closely in that regard. He must have said something though, because a few seconds later Luka explodes: "Oh grow up, Patrick, and leave God out of this. I'm not too interested in fucking anyone. You know that. All I'm saying is that the female body does next to nothing for me."

Marvelous, simply marvelous, Patrick isn't going to leave that one alone, I think to myself on the other side of the door. Luka's laughing hysterically now. "Haven't you worked that one out yet, Patrick?" he yells amid the laughter. "For crying out loud, stop guzzling the scotch, it ain't gonna help. Your brother's still going straight down to hell if those priests of yours can be trusted."

Great, Luka has just very loudly and effectively outed himself to the entire neighborhood. Christ, and Patrick is not going to drop it any time soon; he's bound to be up in arms. Luka isn't having any of it though; he's chuckling maniacally. "What do you want me to say, Patrick?" he snarls. "You want a detailed account of just how repulsive pussies are?"

I would like nothing better than to hear Patrick's contributions to the conversation right about now because he must be close to apoplexy. Whatever he's saying, it's not doing anything to calm Luka down any. "No, Patrick, I'm not gay," he yells. "That would imply that I've actually had sex with a man, and all I ever seem to end up with are James' cast-offs."

That surprises me. I don't actually ask Luka what, or more precisely, who he gets busy with, don't really want to know either, but I'd always assumed that—Christ, I'm such an idiot! It all makes sense now. All that tiptoeing around the Kid, all that anxiety over fucking my whores. The lad must be so confused: twenty-five years old and he's never actually worked up the courage to get what he really wants. A curse on the church and all its henchmen.

He's getting suspiciously calm now. "So you see, Patrick," he says, "I really shouldn't have wanted James' whore all that much. I fucked her anyway, and I don't know why because she didn't belong to me. None of them ever belong to me, but at least I have the decency to wait for James to say it's OK. He didn't tell me this time. Where does it stop? Do I come over there and fuck Annie too? I might as well put us all out of our misery and just shoot myself."

Well if he shoots himself, the dumb fuck ain't doing it in my house, because there's no way in hell I'll clean his brains out of the carpet, I think, and then realize what I'm thinking. This is my brother. How can I even think those thoughts about him when he has done nothing wrong? She was just a girl after all. Just some girl who could tolerate my moods and provide mind-boggling sex when I wanted it.

A woman who got fed up with my chronic lack of interest in being darned like an old sock and decided to throw herself at my brother instead, because Luka can provide an almost identical body and a much less resentful mind. It makes me wonder whether the similarities go beyond physical resemblance. Does he respond to the same stimuli? Did he purr when she ran her nails along his spine? Did he hiss with pleasure when she nipped his thighs just before—Jesus fucking Christ, why am I doing this?

"It doesn't matter, Patrick," Luka shouts, startling me out of my

67

thoughts. "I'll just kill myself and refuse to believe it is really happening. As long as I deny everything, it isn't real!"

I groan inwardly. I have been punished for my sins with a lunatic for a brother, a lunatic who, by the sounds of it, has read Kafka quite recently. I remember too late why Patrick usually doesn't deal with Luka in these states: even though he is quite frantic, he is still capable of his own brand of cold logic.

I'm almost certain that Patrick, at the end of his tether, started to argue church doctrine again, because I'm jolted out of my private misery by Luka, who has stood up from his seat on the porch steps and is yelling down the phone for the entire neighborhood to hear, "There is no god. God is dead."

I collectively curse Nietzsche and Marx behind the door. This is America, where, no matter what his supposed constitutional rights, Luka's announcement that god is dead will have the neighborhood up in arms for weeks to come. This is America, where Luka is free to believe in any god he chooses, provided he chooses a god, preferably a Christian one.

"I hate to break it to you, Patrick, but Berkeley cheated," Luka shouts, snapping me out of my thoughts. "He theorized himself into a corner and simply made a semantic exception for God."

I can't decide whether I should laugh, because Patrick has never been an intellectual match for Luka, whose pleasure reading has the unique ability to bring on migraines in others. Still, as the alpha male, Patrick hasn't had much practice at conceding defeat either, and he believes fervently enough to stand his ground.

When Luka finally speaks again, his tone is fairly calm, but also much harsher than I ever expected. "I'm not even going to point out the logical contradictions in your argument, Patrick," he snarls. "I'm just going to pose a few simple questions: what kind of God would allow a two-year-old child to get hit by a bus? What kind of God would let you leave us? What kind of God would choose to kill Catriona and keep me alive?"

Behind the door I sink to the floor. I shouldn't be listening to this conversation.

I'm walking up the road to our house on not entirely sober legs. I really hadn't intended to go out and get pissed, but Phil and Lenny asked me to go for a pint after work. Micky has been off at university for two months now, and Declan is a big brute of seventeen who can take care of himself, so I thought what the hell, it's just a pint. Well, one pint turned into five or six, and then it was closing time, and I felt a little stab of guilt because I'd told Catriona that I would be home by seven, but it's not every day that I go for a drink with my mates.

I let myself into the house, still kind of wobbly because I'm not used to the alcohol any more, and before I can so much as switch on the light, I hear an unearthly howl and Declan body-slams me into the wall. He's shrieking, a high-pitched wail that makes my bones ache, as he starts attacking me indiscriminately with his fists. Sweet Jesus, I've heard that noise before, once, from a most unlikely source.

He's screaming something, but his words are so indiscernible amid the wailing that I can't make out what he's on about. I don't need to. Someone's dead. Mother made that noise when my grandfather died. I block his blows as best I can, but I don't fight back. Better to let him get it out of his system. After a few minutes he starts growing tired and his caterwauling turns to sobbing.

"You utter bastard!" he screams as he throws himself at me again. "You were supposed to be here tonight."

"I'm sorry," I wheeze, winded from trying to keep out of harm's way. "I went for a drink. Just a drink. I'm here now."

"Yeah, well, you're too fucking late," Declan shouts with renewed vigor as one of his balled fists grazes my kidney. "You killed her!"

It takes me a few seconds to file his words in the appropriate categories of my foggy mind, and then realization hits me and another voice joins in the howling. Holy Mother of God, am I making that noise? My knees are buckling underneath my weight, and the walls are crashing in around me. I'm dimly aware that I'm hyperventilating, driving myself to the brink of unconsciousness. Oblivion would be a blessing right now.

Declan won't allow that though. He has become my equal in strength over the past few years, but tonight he is much stronger than I will ever be. He grabs me and hurls me across the room and forces my head to within inches of Her lifeless body.

I guess death was pretty instantaneous, because it doesn't look like Declan made any effort to revive Her, just left Her there for the coroner. She isn't a pretty sight; nobody who dies like that ever is. Yet She remains the most beautiful woman in the world.

I sink down on my knees before Her and know with absolute certainty that there is no god. No god, however evil, would have taken Her from me.

Declan, all out of punches, gets up and starts heading for the door. "You're the biggest cunt that ever lived!" He shouts before the door slams shut behind him.

On the porch Luka is shouting again. "Shut up, Patrick, and listen to me. You're using an ontological argument, and it's been proven to contain some definite linguistic weaknesses and quite possibly a few logical errors as well."

In the pause that follows, I find myself almost feeling sorry for Patrick. The poor sod is probably trying very hard to prove that god exists while Luka's on a roll.

"I don't give a flying fuck what you call it," Luka exclaims. "It's still an ontological argument, purely based on an *a priori* claim that doesn't meet the fundamental requirements of an analytic proposition, and since your god refuses to prove that he exists, he can't be filed as a synthetic proposition either. There you have it, god vanishes in a puff of Hume's radical empiricism, which he already would have done had Berkeley not cheated to start with."

Patrick seems to be giving Luka a run for his money, because Luka starts yelling again. "Fine, in that case you created your own god. We all make our own gods, and we make the gods we deserve. You and James made me god of your own private hell. I am your god. I am the god you raised, and I will be worshiped."

A few blissful seconds of silence follow and then the phone starts ringing. I have no desire to retrieve the cordless from Luka right now, so instead I head to my bedroom to pick up the other extension. Patrick skips the preliminaries this time. "Were you listening to that little tantrum?" he asks.

"Yeah, I was, and it's a new one," I admit. "He's never gone around claiming he's god before. He usually just sticks to proving that god does not exist. What the hell were you telling him?"

"I accused him of existentialism," Patrick chuckles. "He really can't stand the idea that he could be responsible for his own actions."

"Great idea, Patrick," I moan. "He's going to make me suffer for that one."

"Is he high, James?" Patrick interrupts, changing the subject.

"I don't think so," I reply. "I couldn't smell anything on him and his pupils looked normal. Of course, with Luka you never know."

Patrick sighs, "OK, here's what I think you should do: call an ambulance and call the police if you have to. He needs to be in a hospital."

I swear Patrick can actually hear me shaking my head, because he goes on to say, "You can't put it off much longer, James. He's losing it. This isn't just schizophrenia. This is megalomania. It's delusional. This is our brother turning into Caligula. This is our brother demanding to be worshiped. You've got to put a stop to it."

"Look, if you hadn't started the theological debate in the first place, he wouldn't go around claiming he is a god," I growl. "He's probably just doing it to piss you off, and I guess it's working."

"Speaking of which, since when has he gone around claiming he's a... a homosexual?" Patrick asks.

"You think you could come up with something slightly more clinical, Patrick?" I reply. "He's actually spent the better part of the past seven years reassuring me that he isn't, but I don't give a toss either way. What does it matter if he is?"

"Well, maybe it's just a phase," Patrick mumbles. "I mean, if it's true what he says and he's never actually—"

I don't let him finish that sentence. "You're one of the lousiest hypocrites it's ever been my misfortune to meet, Patrick," I snarl. "You need to get your head out of your arse and tell him you don't care whom or what he's fucking. God knows he deserves a little bit of happiness in his life. I need to go and talk to him, undo some of the damage you've done. I'll call you tomorrow."

I slam down the phone before Patrick can come up with an answer. It's time for my own brand of damage control. I fetch a couple of beer bottles from the fridge and walk back out to the porch, where Luka has calmed down a little bit. He takes a bottle and asks, "You were listening, weren't you?"

"Luka, the entire neighborhood was listening," I say humorlessly. "This isn't really about Sally, is it? Because you know I couldn't care less about that. She was just a toy, a nice toy—I guess you figured that one out too—but a toy nonetheless."

Yes, that's all she was, a toy. An excessively attractive toy oozing sex appeal out of every pore. Did he smell it on her? That unique scent of sin and damnation. Did he taste it? The sweet and enticing flavor of fallen women. Did he scream her name in her embrace? I have to stop thinking these thoughts. This isn't really about Sally.

"Luka, listen to me," I say, "if you're in love, if the chemistry is there, it doesn't matter all that much what the plumbing is like, if you know what I mean. Nobody, not me, nor Patrick, nor Micky, is going to think any the less of you just because of it. We just want you to be happy is all, and god damn the priests and the church and anyone who says differently."

"I am not gay," Luka says defensively. "I can't be."

I rub my eyes and sigh. "Why can't you be gay, Luka?"

Luka sits there silently for a long time before he turns and meets my eyes. "I've been in love with a girl. Once. Never happened again, but I'm still thinking it might, you know. I know I can fall in love with a girl, if nothing else."

"So you're just going to hang around being miserable and not go after any men you like on the off-chance that another girl turns your head?" I ask.

He blushes. "It's never been like that again, with anyone. Never. She was something special. You know that probably better than I do. I'm going to tell you this now, James, because I may never again have the gall to speak, and I've waited ten years to say it." He takes a long draught from the bottle before continuing. "I remember the day I knew for certain I was in love with Her."

I don't want to hear this, but I don't think I have a choice. I suppress the urge to get up and leave and start picking at the label of the beer bottle, while Luka's voice drones on.

"I was fifteen and it was summer and really hot. We were visiting Patrick, back when he and Annie were living in Ealing, and the three of you had been out half the night while Micky and I were babysitting the little one. When you got back it was too late to go home, so we ended up staying there. On Sunday morning we decided to go and kick a football around the park. Micky came too, one of the few times he humored us with his presence at a family activity.

"Of course She was totally inappropriately dressed for it, still in her Saturday night clothes. She was wearing that short red skirt and those black boots with the ridiculously high heels that made Her almost as tall as you are. Nearly broke Her sodding ankles running after the football in those heels, but run She did anyway. Then She was spinning around in a circle in the middle of the park laughing, and you caught Her before She could fall, and all I could think was that it should be me catching Her, because I knew you'd screw it up sooner or later. I just never imagined how much you'd screw up."

Yeah, neither did I, I think, but have the good sense not to say out loud.

The day they bury the body I'm marinated in gin and barely conscious. The past week has been a blur of alcohol-induced nightmares. I only sleep when I pass out from excessive drinking, and when I come to I down a few more bottles until I pass out again. The only reason for my being somewhat upright by the graveside today is that Patrick and Micky have me firmly locked between them and keep me from falling over. I'm too drunk to care much about whether or not I'm making an arse of myself.

There aren't many mourners attending this funeral; it seems our so-called friends don't like to be reminded of their own mortality by Her stubborn refusal to live to the age of twenty-six. Declan isn't there; none of us have seen him since that night. Her mother came over from Cork. Thankfully she's avoiding my eyes because I don't think I could stand the resemblance. I know she blames me for losing her daughter; I blame myself.

Besides Patrick, Micky and myself—forced to attend against my will by two brothers much larger and more sober than me—only Annie is there, standing a little bit away from the three of us, holding her swollen belly. When I first saw her, twelve, almost thirteen years ago with her purple hair and black lipstick, I never had her down as a breeder. Yet there she stands with honey hair and a one-carat rock set in gold on her finger, the look of middle-class motherhood only slightly marred by the safety pin still stuck in her ear. She is six months gone with her third child, reminding me of what I will never have. I try to tell myself I never really wanted babies anyway—I've paid my dues, raised two children that weren't even mine—but even in my current state of inebriety, I know it's a lie. I would have sold my soul to the devil for a child from Her womb.

An old fool in a dog-collar is droning on about a god I no longer believe in, and I shudder, knowing it is only Patrick's tightening grip on my elbow that is keeping me on my feet. How long is the fool going to gab?

Her mother is throwing the obligatory handful of dirt into the open grave now, and I don't know where it comes from, but with an unearthly howl I try to break free and hurl myself onto the coffin to lie there with Her. I almost manage it, too. Micky doesn't expect me to throw my weight around and lets go of my arm, but Patrick has better reflexes. He grabs me around the waist as I'm getting ready to plunge and wrestles me down inches from the hole in the ground.

"*Oh no you don't, lad,*" *he growls into my ear.* "*And now you're going to get up and stand through the end of the show for her mother's sake, or so help me God, I'll make you regret ever having been born.*"

He pulls me up, and for lack of anything better to do, I spew up all over the front of his suit.

Luka and I sit on the porch in silence for a long time. Then he gets up and says to no one in particular, "I'm going to prove that I am a god."

He strides off into the house. I hesitate for a moment, dreading whatever grand proof of deity he is thinking of, and then I pull myself together and follow him through the patio doors.

I find him in the bathroom, mixing up what looks like at least two grams of crank, probably more. He nods at me but doesn't say anything, just methodically continues doing what he's doing. Once the crystals are dissolved, he pulls out six different syringes, dividing the likely lethal cocktail equally between them. I have to swallow hard at the bile rising in my throat and even so, I'm not sure I can suppress the urge to hurl.

Luka turns to me and asks calmly, "The first proof of godhood is immortality, yes?"

I clear my throat and try not to beg. "Luka, don't do this."

"I think I have to," he says just as calmly as before, already tapping his arm to raise a vein. "One miracle for beatification, two for canonization. How many do you suppose apotheosis takes?"

"That's more Patrick's department than mine," I snort, taking hold of Luka's wrist. "And besides, the one miracle rule only holds for the beatification of martyrs."

Luka pulls back his wrist and poises the first syringe atop the median cubital vein. "I should think that Patrick would be the first to recognize immortality as a sign of divinity."

"Please don't," I say weakly as the needle pierces the skin.

Luka ignores me wholesale and depresses the plunger. As soon as he pulls out and recaps the syringe, he reaches for the next, pushing it into his arm a quarter of an inch higher than the first. He closes his eyes and his breath picks up, but he still reaches for the next rig within moments of putting the second one down and repeats the procedure.

After that shot he pauses long enough to turn around and throw up into the toilet, which snaps me out of the lulling stupor of watching the ritual and into action. "That's enough, Luka," I say, firmly grabbing hold of his shoulder. He's had at least a gram by my reckoning.

He shakes, with the aftershocks of vomiting and the strain on his system I think at first, but then he starts laughing, and I realize he's shaking with amusement. "It ain't gonna kill me," he laughs, shaking his shoulders violently to throw off my arm. He turns and reaches for the next syringe without meeting my eyes.

"No!" I yell. "Enough!"

Luka pauses, the syringe already resting on his arm a quarter inch above the last injection site, and quirks an eyebrow. "How else would I prove my divinity to you?"

"I concede," I say quietly, trying to suppress the quiver in my voice. "You are my God." The words leave a bitter taste on my tongue.

Luka sets down the syringe and nods. "Make sure you let Patrick know," he says, slowly walking past me out of the bathroom and keeping a steadying hand pressed to the wall as he goes.

The next few hours pass in precarious silence as Luka rides out his high at the dining room table. Darkness is falling outside by the time he rises and makes his way to the kitchen to rummage through the cabinets until he finds the last bottle of tequila.

Mindful of his usual reaction to alcohol, I sit down with him and end up drinking more than my fair share of the liquor. It's been years since I drank tequila straight from the bottle, and I didn't much like it then either, but I would do anything just now to prevent further drama. Luka doesn't intend to oblige me.

"I'm leaving tomorrow, James," he finally says.

"Oh?" Is all I can muster in return. I have been expecting it for a while now. Luka always leaves sooner or later; he learned from the best, after all.

"I'm leaving tomorrow, and this time I will not be coming back," he slurs. "I'll be heading to Portland."

I raise an eyebrow slightly. Every time Luka visits he insists that San

Francisco is a close second to LA on the list of cities he hates most. Every time he leaves, he swears he will never be back. Every time he comes back he swears it is absolutely, positively the last time. It never is. He hasn't been to Portland since that disastrous dance with heroin more than seven years ago though.

"I've always known I would die in Portland," he says quietly. "Don't ask me how, but I've always known, even before I went there for the very first time. Portland is where Declan Kelly Sheahan is destined to die."

I shudder, and when I raise the bottle to my lips my hand is shaking uncontrollably. I take a long swill, mostly in order to avoid having to talk. What Luka just said shook me to the core. It is the first acknowledgement in years that Luka remembers who he is. It is the first time in years that Luka uses his real name.

I toy with the idea of pointing out that Luka tried to prove his immortality a few scant hours ago but quickly dismiss the thought. I'm almost certain I prefer borderline schizoid to grand displays of transcendence.

"You're out of it," I finally say because it is clear he is expecting a response.

Luka laughs, the sanest laugh I have ever heard. It starts as a growl deep down in his chest and becomes a chuckle and then a roaring, leonine laugh, and I think this is what Luka would sound like if he were ever truly happy. I look at him and his eyes are burning with an ice-cold fire I have never seen in him before and he throws back his head, laughing even more.

"Are you scared, little brother?" he mocks me. "Don't you know that we all make our own destinies?"

Great, delusional again. "You've had too much to drink, Luka," I say firmly.

Luka shakes his head. "I haven't had nearly enough to drink today," he says, "just enough to loosen my tongue a little. I dance on the dark side, James, always have, and She understood that when She handed me the needle for the first time."

I reel back at the verbal slap. I know he's manipulating me, choosing his words carefully for maximum effect. It's working. He has just confirmed what I have so diligently refused to acknowledge. I always suspected that She had shown him the ropes, ever since I saw the clean tracks in Portland. Somebody who knew what they were doing had taught him the fine art of finding his veins, and it wasn't me. I just never wanted to believe it was Her. Until today, I never believed for a moment that She had sunk that low.

Luka looks at me coolly for a moment and says, "And if I perish, I perish."

"Esther didn't die, Luka," I reply, laughing hoarsely. A heretic I may be, but I still know my scripture. "Not with a wrathful god behind her, and you are no instrument of god."

"Ah, but you agreed that I am God," Luka says, smirking.

"So I did," I agree reluctantly, dreading the thought of reconfirming his delusion. "And didn't you tell me only a few weeks ago that a god's only duty is immortality? Didn't you just try to prove your immortality?"

"Perhaps," Luka replies unabashed, "but I never claimed to be a greater deity than She was."

I cannot allow myself to be drawn into an argument over the extent of Luka's supposed divine powers, no more than I can allow Luka to continue drawing Her specter into the discussion at every opportune moment; that way lies madness, for both of us. Instead, I steer the conversation back on course. "I assure you, Luka, you will not die. Not as long as I'm in charge around here."

"And that has always been your problem, James," he says. "You tread on the light side, and you've never understood the attraction of heroin because you won't allow yourself to give up control. She and I, we were only ever happy walking the thin line halfway between life and death, and when death finally claims us we feel relief more than anything else. So I'll go to Portland to find relief, and this time there won't be any desperate business with razor blades or sleeping pills. This time there will only be the sweetness of the needle."

Luka's calm is scaring me. "I'm warning you, lad," I say with much less conviction than I had hoped for, "I'm a phone call away from committing you."

"And put off the inevitable?" Luka asks. "We both know that this is how it is going to end. You've spent twenty years protecting me from myself, maybe it's time you let go."

It occurs to me that Luka may be serious. I have learned to deal with hysterical, delusional, paranoid, even suicidal behavior. Self-possession is an entirely new facet of Luka, and I don't know how to respond.

Luka grabs the bottle from my unresisting hands and takes a sip. "You know, Portland is the reason I'm still alive," he says after a while. "When

I slit my wrists or overdosed, I never really intended to die, because I knew I'd die in Portland. It was always about the pain."

"You're sick, Luka," is all I can say, knowing full well that I'm a hypocrite.

"Sick like you are sick when you get hard just before you're about to shove a needle into your arm?" Luka laughs. "Sick like you are sick when you see my veins? I've seen the look you get on your face when you see the blood pulsing in my arms, and it's pure lust. The way your heartbeat picks up and you almost salivate with desire because of the blue lace bulging through my skin. You get hard just thinking about what it'd be like to stick a needle into my veins, and you dare to tell me I'm the one who's twisted?"

"All right," I admit, "point taken. Still, if pain is what you wanted you could have just asked me or Patrick to kick the shit out of you; most of the time we would have been glad to do it. Besides, you came a little bit too close to dying on a few occasions."

"No point in having near-death experiences without the near-death part," Luka shrugs.

"What news! Stop the presses!" I say, trying for sarcasm, but even I can tell I only sound bitter. I know he enjoys pain, that has always been blindingly obvious. His entire adolescence and adult life have been characterized by a constant pursuit of pain, and it wasn't the kind of pain I seek for myself in the bedroom. There never has been anything remotely sexual about the pain Luka is after. When he isn't inflicting pain on himself in the form of self-mutilation, he actively picks fights with the meanest, largest rednecks he can find, and he savors the bloodbath that follows.

Luka jumps out of the cab of a truck at the Gilman Street exit just as the sun is setting over the Bay. "Home, bleeding home," he mutters underneath his breath as he starts walking toward downtown Berkeley. He likes to swing by Telegraph Avenue on his way to my house in Oakland, just to remind himself of how much he hates Berkeley.

He picks a group of likely looking college kids, probably frat boys, walks up to them and starts staring, never breaking eye contact. It takes no time at all before they start responding, posturing defensively, so Luka adds a disconcerting leer from the bag of tricks. He is a master at this game.

Soon, posturing turns to insults, and Luka matches them, grinning like a maniac until the first frat boy loses his temper and lunges at him. He parries quickly and follows up with a point-blank punch to the boy's face. Within seconds, the other kids start laying into him while Luka laughs at the sight of blood spurting from the frat boy's nose.

He isn't really fighting back because that would defeat the purpose of the exercise. He throws a few punches in the general direction of one of the kids, just to put on a show, with no intention of doing any more damage than he has already done. They've already been provoked; time to lean back and enjoy the onslaught of fists.

The biggest guy, who looks like he got into Berkeley purely for his prowess on the wrestling team, eventually gets fed up with Luka's demented chuckle, picks him up bodily and slams him head-first into the street. That's when the lights go out.

When Luka comes to a minute later the college kids are gone. "Bugger," he mutters, gingerly feeling his shattered jaw before picking up his pack and starting to walk down Telegraph toward the bus stop.

Forty-five minutes later I open the door to Luka who is grinning sheepishly through the caked-up blood on his face. He smells like he hopped a few trains on his way from Texas to California before hitching a ride up I-5. "I hate this town," he mumbles by way of saying hello.

I look at his smashed-up face and sigh. "How many?" I ask.

"Four," he mumbles, "I won the fight though."

I raise an eyebrow skeptically. Luka doesn't look like someone who just won a fight.

"Really," he mumbles. "We were fighting and then one of them threw me in the street and when I woke up they were gone, so I won the fight because they ran away."

I sigh again and pick up my car keys. "No shit, Sherlock," I say. "Get in the car. We're going to Highland so they can wire your jaw shut."

"You know, I can't purposefully kill myself," Luka says, pulling me out of my thoughts. "I mean, it must be the years of parochial schools or something, but when it comes down to it, I can't actually go through with it."

"Could have fooled me," I mumble through the tequila haze.

"I'm serious, James," Luka says, "I've thought about doing it properly you know, in a way that doesn't involve a drawn-out death and the possibility of being saved by a bunch of over-eager brothers, but I could never bring myself to do it."

"Why not?" I ask.

"Because I would never put you through the pain," he says quietly. "I'm going to Portland because in my dreams I have seen myself overdosing there, and if I die by accidental overdose, it doesn't count as suicide. I'm going to Portland because if I were to kill myself intentionally, I'd have to kill you and Patrick and Micky first."

That's when he passes out.

As soon as I'm sure he's out cold, I go to my bedroom and pick up the phone to dial Patrick's number. I no longer care what time it is in England.

"I can't take this anymore, Patrick," I shout down the phone seconds later, albeit sotto voce since I have no intention of waking Luka in the living room. "Twenty fucking years I've been putting up with him, and I've had it. I refuse to take another day of the hysteria and the drama and the suicide threats. You took the easy way out, left before he was five. Well, he's twenty-five now, and all I have to show for my pains are two badly scarred arms and ruined teeth."

"Calm down, James," Patrick says. "What's he gone and done now?"

"For starters, he's conclusively proven that he is god. Don't even ask," I yell, hysteria edging into my voice. "Then he cleared me out of tequila in order to tell me that he was going to Portland to die. Oh, and in case you were wondering, all his near misses were just staged for the benefit of deriving some twisted masochistic pleasure."

"Yeah, I wonder where he gets that one from," Patrick interrupts caustically.

"Screw you, Patrick!" I shout. "My sex-life has never been, nor will it ever be, up for discussion with you. I called you to tell you I am through with caring for him. Starting tomorrow, I will not lift another finger on Luka's account."

"Call Dad," Patrick replies.

"Yeah, because he's likely to leave the new perfect partner and the new perfect children to go chasing after Luka," I laugh. "You don't seriously think he's up to more than a token weekend every six months any more now than he was thirty years ago, do you?"

"What would you have me do?" Patrick asks quietly.

"Take over."

He sighs. "I'm an ocean away, James."

"No further than I was when you sent me chasing after him," I yell, frustrated.

Patrick laughs. "It's hardly fair bringing that up so many years later."

"Neither is that goddamn debt I supposedly owe you that you keep on dangling over my head, Patrick," I shout. "And you're going to have to call that in this time, or else he's out on his ear."

There, I've said it. Took me the better part of a decade but I've finally told Patrick what he can do with his goddamn debt: use it to keep Luka alive or stick it up his sanctimonious arse. Either which way, I am through taking this shit. It's somebody else's turn to pick up the pieces in Luka's wake now; I've been doing it long enough.

Patrick doesn't say anything for a long time. I'm not sure whether he is waiting for another outburst or whether he is actually thinking about what I've said. The longer I wait the more I think it might be the latter: it always takes a while for Patrick's brain to grind into gear.

"That debt will be claimed at a time of my choosing, Seamus, not a minute before," Patrick finally utters, and I wince at his use of the Irish variant of my name. He hasn't called me Seamus other than to tease me in a very long time.

"Well then you better get your hairy, fat arse on the next transatlantic flight to SFO, because you've got a package to pick up," I yell and immediately know I shouldn't have said it. Personal attacks are the last resort in a drunkard's argument, even Patrick knows that.

"Exactly how much of the tequila did you drink, James?" Patrick asks quietly.

"Fuck you, Patrick! This isn't about how much I've had to drink," I say, but the fight has gone out of me. "This is about the kid you left wailing for three nights straight while you ran off to have a life. This is about the kid you left who has never been the same since, and this is about me. I was ten years old, Patrick. I was ten years old and you left me to care for two boys barely out of their diapers." I pause to catch my breath, "How do you explain that to your children, Patrick?"

Patrick growls. "Don't make this about me, James," he says quietly. "Nobody forced you to take care of them, just as nobody is forcing you to take care of him now."

"Oh yeah?" I shout with renewed vigor. "If I remember correctly you

81

practically beat me onto that airplane when you sent me looking for him. How do you think I wound up living in this godforsaken country?"

Patrick sighs. "That was years ago, James. Nobody forced you to stay, but you couldn't face returning to London. You were looking for an excuse, any excuse, that would keep you as far away as possible."

"If it weren't for him, I could have gone somewhere else," I reply, "somewhere new and foreign. I could have disappeared again, you know."

"To spend the rest of your life running from ghosts?" Patrick asks.

"Oh no, Patrick, we are not going there. You are not going to turn this into a treatise on exactly how I have failed to deal with my problems. This is still about Luka. Still about the fact that you never so much as lifted a finger. You expected me to pick up the pieces," I yell.

"You were never responsible for him, not when he was a child, and certainly not after he turned eighteen," Patrick maintains. "You chose to take Luka and Micky on as a personal project."

"What was I supposed to do, Patrick? Hope that Mother would acknowledge their existence? Wait for a mythological wolf to show up and suckle them? I had no choice after you up and left. I hope it was worth it for you, because I sure as hell haven't had a life since." I'm starting to feel a knot in my throat, and I fight it desperately. I'm quite aware that my actions and reactions in recent weeks have all but convinced Luka that I'm a big girl's blouse and I don't really give a damn, but I swear it will be a cold day in hell before I break down and start bawling in front of Patrick.

"It wasn't exactly Walt Disney's wet dream of a childhood for me either, James," Patrick says acerbically. "I did the best I could for years, taking care of you and Luka and Micky, and then I grew up and left, and I didn't leave because I wanted to abandon you, I left because that's what people do when they grow up." After a few seconds he adds quietly, "It's what you did when you grew up."

He's right, of course. When it came down to it, I was no better than he was, probably worse. I ran off with Her as soon as I could and didn't leave so much as a forwarding address, but that's not what I want to hear right now, so I change the subject. "You know what he told me today?" I ask bitterly, noting the barely suppressed sob in my voice and wondering whether Patrick can hear it too. "He told me the only reason he hasn't killed himself in a foolproof manner is because he would have to kill you and Micky and me beforehand."

Patrick sighs. "James, you know as well as I do that it's one of his mind-fucks," he says. "We both know that whenever he hurt himself he was deadly serious, a couple of times he barely pulled through, and he's never displayed any homicidal tendencies whatsoever."

"What if he's telling the truth?" I whisper.

Patrick is quiet for a long time, then he asks, "Are you going to tell me what's really bothering you or do you want me to guess?"

Damn him! How does he do that? How does he read between the lines even before I know that there is something to be read there? "I don't know what you're talking about, Patrick."

"Yeah, and I can tell when you're lying," Patrick says.

"He's been trying to talk about Her," I grind out.

"Good, someone has to," Patrick replies coldly. "How long do you expect us to pretend it never happened?"

"He told Sally about Her. That's why she broke up with me," I complain.

Patrick laughs. "Let's be honest about this, shall we?" he says. "The little strumpet dumped you because she finally came to her senses and worked out that you weren't just any old fixer-upper. Now you're beyond pissed off because Luka managed to give her something you couldn't."

"And what might that be, Patrick?" I ask, my voice dripping venom.

"Probably nothing more than to hold her after, James," Patrick replies. "Because we both know you're too twisted up inside to ever do that. So there you have it, what you're really upset about is the fact that Luka fucked your whore and probably left her feeling better than you ever did."

"Don't call her that," I snap, "and anyway, it's nothing to do with her. I was through with her, and you know as well as I do that Luka always gets the crumbs."

"So why are you upset when I call her your whore?" Patrick counters.

I'm gob-smacked because I realize that for the first time in years I really object to the title routinely bestowed on the women I choose to sleep with. Maybe it's because she's in love with me, or maybe it's because she put up with a lot more than most of them put up with, but I don't think she deserves being called a tramp. She is Sally: beautiful and angry and sexy certainly, but not cheap. I'm not in love with her, never was, and I've been pushing girls into Luka's arms for years. Why do I have to keep on telling myself that?

"That thing you're feeling," Patrick says quietly, "is jealousy."

I shake my head. "How could I be jealous when I don't care about her?" I ask him and know the answer even before Patrick drives it home.

"It's not about the whore, silly," he says. "It's about him."

I laugh nervously. "What the fuck are you going on about now, Patrick?"

"Shut your mouth and listen," Patrick replies angrily. "You're talking to the one person who knows you better than anyone else. I've been watching you your entire life, I changed your diapers for God's sake, and I know exactly how your mind works."

"Fine," I say sarcastically, "analyze me."

"Not much to analyze," he says. "For years, I watched you take care of those boys like a mother hen even though you were nothing but a child yourself, and then She crossed your path and everything changed. You abandoned the only two people you cared about to run away with Her. I watched you worship Her; don't try to deny it. She played you like a fiddle, and you were consumed by a compulsion to make Her happy. You did everything She asked and kept Her on Her pedestal even after She became a scrawny, pale imitation of Herself. Hell, you clung to Her corpse until I pried you apart and then tried to throw yourself in Her grave."

I'm getting impatient. "What is the point you are trying to make?"

"My point is that you have an impressive history of focusing all your attention, all your affection, on one person and one person only," Patrick continues. "Micky never forgave you for abandoning him, but Luka was different. Luka needed someone to cling to because he couldn't survive without that attention. So after Her you focused all your attention on saving someone who didn't ask—didn't want—to be saved. You live for his visits no matter how brief, wait for his early-morning phone calls no matter how deranged. You're consumed by the desire to give him something resembling a normal life. That's why you force your discards on him; throw him crumbs, so he will come back.

"Except he's changed the rules of the game without consulting you, hasn't he? This time, he took a woman without being pushed into it. He wasn't drunk and he wasn't high and sex wasn't forced on him. He took her because he wanted to. He took her of his own free will, and you're jealous because you think that maybe he doesn't need you anymore like you need him."

I should be protesting now, telling Patrick just how much of a wanker he is. Instead I'm trying to drown out the voice at the back of my mind that is screaming yet again. Howling in pain, because if Luka doesn't need me anymore, if Luka has truly raised himself to godhood, who will adore me in the years to come?

Patrick senses my confusion. He makes a sound, halfway between a whistle and a sigh. "Sweet Jesus," he mutters, "I've finally sussed it out. As of today you are not his god anymore."

"When did you start talking so much rubbish?" I say. "Luka is the bane of my existence; without him I could really have made something of my life."

Patrick is quiet for a moment, and when he speaks there is unbearable sadness in his voice. "Luka is the sole reason for your existence. Without you, Luka would have lost his struggle with the razor long ago. Without Luka, you would have succumbed to the needle. You have kept each other alive for twenty years because you're faces of the same coin and neither one of you could survive long without the other."

"Oh I do love it when you get all metaphysical with me, Patrick," I reply, "but I think you had better leave the pontificating to religion vendors and others trained in the fine art of thinking."

"Personal attacks aren't going to change a thing, you know," Patrick says calmly. "I may not have your brains, but you know damn well that I'm right about this: you need Luka just as much as he needs you."

"Fine, whatever," I say impatiently. "If it's all the same to you I think I've had enough of the armchair psychology and cryptic aura readings for one night. Think I'll turn in and try to get some sleep. After all, looks like I'll be driving to Modesto tomorrow morning."

"Modesto?" Patrick asks.

"Yeah, apparently it's really easy to hitch a ride out of Modesto. Remember? Portland? Death-wish?" I say sarcastically.

"Good night, James," he says. "For what it's worth, I don't think he'll die in Portland any time soon."

And what would the tosser know about that, hiding five thousand miles away?

7

Drift: Press One to Accept the Charges

The first time the phone jolts me awake at Luka time—2 in the morning—is barely thirty-six hours after I drive him to Modesto. I grab the phone and oblige the computer voice by pressing one to accept the charges.

"So you're alive, then," Luka whines. "OK, it's official. I'm losing it. I'm a wingnut."

"Why wouldn't I be alive, Luka?" I sigh.

"I don't know," Luka wails. "I just had this feeling that something horrible happened, and I thought it was you."

"It's OK, Luka, I'm fine, really, just sleeping in fact," I say in the most soothing tone of voice I can muster at such an ungodly hour.

He's sobbing now, "James, you've got to call Micky and Patrick, make sure they're OK, I can feel that something happened. Really, I'm not crazy, I have this bad feeling that things aren't right."

I try to decide which is worse, the fact that I have no idea whatsoever what time it is in Singapore, where Micky was chasing numbers last I heard, or the fact that Luka is asking me to call a brother I haven't talked to in years, a brother who detests me.

All Micky feels for me these days is hatred. No, not hatred exactly, because hatred indicates love and a thousand other emotions equally strong. Micky hasn't hated me in a very long time. Luka hates me as much as he loves me, throws fists at my face as often as he plunges himself into my arms, because he still needs me. Micky hasn't needed me in an equally long time. Even those last few years he was living with me he didn't truly need me, he simply needed the façade of a legal guardian for propriety's sake. Since he doesn't need me he can allow himself to detest me, to resent me for all I did and all I failed to do.

"I'll call Patrick," I say, "but please don't ask me to call Micky."

"You have to," Luka howls. "Please, James, I know something is wrong. You don't have to talk to him, just call and make sure he's alive."

I have to laugh at the ludicrousness of it all. "Luka, calling someone you haven't spoken to in three years to ask whether they're alive is not the greatest opening line of all time," I reply. "Especially not when your last meeting went the way Micky's and mine did."

"James, please," Luka pleads.

"OK," I relent, "I'll call Patrick and ask him to call Micky. Give it a couple of hours and then call me back."

Luka sobs down the phone a little longer without saying anything much and then hangs up.

I'm at Uncle Paulie's wake, and it feels very much like a family reunion. Not that we have any real sense of family, but with the exception of Luka, who is AWOL again and doesn't know about our uncle's death as of yet, we're all here to pay our last respects or get mind-numbingly drunk. In practice there is no real difference between the two.

Funerals and wakes are really the only times all of the Sheahans meet these days. I suppose Patrick and Micky also attend christenings and weddings, but I boycott both on the grounds that I see little use in travelling thousands of miles only to find that one set of cousins isn't talking to another on account of what Auntie Tess said about the virtue, or lack thereof, of Uncle Diarmuid's youngest daughter.

Our family has a long tradition of suspending its internal squabbles for the burial of one of its own, though, so I suppose funerals are a chance for everyone to get together and start next year's strife. As far as I'm concerned, the only two reasons I have for attending are Patrick's implicit threats and the fact that Luka and I amuse ourselves by placing bets on which family member will throw the first punch.

I surreptitiously down a glass of finest Irish whiskey, another good reason to attend these sorry affairs, while Patrick isn't looking. His James-radar must have gone off though, because he sidles up to me and whispers in my ear, "I'm watching you, lad, and if you decide to start behaving like the prat you usually are, I'll kick your arse from here to Cambridge."

I snicker, because we have been playing this game for years and sometimes I think it's worth attending my relative's funerals just to see how much I can rile Patrick. Of course, I'm half-convinced he only forces me to come because it gives him a chance to let off steam. "I never plan on freaking out, Padraig," I say, knowing full well how much he hates it when I use the Irish variant of his name, "It just kind of happens."

"It usually happens after the better part of a bottle of whiskey," Patrick growls.

"Well, I need something to take the edge off the open casket," I say. "You are aware of the fact that I really don't like funerals? I mean, the last six disasters tipped you off, right? I can't fathom why you insist on my presence at these charades, but the least you could do is let me enjoy the hospitality. At any rate, I would watch Micky if I were you; I've got five quid on him throwing the first punch."

"You and Luka are still playing that game?" he asks incredulously.

I nod. "Yeah, Luka's got a tenner on Auntie Tess."

Patrick bursts out laughing but quickly lowers his voice when a couple of black-suited cousins throw him angry looks. He heaves slightly, suppressing his laughter, and fishes his wallet out of the breast pocket of his suit. "All right, put me down for ten on Father O'Riordan."

I pocket the ten and go off in search of more whiskey and Micky. Since Luka isn't around it's my turn to cheat.

Half a bottle later, I feel sufficiently fortified to face my youngest brother. I spot him across the room talking to Annie. It has been a couple of years since I saw him last, a couple of years during which he shed the baby fat and grew into an even meaner-looking bastard. I have to remind myself that the plan is to have Micky throw the first punch, otherwise I might well have gone up and decked him right there. As it is, he favors me with an icy stare and asks, "What do you want, James?"

"Is that any way to greet the man who raised you?" I respond caustically.

"You mean the man who spent half his life sticking needles into his arms while worshiping a strung-out whore?" he counters. "Just for the record, James, who do you think dealt the final deathblow to Declan? Who broke him? She or you?"

My fingernails are digging into the palms of my hands as I restrain myself from throttling Micky. "Poor deluded Declan," he continues, "so in love with the cailleach. *Do you think it ever occurred to him that for a fiver he could have had Her?"*

I won't be able to stop myself much longer, and I've got twenty-five quid riding on Micky throwing the first punch, so I aim my next remark below the belt. "How about you, Micky? Managed to lose your cherry yet?"

Seconds later his right hook hits me square in the jaw, and I start cackling maniacally as I lay into him. Fists are flying and bruising and demolishing the room, and I suppose Patrick will appear any second now to wrestle us apart, but until he breaks us up, everything is as it should be, and I am grateful for it.

"You have a collect call from *pick up the sodding phone, git*. Press one to accept the charges."

I can instantly tell he's out of it, even before he says a single word. It's been two weeks since he called, and I have been sick with worry ever since. "Luka, where the hell are you?" I ask.

"At a gas station somewhere in Arizona," he drawls out with difficulty. "I'm in a car full of kids heading to Mexico."

"What are you on?" I ask, skipping the small talk.

"The stuff that dreams are made of," he chuckles. "I've decided to join the dark side for a while."

I tell myself to stay calm. Luka is toying with me, relentlessly taunting

89

me with the specter of heroin, seeing how much I can take before I crack up and tell him he cannot die because I need him. Christ, when they wrote the dictionary they placed a picture of Luka and me next to the word 'co-dependence.' They ought to have done that, at least.

I hate him so much because every time he goes off on one of his heroin binges, I can feel the ties between us snap a little more. Each time he calls to tell me just what he is ramming into his veins I wonder whether it's the last time I will hear his voice. Each grueling day between late-night collect calls I wait for the other call, the call from a sheriff's department or coroner in a town I have never heard of, to inform the next of kin that they have identified the corpse, and when the call doesn't come, the foremost thought on my mind is that they haven't found the body yet.

I hate him so much because he is all I have left and he exploits the knowledge mercilessly. I hate him so much because he is all I live for and he constantly tries to escape life's shackles. I hate him so much because he is my creation, the boy I took and somehow broke and then rebuilt into a ramshackle replica of myself.

"Luka, be careful," I say. What else is there to say?

He laughs in response, "Don't worry, I'm nowhere near Portland," he says, "and we both know I won't die anywhere else."

A pregnant pause follows, but I can't think of anything to say that wouldn't embarrass us both, so I remain silent and curse myself for it, as this could be the last time I speak to him.

"Anyway," he says when it becomes clear I have nothing left to say, "the guys are getting ready to go again, so I'll talk to you later."

Cold hands are stroking my back impatiently as I wake up. The curtains are drawn but it looks too bright outside. "What time is it?" I ask turning around.

"Almost one," Cat says as she turns her attention to my thighs.

"Too damn early," I mutter.

I've been working nights for several months now, not because I enjoy going to sleep just as the sun comes up, but because of the night differential and the fact that we are desperately short of money. Cat doesn't concern herself with mundane pursuits such as putting food on the table and buying school uniforms for boys who never stop growing and has settled into a comfortable life on the dole. Consequently, she is bored most of the *time and takes delight in waking me when I should be sleeping.*

Her head dips below the blanket, and suddenly I'm wide awake. I whimper, because Cat has the ability to transform me into a purring heap of limbs with her oh-so-talented mouth. She's lapping at my thighs, and all the arrogance and anger and malice in me is swept away with each little lick of her rough tongue. I close my eyes again and moan as her mouth fastens around me. Cat is my drug, my heaven and hell, my paradise, and my heart bleeds because I am none of those things to her.

As the anger and self-pity reclaim me, my hips start rocking, driving me deeper into her mouth. She relaxes her throat while I clench my eyes shut to prevent the tears from flowing because I know I'm not the only one she does that to, know that in all likelihood I never was. I'm a meal ticket, a worshiper, a lover even, but never the object of her love. Her love has always been pledged elsewhere.

"Cat, I'm going to come," I say urgently, seconds before the climax washes over me. She doesn't withdraw like she would in the past, doesn't spit the semen onto my abdomen, she swallows and doesn't even gag. Then, before I can go limp, she crawls up my chest and slides my dick into her cunt. I whimper again as she starts thrusting her pelvis into mine. I open my eyes and gaze at her pinpoint pupils before looking to her thin, white arms bracing themselves against the mattress. I see the fresh tracks and know this is a thank-you fuck for the twenty I will find missing from my wallet later.

I shut my eyes, not wanting to look at what she is, what she has become, what I made her, hoping that if I refuse to believe everything will be all right for a while.

With my eyes closed, I feel the rage inside me building to a crescendo at yet another solemn promise broken. My eyes still shut and my fingernails digging into her waist, I roll her over and start thrusting fast and deep, thinking that if I pound her into the mattress hard enough I can still the urge to pummel her face with my fists. Why did no one ever tell me that love is messy and complicated and painful? As the rage boils over I ram my fists into the headboard which tumbles to the floor.

Afterwards, as I'm lying there spent and confused, experiencing a plethora of emotions ranging from adoration to revulsion, she nuzzles my neck in contentment. Suddenly the rage is gone. "How much, Catriona?" I whisper.

"I'll pay you back soon as I get the next check," she replies. "I saved *some for you too."*

I suppose I should be grateful for that at least. I'm still angry, of course, but Cat knows just how to play me, always has. Kiss me and lick me and suck me into submission and then dangle the proverbial carrot in front of my face. Oh, Cat knows how to tempt me, knows how to tread me into yielding; she's spent long years nurturing my weakness, after all.

Minutes later we're in the sitting room, me only in my jeans, Cat clad in underwear, and I'm mixing up. There's no question in her mind that I'll share with her, still the hunger in her eyes. I always do. When she's sated, sprawled on the couch barely clinging to consciousness, I raise the needle to my own arm.

Micky and Declan burst into the room as I push the plunger. There's no escape, no way for me to hide what I've carefully hidden from them until now. All I can see in Micky's face is resentment and maybe a trace of hatred before he runs out of the room. Through the fog in my mind it registers that our relationship is changed forever. I'm dimly aware, despite the heroin haze, that Micky will never look up to me again. Declan just stands there, watching me as I pull the syringe out, and his eyes greedily follow the single drop of blood that runs down my arm. My world shatters at what I see in his gaze; I have seen that look before, see it on Catriona's face every day—yearning, desire and lust for the needle.

"I don't feel so well," Luka stammers without realizing that he switches languages halfway through the sentence.

I clutch the phone tighter in my fist, trying to will myself awake. All I can think is, oh fuck, he's totally out of it, and then I remember that I have to keep him talking, have to keep him conscious, until he's out of danger. "Tell me what happened," I say slowly as if I were talking to a child.

"I was hitching a ride and we stopped at a rest area and I found these pills by the side of the road, so I took them," he explains haltingly, still having trouble distinguishing between different languages.

I reach for the Merck Index, my own personal bible these days, that has lived next to the phone since the first time he pulled this stunt and ask, "What were they?"

"How the fuck am I supposed to know?" Luka whines, all in English this time and much easier to cope with than the jumble of languages in the last sentence.

"What did it say on the bottle?" I ask, exasperated.

"They weren't in a bottle," Luka replies.

"You fucking idiot!" I shout. "How could you be so stupid? Those pills could have been anything!"

Luka laughs hysterically, "I'm thinking horse tranquilizers myself," he says. Then, slightly more panicked, he adds, "I think I need to pass out."

His agitated statement reins me in from the brink of fury. I don't have time to be angry now; I have to keep him talking, make sure he doesn't lose consciousness before I work out where he is. "Work with me here, Luka," I say. "Where are you?"

"At a pay-phone," comes the deadpan response.

"Let's start with city, state, and street if you know it," I say, trying to sound reassuring, no need to fuel his hysteria.

He's silent for a long time, his raspy, irregular breathing the only indication he is still conscious. "Come on, stay with me, Luka," I urge him.

"Ogden, Utah," he finally stammers. "A gas station, lots of lights, I don't think I can stay awake any longer, James."

"Yes you can," I say, "You've stayed awake through much worse. Look around you, see if there are any street signs."

"All the lights," Luka mumbles. "Pretty lights."

Damn, he's hallucinating. "What kind of gas station, Luka?"

"Kind of like Vegas," Luka whispers. "Do you think there's still a bench warrant for my arrest in Vegas? Maybe I'll go to Vegas tomorrow."

I'm losing him, probably won't be able to snap him back to reality, so the only option now is to keep him talking. This is going to be one hell of a phone bill. "Tell me 'bout Vegas, Luka," I prompt him.

"All those colorful lights," he mumbles. "I see tracers every time. I want to see the tracers, James. Gas station lights are kind of like that, feels like you're tripping, 'cept they're not as pretty as the lights in Vegas."

"Stay with me here, Luka," I plead. "Tell me how pretty the lights in Vegas are."

"So sleepy," Luka mumbles. "Don't wanna talk anymore now. Need to lie down. Watch all the pretty lights."

He doesn't hang up, but suddenly I can't hear his breathing anymore and I have no idea whether it is because he stopped breathing altogether or whether he simply walked away. All I know is that somewhere in

Utah a gas station pay phone is dangling off the hook.

I haven't slept much the last few days, and today is no exception. I spent half the night listening to Luka rambling on about how much he hated the Bay Area and how he had to get out of California, and then, after he had mercifully passed out, I spent several hours making phone calls and arrangements to fulfill his wish. Now I'm sitting on the couch, watching him, waiting for morning.

He's lying there on the living room floor in his sleeping bag, because he couldn't get used to sleeping in a real bed again, and I study the runes he cut into his arms a few days ago before my eyes are distracted by a flash of black on his chest. I reach out slowly and pull his shirt aside, careful not to wake him. With the shirt out of the way, I get a full view of the home-made tattoo.

My hand flies to my own chest, the spot right above my heart where an image was engraved into the skin when I escaped Patrick's house still mad with grief. The tattoo Patrick hates so much he never could bring himself to look at it. What would Patrick think now, I wonder, if only he knew that Luka is growing more and more into myself with every day that passes?

I force my eyes back to his breast. The cuts are new, angry red welts. I wonder briefly what he used for ink. Not that it matters much, I decide, even if the black substance doesn't prove permanent, the scars will remain. I slowly trace my finger along the letters Luka has carved into his skin: H-A-T-E.

Luka's wrist healed quite nicely, but his mind is a different story altogether. I'm starting to think that his mind is beyond hope, and the welts above his heart only confirm my opinion. Who is the word directed at? I know better than anyone else how much reason he has to hate, how much we all failed him, how much I failed him. Come morning I will fail him yet again when I pack him into a Greyhound bus to Philly, where our uncle and aunt are waiting for him.

He looks sweet when he's sleeping, oddly relaxed and so much younger than his eighteen years. It reminds me of when he was a little boy, all golden-haired and wide-eyed, curled up in my lap or clinging to my neck for what seemed like hours. I want that boy back.

I know when he wakes, though, things will be much like they were yesterday and the day before and the day before that, a mindless routine of accusatory looks and self-inflicted wounds and hateful words never quite vocalized, and I know I must be strong this time and send him away because California is slowly killing him. I know I am to blame for that, and maybe Patrick, to a lesser extent, because we insisted on keeping him alive. I wonder for the millionth time what right I had to play god. Who gave me the right to save him when he didn't want to be saved?

When the sun is up, I carefully shake him awake. I tell him to pack up his things, because I intend to give him what he asked for, a ticket out of California, a chance to get away from me, a chance to start over somewhere without the constant reminder of my face. This may very well be the first selfless act I ever performed, sending Luka to live with Uncle Diarmuid where he can be whole again if he so chooses. Alternatively, I may be completely self-absorbed, ridding myself of Luka and all the responsibilities that come with him. Whatever the case may be, Luka will get his ticket out of California.

I drive him down to the Greyhound station, briefly stopping at the grocery store to buy his supply of soda and cigarettes. At the station I slip him fifty bucks for food along the way before going up to the ticket counter. "I need a one-way ticket to Philadelphia," I tell the clerk.

"OK, the next bus would be the one p.m. non-stop to Chicago," the clerk says after consulting his computer terminal. "In Chicago you'll transfer to a bus going to Cleveland, Ohio, and in Cleveland you'll have a four-hour layover before catching the bus to Philadelphia via Pittsburgh."

"Fine, how much?" I ask.

Before the clerk can answer, Luka starts talking agitatedly. "Can't take that one," he mutters. "Can't get on a bus that goes through Ohio."

The clerk looks unfazed. It would appear that Greyhound is the preferred mode of travel for quite a few people with mental instabilities. "You'll have a hard time getting to Pennsylvania then," he tells Luka. "The direct routes all involve going through Ohio."

"Excuse us for a moment," I say with a forced smile and grab Luka's arm to drag him out of the ticket line. "What problem do you have with Ohio, exactly?"

"It's a well-known fact that Ohio does not exist," Luka explains. "The entire state is merely an invention to make up a nice round number of states. It's a conspiracy."

"Luka," I sigh, "let's assume for a moment that you are right and Ohio doesn't exist. Wouldn't that solve all your problems?"

"Why?" he asks.

"If you are right and Ohio doesn't exist, then you yourself will cease to exist the minute you cross the state line," I say. "Think about it, Luka. If you're really as tired of life as you always claim to be, wouldn't it be great if you could end it all by travelling to a state that doesn't exist?"

Luka stands there with a huge grin on his face and nods, "Let's do it, then," he says enthusiastically. "One-way ticket to Philly via Cleveland."

After several weeks of not hearing anything from Luka, I return home after a night out with some friends to find the message light on the machine flashing rapidly. I hit the play button.

"Dude, it's Phoenix. You'll never believe this, but I just saw your brother in the City," an acquaintance shouts into the recorder excitedly. "Except he didn't recognize me. He bit me in the nose. I mean, can you believe it? He actually bit my fucking nose. He's in a bad way, man, like he didn't have any shoes, and he lost most of his stuff, and I'm not even sure he knows where he is. Anyway, I'm taking him to the Taco Bell on Market, it's right between Powell Street and Civic Center. I'll try to keep him there, but I really don't know how long I can do it, so you better come over here as soon as you get this message." Beep.

"James, it's Phoenix again. Where the hell are you? Luka wants to hop a train to Portland tonight, so I'm going along with him, making sure he stays out of trouble. I'll call you when I can. Take care." Beep.

"I'm going to die," Luka states simply and his voice is like nothing I have ever heard before. "I am so sorry, James. I am so sorry. It was all my fault. I was buying that night. I watched Her die. I couldn't do anything; it was too quick. She wasn't alone though. I held Her, told Her we loved Her. I am so sorry. Please forgive me. I love you." Beep.

"Come on, Seamus, nobody ever looks like their passport picture anyway," Cat purrs. "All we have to do is dye your hair a little, and then we'll have the whole summer to ourselves."

"What about Declan and Micky?" I ask.

"It's just a few months," she shrugs. "They'll be fine. You could always ask your brother to keep an eye on them. OK, now raise your chin a little."

"Why?" I ask.

"Because you love me, because you want to be with me, because I want to be somewhere warm and sunny and I would like you to be there," she pouts. "Turn a little to the left, not too much, just a couple of inches."

I'm acutely aware of the effect that pout is having on me, or at least parts of my body that are only marginally under the control of my brain. Damn her! Why does she always have to move in for the kill when I'm at my most vulnerable? Time to be reasonable. "Look, all I'm saying is that it's easy for you to do, you're over eighteen, you can do whatever you want, but I can't just up and leave for a couple of months," I protest.

She throws the passport at me. "According to this you're eighteen too. Nothing to stop you, no way to find you—they probably won't even notice you're gone. When was the last time your mother noticed anything?"

She's right. The number of times Mother has acknowledged my presence over the past few years can probably be counted on the fingers of one hand. Maybe I can send Micky and Declan to stay with Nonna in America. No, that would raise too many questions about why I wouldn't be there. The logical choice would be Patrick. Problem is, Patrick has gone missing again with his drummer. Well, not missing exactly, because I know where he is from the random postcards we get, but definitely not available for babysitting. His last communiqué had him in Australia for a few more weeks and then back to Berlin where he has been living on and off for a few years. Apparently Berlin is where the music scene is these days.

"Seamus," Cat urges in a sulky voice, treating me to one of her puppy looks. "Think about it: the sun, the sea, plenty of bar work, it could be paradise on earth. You can always come back if you don't like it."

I'm still torn. I want to go, desperately so, but there are Declan and Micky to think of. There are always Declan and Micky to think of. Maybe I can get them to stay with Patrick for a month or so, come up with some piffling excuse about how it would help their German. If Patrick takes them, no one need ever know that I'm not there with them. Patrick will cover at least for a few weeks if I ask nicely. A few weeks of freedom from responsibility, a few weeks of taking in the Greek sun. Surely he wouldn't begrudge me that? It's not as if I would be gone forever, just a few weeks, a month on the outside, a little vacation from playing mommy to Declan and Micky.

"I'll think about it, OK?" I say. "If Patrick agrees to take them while I'm gone, I'll go with you, at least for a little while. Now are you still drawing, or can I move now? When you asked me to pose for you I didn't *think I would be so naked or so chilly."*

It has been three weeks since I returned to those messages. I've had three weeks to prepare myself for this, but my heart still starts racing when I hear the computer voice. I take a deep breath and collect myself, then I push two. I will not accept the charges. He tries to call three more times that night; each time I resolutely push two. Then he gives up, at least for the time being.

I must have drifted off to sleep at some point, staring at the offending phone, because its ringing jolts me awake around sunrise. I pick it up, determined to refuse the charges if it's Luka again. "Why the hell aren't you accepting Luka's calls?" Patrick shouts by way of saying hello.

"I don't want to talk to him," I say hoping that my tone of voice indicates finality.

"Oh. Well, he's fine, I think," Patrick says, confused. "Although I use the term loosely. I gather he's in Davenport, Iowa, with some guy with an insane name. Albatross or something."

"Phoenix," I reply.

"Yeah, that's him," Patrick continues. "Apparently Luka lost most his stuff, his ID and his shoes, but he doesn't care all that much since he's acquired denim overalls, a straw hat, and quite an impressive number of tools."

I have a feeling I know where this is going, but I'm forcing myself not to care.

"James, he's planning to do a Huck Finn," Patrick mutters. "He's sitting there in Davenport with that nutter Dodo, and they're planning to build a raft and go down the Mississippi. They've got it all worked out too, reckon they're going to hit New Orleans in time for Halloween."

He pauses, waiting for me to say something, so I grunt in a non-committal sort of way. "He's called Phoenix," I say, trying to divert Patrick's attention away from why I'm not talking to Luka. "Though Dodo might be strangely appropriate, as in 'dead as'."

"You must be out of your mind," Patrick replies irately. "You haven't listened to a word I've been saying. I mean, I told them about the likelihood of there being locks and such, but they are determined to go through with this."

"It's his life, Patrick," I say, because I have to say something. "It's none of our business. Just let it be."

"What happened, James?" Patrick asks, genuine concern in his voice. "Why are you not talking to Luka? I asked him, and he doesn't know, doesn't remember much since leaving."

"Figures, otherwise he wouldn't have tried to ever call me again," I mutter.

"He's upset, James, doesn't know what he did wrong. I told him I'd talk to you." Patrick says.

I'm quiet for a long time, trying to figure out how much Patrick knows. Our little exchange in the alley outside that pub in Stepney eight years ago keeps on playing over and over in my head like a broken record. Something he said that night. I intuitively search for the words he didn't say, try to read between the lines. What was it I didn't pick up on that night? I can't remember. The passage of years and the mists of alcohol make it all seem like a dream. Yet there was something he said... *Luka loved her just as much as you did, and right now he's hurting more.*

"I know, Patrick," I say. Let him work out the multi-faceted meaning of that statement.

Patrick isn't playing with me though. Infuriatingly enough, he has an unerring instinct for when to play games and when to dig for the truth. "What is it you think you know?" he asks.

"Luka was convinced he was going to die," I say quietly. "He sought a confessor, and priests being generally unavailable at two o'clock in the morning, he chose to confess to my answering machine."

Ah yes, Patrick knows. His silence is all the confirmation I need. Patrick has probably known all along. Luka called him that night. I had always assumed it was after he left the house, but I'm starting to think that it was before I ever got there. Patrick would have told Luka what to do. A long time later, I hear a sound I haven't heard in years: Patrick is lighting a cigarette.

"How long have you known, Patrick?" I ask, my voice shaking. Whatever semblance of composure I managed to maintain is quickly slipping from my grasp.

There is another pregnant pause, and I think I can hear the slight clink of ice hitting glass, Patrick hitting the Scotch. "Listen to me, James," he says, sucking hard on the cigarette, "It wasn't Luka's fault. He called me, and I had him swear on his grandfather's grave that he would never tell anyone what really happened that night. I had to protect him, James; I owed him that much. If you are going to blame anyone, blame me."

"You weren't the one buying that night," I shout.

"So She took Luka for a ride and used his money. Didn't matter then, doesn't matter now," Patrick says. "If it hadn't been his money, She would have stolen it out of your wallet, or—well, gotten it any other way She knew how."

That last one is a fast catch; it wasn't what he had meant to say. What did you really want to say, Patrick? That She would have sucked someone off, gone for a quick shag behind the pub? I know what you all called her behind my back, *cailleach ag caitheamh mo chuid airgid*, wasn't it? I'm under no illusions as to where that money came from when it wasn't coming from our wallets; I smelled it on her every time. There is a unique scent to sex and to every single male on this planet. I know that better than most. My capacity for make-believe died right along with Her, but with the exception of Micky, who has his own reasons, my brothers are still careful to maintain the myth.

"I am fully aware of how She got the money so stop pussy-footing around," I yell. "He still bought that night and then didn't know what to do when it all went wrong. If I had been there—"

"You couldn't have done a thing," Patrick interrupts. "It was too strong, too quick. Even you couldn't have stopped it, and even if you could have, just for the sake of argument, it would only have been a short-term solution. It still would have happened eventually. She made Her own choices. She was bloody-minded like that, always did what She wanted."

"I had a right to know!" I shout.

"Luka deserved a life!" Patrick shouts back.

"Yeah and look what he made of it," I scream.

"We both know who's to blame for that, James," Patrick replies. "She dragged you both down with Her. The only thing I don't understand is how Micky got away. I should have wrung Her bloody neck years before, but all I could do in the end was some very limited damage control, protect you and Luka; it was all that was left once She was through with you."

"She was my wife!"

Patrick sighs. "She broke every vow She ever made."

"I spent eight years thinking She died alone," I whimper.

"I wish She had," Patrick spews out, "maybe then She wouldn't have taken Luka with Her."

"I loved her, Patrick."

Patrick considers this for a moment. "Grow up, James," he finally snaps. "You don't know what love is. You worshiped her, certainly, were obsessed with her, probably, but neither of those amount to love. Love works two ways, you know, and She was incapable of loving another human being. I think you knew that all along. In the end you only married Her to prove to me that you could be blissful and happy, that you could have the sort of life I had. You were too young, too confused, and too hell-bent on competing with me to know any better. You never even considered marrying her until you found out Annie and I were starting a family. That's what it was all about: do it better than Patrick, marry the girl instead of living in sin. You were trying to prove that you could have a family yourself."

"What could you possibly know about family?" I snap. "You were the one who broke this family apart."

"Then maybe it's time I fixed it," Patrick says.

"You are twenty years too late," I reply.

"I refuse to believe that," he says. "I know I made mistakes, failed you, but I know if you give me half a chance I can do something about it."

"I am thirty years old, Patrick," I respond. "There are two decades of pasts that neither one of us can undo, no matter how much we would like to."

"When you left, we had to clear out your flat," Patrick suddenly says, apropos of nothing.

"Yeah, so?"

"I took some of your books, and I've been reading my way through them whenever I had a moment," Patrick admits in a mortified tone of voice. "It's not something that comes naturally to me, never has, but I figured I should at least give it a try."

I'm puzzled. "Your point being?"

Patrick sighs. "I've started to enjoy it. I'm not saying I'm as much of a reader as you are, by any means, but over the years I've come to think that even though I didn't like reading in school, the future isn't always defined by the past. It isn't as clear-cut as all that."

Is he trying to blindside me into agreeing to something? I gear up into defensive mode and scoff: "I'm delighted you're trying improve your mind, Patrick. Maybe you should try to re-read 'Jane Eyre' a few more times to wholly appreciate it. No, better yet, go re-read 'Wuthering Heights' and picture yourself as Heathcliff. That's what I usually do."

"Heathcliff? You think of me as Heathcliff?"

I'm enjoying this. Patrick is getting flummoxed. "Yeah. Well, tall, dark, brooding, ripping families apart, what can I say?"

"Can the sarcasm, lad, it doesn't become you," Patrick snarls. "As I was saying before you interrupted me, I've grown to enjoy some of those books."

I can't help it but snort. Patrick, illiterate as ever, probably got stuck on D.H. Lawrence and a couple of volumes of Henry Miller I may have left lying around there. "Found the porn amongst the literature then," I needle him.

Patrick laughs. "That too. James, all I'm saying is that sometimes you have to let the past be just that, past. Nothing can ever change what happened, but that doesn't mean you can't change," he says hurriedly, afraid that I will interrupt him before he has a chance to say his piece. "You could still do all the things you dreamed about. Become a writer, marry, have children—you're not too old for any of that."

"I am a writer, though be it a bad one," I mutter, "and I've been married."

Patrick sighs. "Look, what I'm trying to say is maybe you should come out here for the summer, spend some time with us, let me try to fix things. I was going to take the kids to the old country for a while, give Annie some well-earned rest, show them where their grandmother came from. You haven't been there since independence. I think you'd like it. Spend some time in Europe; maybe it'll give you a chance to straighten things out, think about where you want to go from here."

He must be out of his mind. "Patrick, I've obligations over here," I stammer, trying to think of a polite way of saying no.

"Bollocks," Patrick laughs, "you just finished a writing contract and the only other obligation you have over there is Luka, and you've already made it clear you don't want to talk to him. Come on, give it a try. I'll even pay for the airfare."

Shit, he really wants me to come. Why? Is this about guilt? About having kept the truth from me for so long? Oh fuckiddy-fuck-fuck-fuck, he's trying to turn me into a project, finish the job that Sally and Luka started in their folly. He wants to force me to confront my demons, and I don't think I'm ready for that. "Patrick, I can't..." my voice trails off.

"I promise you I won't mention Her," Patrick assures me. "I won't say a thing unless you bring Her up first. Scout's honor."

Christ, what do I say now? What other excuse could I possibly have for not visiting, especially if he'll pay for it? "What makes you think I would like to spend the summer with your brood?" I ask, thinking five kids is a damn good excuse for not visiting.

Patrick laughs. "James, you're the only grown man I know who will play with Barbies just to keep Siobhan happy. You know, it's been two years, but she still asks after you almost every day. It's not easy for her, having four brothers. It's part of the reason we decided to try for another girl."

"You realize you are almost certainly going to have another boy instead," I reply. "We aren't exactly known for our productivity in the girls department."

"Yeah, well, I reckon if we skip the usual three-year break, we might just be able to squeeze in number seven if this one doesn't pan out," Patrick says. "Come on, James, do it for Siobhan if no one else."

"You realize that's psychological warfare," I say, "using a little girl to blackmail me."

"I'll buy some new Barbies," Patrick offers.

"Think you'd be able to get a doll that looks like Sarah Michelle Gellar?" I joke.

"Who?" he asks.

"Actress on Buffy, fights demonic creatures—never mind."

Patrick laughs, "Are you trying to change my mind about letting you anywhere near my daughter?"

"All right, all right, you win," I grumble. "Just as long as we both understand that I'm doing this for Siobhan and not for you. The poor girl needs someone to play with."

8.

Oracle: The Son Shall Marry His Mother

I'm on the Heathrow Express hurtling toward London, all the while asking myself why I ever agreed to come here. I know the answer to that at least; London is my siren just as the Bay Area is Luka's and Berlin is Patrick's. There are cities I have used and abused, made my own for the duration, cities I have never returned to once I was through with them. There are cities I have loved with a passion, but there is only one city I hate with equal fervor, and that would be London. She exerts an unbearable attraction on me, pulls me in like a black hole pulls in matter. Wherever I have gone in the course of my life, eventually I am always drawn back to her. No matter how many times I swear I will never return, I find myself rushing back to her to drink in her stink and her sins and her glory.

I suppose boys with no clear sense of belonging, who carry passports of different nations purely as a means of travelling, would have to pick a city, any city, to call their own. London is the whore between whose thighs I tasted sin. In her womb I learned to booze and brawl and bet on horses. In her embrace I learned to make a woman mine and dance with death. In her heart I learned the true meanings of grief and guilt and redemption. In her eyes I watched my reflection change from boy to man. London made me, betrayed me and expelled me, but no matter how often I leave, like a fool I return each time my siren calls.

Before the train pulls into Paddington, I know with absolute certainty I should never have left. The city calls out to me, beckons me, seduces me with her vulgar charms. Instead of going straight on to King's Cross and catching the first train that stops at Durham, I decide against all reason to stay in London for a few days. My mistress calls out to me and I obey her wish; I find myself drawn toward my mother's house. I've always known that Luka isn't the only one who enjoys pain; I'm a glutton for punishment.

Before I know it, I'm standing in front of the house, jet-lagged, travel-sore, and in desperate need of a bath. Probably not a good time to get apprehensive, I decide. I made it this far, I might as well go and knock on the door. She's my mother; what is the worst she could do? Why am I so scared?

We've gotten into an awkward routine of Sunday morning phone calls. Not peace exactly, but détente, the weekly exchange of pleasantries. Never intimate, never personal, but words nonetheless, which is more than can be said for the preceding twenty-five years. As I'm standing there staring at the house I spent the last few years of my childhood in, I'm acutely aware that talking across the safe distance of five thousand miles and facing my mother in person are two entirely different propositions.

I'm about to pick up my bags and head back toward the tube station, go running, tail between my legs, for the safety of Patrick's semi in Durham, when the door opens and she stands there on the front steps, smiling faintly. "Will you come in, James?"

I look at her for a moment. I remembered her being taller and sturdier.

It is hard to associate this diminutive old lady with the woman who gave birth to me. Patrick will be thirty-eight in a few weeks, that makes her what? Fifty-nine? Sixty? Her long black hair is streaked with gray now, but her eyes are as clear and blue as they were forty years ago. The eyes my father fell in love with, or so he claims. She is still beautiful, regal even, and still so very distant.

I nod, pick up my bags, and follow her inside. No escape now. I put my bags down in the hallway and follow her into the kitchen. "How is your father?" she asks.

"Good. I saw him a while ago when he breezed through on his way to a conference at Stanford. I met his—" I swallow the last part of that sentence, no need to describe my father's sexual peccadilloes to his lawful wife.

She sighs. "It's all right, James," she says. "I haven't talked to him in more than a decade, and even I didn't expect him to spend the rest of his life by himself. Is she pretty?"

Is this the right time to be truthful, I wonder? Lying across an intercontinental telephone line is much easier than lying in person though; diplomacy might be the right choice here. "She's young," I say. "Well, not young exactly, probably around Patrick's age. Assistant professor at MIT, got a couple of kids, and I suppose she's pretty in an all-American kind of way." I hesitate for a moment before diplomatically adding, "Not as beautiful as you were."

That makes her smile. I must be doing something right. If Patrick could see me now, he'd have to revise his whole theory about the inbred lack of tact in us Sheahans.

"How's Declan?" she asks.

I flinch at the use of Luka's old name. "Mother, he's been calling himself Luka for eight years. Don't you think it's time you called him that too?"

"I'm sorry," she stammers. "It's just, well, it was your grandfather's name."

"That's why he chose it," I say in my most reasonable tone of voice. "I haven't talked to him in a few weeks, but I think he's fine. Travelling somewhere down south, I think." I carefully omit the bit about building a raft and going down the Mississippi in search of a Mark Twain fantasy. Being our mother demands a certain amount of repression, but even I know not to push the boundaries of denial.

I shrug off my jacket and sit down at the breakfast bar. An uncomfortable pause follows.

"How did you know I was coming?" I finally ask to break the silence.

"Patrick rang, told me there was a possibility you would stop by," she replies. "Are you hungry? There's some roast lamb and some home-made ajvar, much better than that preserved stuff you kids eat these days."

"Maybe later," I say. "I'll have a drink, though, if that's OK."

She nods and pours me a glass of wine. "He brings the kids down to see me every few months, you know," she says, and she's talking to herself more than she is talking to me. "Their other grandmother practically lives with them, but then I suppose I would never have made a very good babysitter myself."

I can't think of a response that wouldn't be hurtful. The animosity between Mother and Annie was mostly of Mother's design. No one expected her to be open-armed, but then again, had she been slightly less combative, Annie may be more inclined to have her in her children's lives. Mother is lucky, really, that Patrick has this insane desire to ensure his children know their roots and drags them down here every few months. If it were me, I don't know that I would be as kind.

"Oh, you know Annie," I say, sipping the wine. "Overprotective of her brood, she is. Who would have thought that twenty years ago?"

Mother nods. Her eyes travel up my bare arms, and I can feel myself blushing. I try to take care of them, I really do, but after more than a decade there are bound to be scars, including a couple of bad ones from abscesses drained in a make-shift manner in the privacy of my bathroom. Denial is all fine and good, but even denial can't surmount hard evidence. Her eyes lock with mine for a second before she smiles faintly and looks away. "With the benefit of hindsight, I have to admit that I objected to the wrong girlfriend entirely," she states and walks out of the kitchen.

I'm standing in the street outside one of those large Victorians in Ealing that have been converted into flats, trying to get up the nerve to go and ring the doorbell. I'm back in England. I spent the better part of the last two months hitchhiking my way back from the far side of Europe, and God only knows what possessed me to return to this rain-plagued country. It took me another day to find out that Patrick was back in England too.

Then I called in a lot of favors to get an address, which brings me to this nice suburban street in west London, feeling apprehensive.

I have a feeling Patrick will give me the walloping I so richly deserve, but it starts to drizzle and I hate the rain, so I take a deep breath and walk up to the door. It takes him a minute or so to answer, and the look on his face when he sees me is worth anything he could possibly do to me. What he does though is a complete surprise: he pulls me into a rib-cracking embrace, and it doesn't look like he'll ever let go again. When he finally steps back a few minutes later I wheeze, trying to draw air back into my lungs.

"So you're alive, then," he says.

"Yeah, well, us Sheahan boys are hard to get rid of," I grin sheepishly. "Can I come in?"

He waves me into a living room filled with the ghastly twenty-year-old furniture common to all flats that come fully furnished. Then he steps over to the sideboard and downs a few shots of Scotch in quick succession, his only guilty pleasure these days it seems, before turning to me and asking, "Where the fuck have you been for the past two years?"

"Greece mostly. Cyprus, Turkey, Lebanon, Italy," I shrug. "I lost track after a while. It's easy to lose yourself when you're drifting across a continent."

"You could have sent us a postcard," he says angrily, "let us know you were fine."

I shrug again. Truth be told I came close to it many times. Almost walked into an embassy a few times too, for that free ticket home, but I never did because it would have been tantamount to admitting defeat. Patrick left and never looked back. Oh, he came to visit and such, but he never came running with his tail between his legs because the world turned out to be more than he had bargained for. That's why I never gave in to the urge to run for my mother's apron. In the end I did all right most of the time, merely survived a few times, did some things I'm not too proud of, had the adventure of a lifetime. So why the hell am I back here?

"Well, are you going to tell me about it?" Patrick asks.

So I tell him, the highly edited version at least. No need to spill the whole truth unless it becomes absolutely necessary. I tell him of summers spent working bars, I tell him of winters spent hiring onto ships, I tell him about two years of waking up next to that beautiful creature each morning which somehow made it all worthwhile. I think he understands too, knows *that after that first summer of freedom, I simply couldn't go back, couldn't return to Mother's house. It hasn't been that long since he tasted freedom for the first time.*

From the look on his face I know he's reading between the lines, listening to all the stories I won't tell. I don't mention the days I spent in jail for beating some Italian wanker to a bloody pulp because he had the audacity to fuck Catriona against the hot brick wall of a nightclub. I don't talk about the night she totally lost it and tried to stick a carving knife through my chest; he'll probably notice the scar sooner or later anyway. I'm sure he hears the stories I won't tell, but he has the decency not to ask too many questions.

"Where's Catriona?" he asks when I finish my story of hitchhiking across Europe to get back to England. I guess he sees my eyes clouding over for a moment, because he steps up to the sideboard, gets me a glass of Scotch, and adds, "If you don't mind me asking."

I shrug. "She flew out to Ireland a couple of months ago," I say. "Her father died, and she just packed up one day. She left me a note with her mother's phone number, said I should call her if and when I returned to England."

I don't know what I expected him to say. He's never liked Catriona all that much, and I thought he would come off all high and mighty hearing that she packed her bags and left me without so much as a word. He doesn't.

"A little over a year ago, after she turned twenty-six, Annie decided it was time to grow up," he says quietly. "Said there were things besides music, things she wanted to do, like go to university, get married, have children, and buy a house. She quit the band one day and packed up and told me she was moving back to England, and I could come if I wanted to and get those things with her or I could stay in Berlin, but either way she was going home."

"Looks like you chose middle-class boredom," I say.

"Yeah, and you know what? I don't even miss the old life too much because I still have her, and if middle-class is what she wants, then middle-class is what I'll give her, come hell or high water," he says. "I've never been much good at saying what I feel in my gut, but I try to show her what I can't find the words to describe, try to show her how much I—"

He never finishes the sentence, can't bring himself to, I suppose. There he stands, almost a decade down the road and can't even say the words.

"You're a coward, Patrick," I say dryly.

He laughs. "Runs in the family, then," he says. "I can't honestly say I like Catriona, but if you love her, if she makes you happy, you should call and tell her that."

I shrug. "Maybe I will," I say.

"First you have to call Mother though," he says, "let her know you're all right."

"Why?" I ask.

"She's your mother," he says. "You owe her that much. You can stay here as long as you need to on condition you call her and tell her you're alive and well."

"Fine," I say. "Later."

The next morning Patrick shakes me awake at some ungodly hour, and he's in a foul mood. We stayed up late drinking, and he probably didn't get as much sleep as he's used to. He's standing there in his dress shirt, the tie hanging loosely around his neck, holding a cup of black coffee. When did he make the transition from punk to suit? I blearily look around, take in the couch and the coffee table and Patrick scowling at me from the kitchen door, and I remember.

"Have you called Mother yet?" Patrick's question jolts me out of my reverie.

Being not quite awake enough for verbal responses, I simply shake my head. Patrick slaps me lightly across the back of my head as he walks off toward the bathroom and says, "I meant what I said, lad, if you don't call her and face the music I'll have you out on your ear."

I grin at the threat and turn around to go back to sleep, feeling a lot happier than I've felt in years.

I dump my bags in the room that was mine fifteen years ago. It isn't anymore, of course; any trace of my occupancy has long since been removed. I wonder briefly how long she waited to see whether I would return before she cleaned out the room. Patrick's room barely lasted a week, but then she was furious; smashed anything worth smashing in hysteria. By the time I left there was no anger, just complacency. Perhaps that's the reason for my jealousy. Patrick was her first-born. Not that she showered him with interest, but he did anger her on a daily basis, and I was starved for attention, however negative. To this day I am envious of

Patrick.

After a long bath, I make my way back to my room, briefly pausing at the door that leads to Micky and Luka's old room. On a whim I push open the door and peek inside. Their bunk beds survived the years, it seems, but that is the only reminder of them. I quietly close the door. The whole house seems strangely dead and much too big for one person. I sometimes wonder why Mother never sold it after we all left. The house was large, even when there were four wild boys racing up and down the stairs; it seems excessive for one person.

When I return downstairs I find her sitting at the dining room table marking papers, a bottle of wine at her side. She points at the mantelpiece. "I've found you some keys," she says. "Do you know how long you'll be staying?"

"Not sure," I shrug. "Patrick probably told you we're heading to the old country next week. I thought I'd go to Durham beforehand, but it seems silly to go up there for a couple of days just to come back down here to catch a flight out of Heathrow. Might just hang out here."

She nods. "There's a copy of *Time Out* on the coffee table. There are a few good plays on right now; you might want to think about seeing a few shows. Also, there's a Cleopatra exhibit at the British Museum you might want to catch."

"I'm not sure I ever stopped boycotting the British Museum," I grin. "Bunch of goddamn thieves."

She laughs and gets up to fetch me a glass from the kitchen. As she hands me the glass and pours the Merlot into it she asks, "Published anything lately?"

"Quite a bit of porn masquerading as romance novels," I admit. I see the look on her face and quickly add, "Published under several pseudonyms, of course. It's ludicrous, but it's the most lucrative market as far as fiction is concerned. Haven't done any serious writing in years though."

"You should start again," she suggests. "You were incredibly talented, even when you were a little boy."

"After *Gethsemane* there simply wasn't anything left to write about," I say. "One of the first poems Luka ever wrote, and it was a bloody masterpiece, said everything I ever could have wanted to say more eloquently than I had ever dared to dream. You know he doesn't really write anymore, never published anything else. How could he? He'd already said everything. I still wish I could have written it myself." I frown at the memory. "It's unfair, really. There I was trying to be a writer, and Luka gets bored one day and turns into a latter-day Rimbaud in a matter of minutes."

"Rimbaud quit writing by the age of twenty," Mother replies, and the analogy isn't lost on me. "You were the one with all the talent, James. Don't throw that away because Luka experienced a moment of inspiration."

I wonder whether Patrick asked her to have a pep talk with me, whether this is all part of Patrick's grand save-the-loser scheme. "You're talking to the wrong son," I say tersely. "Let me give you Patrick's phone number."

Mother smiles sadly. "James, I have even less of a right to tell you how to lead your life now than I did fifteen years ago, but—" she closes her eyes before continuing, "Patrick is ordinary, simple. He has his family, and he has faith. It is enough for him."

I flinch a little at the brutal dissection of Patrick's character. Yes, Patrick more than any of us is more brawn than brain, content with his middle-class life. He never questioned his God or the Vatican, never questioned his role in society. Even while throwing stones at police he was rebelling against his parents, his upbringing, more than he was rebelling against the system.

Patrick sees the world in black and white, and it has served him well. He never had to choose what was what; somebody else had already made those choices for him. Tell Patrick that which is right and that which is wrong, wrap it in fancy words, and he will believe and act accordingly. In Patrick's worldview, Occam's razor strikes and white is right and black is wrong; he is content with that, at peace.

What good did shades of gray ever do Micky or Luka or myself? For Micky, the world is made up of numbers, a series of formulae and equations so much tidier than words or human beings could ever hope to be, and it's not the numbers' fault that carbon possesses certain unpredictable qualities. Life is only temporary at best though, so he tolerates it and spends his waking hours pursuing the perfection of universal constants.

Luka, now there's a thought. Never in a million years will I be capable of understanding just how he sees the world. Where Patrick is capable and Micky and I are smart, Luka is a bloody genius when he manages to think straight for more than five seconds. I'm half convinced that intelligence is inversely proportional to mental stability every time he and I really talk. His is a world of abstract ideas and theoretical concepts, a world of pure reason, the universe a logic table waiting to be sketched.

They never asked how I see the world. Why would they? Patrick hasn't the sophistication to ask or the patience to listen to an incomprehensible answer. Micky only cares about his precious numbers, and at any rate, he hasn't said more than five words at a time to me in a decade. Luka? Well, whenever he gets over himself long enough to actually have a decent conversation, he doesn't ask because he knows I want him to. Luka is the king of the mind-fuck, and he savors the role.

Maybe he doesn't ask because he knows I would lie to him, would never admit that I perceive the world as nothing more than a gray expanse. White and black mingled long ago, got tangled so intricately into a Gordian knot that they've lost all distinction. Sometimes I think that if I really put my mind to task I could untie that knot, could work out by sheer force of will which strands are right and which are wrong. But I am not Alexander; I never bore a sword, never quite managed to fulfill prophesies through the use of cold steel, though I've tried. God, I have tried.

No, Patrick had it sussed all along, knew never to question, never to doubt. "Patrick is the only one of us who got it right," I snarl, my voice dripping venom. "He got everything he wanted: the girl, the kids, the nine-to-five life, and the mortgage."

"You would have been just as miserable as I was with those things, James," Mother says quietly. "You are different, better; you have imagination and passion and drive. You questioned authority, society, and God from the moment you could formulate the questions. You never took no for an answer. You had it all, and then you gave it all away for the sake of a girl who didn't deserve the sacrifice."

Now I know Patrick is behind this little chat. The back-stabbing Judas may have promised not to mention Her, but that didn't stop him from instructing Mother to have this talk with me instead.

"Nothing personal, Mother, but I am not prepared to discuss Her with you any more than I was prepared to discuss Her with Patrick," I say, seething inside. Why would she choose our first real conversation in years to raise the one topic that is beyond the pale?

She opens the French windows and walks out into the late afternoon sunlight, pulling her cardigan close around her shoulders. She really does look like somebody's grandmother—she is somebody's grandmother. I have trouble with that concept. I follow her out onto the porch because it seems like she's expecting it and because I'm probably not allowed to smoke inside the house, and I do feel the need to feed at least one habit.

"I have wondered for years whether it was all my fault," she says while I light a cigarette. "I was never a model parent. I know that. I was part of the first generation of women who were extended equal rights, the first generation of children who were educated, regardless of gender or economic background. Say what you like about socialism, but for a peasant girl like me it provided opportunities and rights my own mother could only dream of. I never really thought about having children before getting pregnant with Patrick, never felt the urge to be a parent."

"Then why did you continue to get pregnant?" I ask without thinking. That was harsh and uncalled for, however relevant.

"It was 1962, James. Getting yourself pregnant in those days meant getting married, especially if you were Catholic. I was lucky your father took my side when it came to schooling. Everybody else was all in favor of my quitting university and staying home to have babies..."

I know the rest of the story; it has become part of the family legend. I suppose I never did the math, never worked out the discrepancies between my parents' wedding date and Patrick's birthday. It never occurred to me to do that. It explains a lot though, explains some of the bitterness and resentment and our parent's rocky relationship. It does not explain why they continued having children. Shaky though my sex education—courtesy of 80-year-old Sister Mathilda, bless her soul—was, I'm fairly certain that by the time I came along right around Epiphany in 1971, there was plenty of contraception around.

She answers the unvoiced question. "We decided to have you. I had finished my Ph.D., and we both were from large families. It seemed cruel to leave Patrick an only child, and I really wanted a little girl."

That's part of the legend too. Mother was so convinced she was having a girl that she only ever picked out girls' names. It fell upon my paternal grandfather to name me, like he eventually would name Luka and Micky, leaving us all with solid Irish names, names we all rejected and abandoned in our quest for anonymity.

"I always thought that girls would be intuitive, but I had no idea what to do with four boys," she continues. "And I know I made mistakes, especially with Patrick. Everything was going to be different with you. I told myself I had learned from my experience with Patrick, told myself that I would welcome your girlfriends when they came, and then I saw Her when you snuck Her in the first time, and it all turned into some sort of Freudian joke, or maybe a nightmare."

"Why?" I ask, totally bewildered.

"You really don't know?" she asks.

I shake my head. "I'll show you," she says. "Wait here for a minute."

She goes back inside the house, and I dig my cigarettes out of my pocket, out of habit more than anything else. I manage to smoke about half of a cigarette before she returns, handing me a black and white photograph of Her.

"Where did you get this? I've never seen it before," I ask, shaken but much better prepared than I was for Luka's picture a few months ago.

Mother takes a deep breath and closes her eyes. "That's not Catriona, James. That's me at seventeen."

The first time I see her smoking outside the art college I think she's an illusion, because I have never seen such perfection before. As I detour past the college for the next three weeks and see her smoking and laughing and sparkling with her friends outside, I realize that she is real. The reaction in my trousers every time I see her is easy to interpret, but it takes me three more weeks to identify the feeling in my stomach. I consult Ovid and Shakespeare and a hundred other authorities on the subject before I resign myself to the idea that the motion sickness I experience while standing stock-still when I see her might very well be love.

Bugger! Coming from a family woefully under-supplied in the girls department, I have absolutely no idea how to go about asking one out. Somehow it gets through my pink-hazed stupor that she probably wouldn't appreciate being wrestled to the ground, which is how I routinely express my affection for Declan and Micky. The fact that she goes to the art college also indicates that she might be a few years older than me. The odds are not in my favor. Where the hell is Patrick when I need him? Oh yeah, gallivanting around Germany with the little drummer girl. Looks like I'll have to work this one out from first principles.

I vaguely remember somebody telling me that first impressions are important, so my first stop is a ridiculously expensive hairdresser, not a barber, where my head gets updated to the spring fashions for 1986. Then I blow an outrageous amount of money on a new wardrobe, and spend two more weeks trying to pluck up the courage to talk to her.

She saves me the trouble. "Oi, Blondie," she hollers and grins when she sees me blush. I swear one of these days I'll have to pull a Patrick and dye the hair. "Relax," she continues, "I was just wondering if you had a light."

I make a show of patting down my various pockets although I'm perfectly aware that I have a matchbook in my back pocket. Still tongue-tied I pull it out and hand it to her.

She smiles as she lights her cigarette and hands the matches back to me. "Ta, love," she says as I start walking away, breathing a sigh of relief at the relative lack of embarrassment of this first encounter. I'm halfway down the street when she hollers, "Has anyone ever told you you've got a cute arse?"

I spin around, and I swear if my mind weren't doing cartwheels because she thinks my arse is cute, the ground would swallow me up whole. As it is, I do the only thing I can think of to hide the blush. I run back up to her, grab her face, and plunge my tongue into her mouth.

You know you've had too much of a classical education when you notice Greek tragedy punching you in the face, I realize as I heave over a flowerbed. When I finally stop throwing up into my mother's roses, the sun is starting to set. I would like to think, at least for the moment, that the unbearable nausea is the result of sleep deprivation and jet-lag rather than a reaction to the Sophoclean turn my life has taken. Mother didn't really expect this reaction either; she excused herself long ago mumbling something about going to vespers.

I walk back into the kitchen and open a few cupboards randomly until I find the hard liquor. I rinse my mouth out with cooking brandy and study the labels of the various bottles trying to decide what to get smashed on. On the whole I think I'm taking the revelation that I have apparently spent my entire life fucking my mother's clones better than most.

I haven't punched anyone or anything yet, I haven't proclaimed myself a god, and I haven't slit my wrists, which leaves me leagues ahead of a typical Sheahan reaction. In fact, all I'm really planning to do is get so mind-numbingly drunk I won't be able to remember any of this in the morning. After a moment's contemplation I select a bottle of vodka and break the seal. I don't bother with a glass.

A few fingers into the bottle, I start to relax a little and move into the living room. Sitting there, sinking into the overstuffed couch with the bottle firmly attached to my mouth, I remember why I usually don't drink by myself. A drunk James Sheahan only comes in two flavors: belligerent or brooding. Since there is no one around to pick a fight with, the liquor goes straight to the brain and triggers the thought processes usually responsible for extended periods of self-piteous reflection.

I wonder why I'm so disturbed by the realization that I'm attracted to women who look like my mother. After all, my mother has always been strikingly handsome, if not beautiful; I am also painfully familiar with the old adage about all girls marrying their fathers, and there must be some truth to all that feminist rot about equality of the sexes. If I were to be truthful, and considering the amount of vodka I've had on an empty stomach it would be hard not to be, I'd have to admit that the real reason I'm so upset is not that my mother is unattractive, but that I have never liked her very much.

This raises the ugly point that I haven't liked any of the girls I have slept with much either. I bed them because they look like Her, lust after them even, but after the sexual frustration has been vented successfully, I'd rather they are gone by morning. Suddenly, I'm terrified that I may not have liked Her either.

I loved and hated Her with equal passion; I worshiped Her, was obsessed with Her, but none of those emotions are dependent upon my actually liking Her. I'm desperately trying to remember something, anything, I liked, but I can't. I can remember a million things I didn't like about Her, but when I try to think of something I liked, all I remember is the pain, the betrayal, the sorrow, and the hatred.

In the foggy recesses of my mind, it dawns on me, not for the first time, that love may have died early on in our relationship—if it ever was truly there to begin with. After that came near on eight years of making each other pay for every little transgression, slowly, painfully, dissecting each other's hearts without ever unleashing the furies within.

Invoking love as an excuse, we mercilessly dedicated our waking moments to making each other miserable. I didn't like Her, because once love dies all that remains are the need for vengeance and the ghosts that will chase you to the ends of the earth and beyond, the ghosts that still haunt me.

Contemplating the last few fingers of liquor remaining in the bottle, I think to myself that the one thing I really liked about Sally was the way she would unbridle her fury, ride it out until it dissipated into the night. In a moment of clarity, it occurs to me then that in the sixteen years I have spent consumed by a woman I didn't even like, I may have let the only woman I did like slip away forever, and then there are tears running down my face.

I quickly down the rest of the bottle and wipe the wetness from my face. This is the liquor talking, bending lies into truth. No matter what my intoxicated mind screams at me now, when morning comes I will know again how much I loved Her and how little I cared for Sally or any of her predecessors. If I remember at all, I will cringe at the memory of these treacherous thoughts conjured up by too much alcohol. Ah, but *in vino veritas*, the traitor in my subconscious whispers to me.

Mindful of being in my mother's living room, I do not act on the urge to throw the empty bottle against the wall. Instead, I collect myself and will myself to stop thinking. I know what I need to repress all thoughts of tonight. I get up and grab my jacket from the kitchen, the keys from the mantelpiece, and walk out of the house in the direction of the nearest pub. Tonight I will find myself a girl, tall and blonde and vapid, with tits instead of brains, the antithesis of all I have ever wanted in a woman, and I will fuck her until my mind is purged, even if only to prove that I am quite capable of fucking something other than my mother's clones.

In between mixing drinks with highly unlikely names, I try to scan the dance floor for Catriona. As long as I can see her gyrating to the music, I know at least that she isn't gyrating against somebody's crotch. She was wasted last time she came by the bar a few hours ago, and I'm pretty sure she's getting her drinks on the other side of the room because I would have cut her off long ago, thus disregarding the rule that if they can stagger up to the bar they can have another drink. I see her periodically on the far side of the dance floor as I continue to mix drinks until closing time.

When I start cleaning up the bar, there are only a few stragglers left on the dance floor, and I can't see Catriona among them. I start to rush the cleaning job in order to clock out and find her and take her home before she has a chance to do something stupid. Ten minutes later I start scan-

ning the dark corners I couldn't see from the bar.

I find her eventually sitting on the lap of some tall idiot whose got his hand up her skirt and his tongue wrapped around her tonsils. Once upon a time I might have hit the guy, but the novelty of ramming my fists into some poor tosser whose only fault was to succumb to Catriona's drunken advances wore off after the first dozen times or so. Instead, I lift her off his lap and start carrying her out of the club, shrugging off his protests with a mumbled, "Sorry, mate, she's my girl."

I hear him laughing behind me, shouting after me, "Half an hour ago your whore was sucking my dick!"

I stop halfway across the dance floor, and if it weren't for Catriona clinging to my neck and slipping in and out of consciousness, I would probably go back and give him a good seeing to. As it is, all I can think about is getting Catriona home before anything else happens; she's just too wasted. So I concentrate on putting one foot in front of the other and holding on to Catriona as I walk out of the club.

It's cool outside, that time of night just before sunrise when the temperature falls to its low for the day, with a strong northerly wind blowing in from the ocean. The meltemi monster, they call that wind here. Catriona, in her skimpy outfit, is shivering a little and sobering up somewhat. At least she's conscious. I'm still carrying her toward our room, of course; it would be too much to hope that she could walk of her own accord, but she's smiling and nuzzling my neck.

I curse underneath my breath because my body is reacting to her no matter how much I would like it not to. If I weren't so pathetically in love with her, I would have left her there, I think, but the thought of her sleeping with the tall idiot is a thousand times worse than the knowledge that she was giving him head, so the white knight came to the rescue. That doesn't mean I'm not angry. I'm fucking furious. I have a hard time just looking at her right now, and she's trying to fix things by kissing my neck.

When Catriona is wasted she gets horny, tries to sleep with anything that meets the minimum requirements of two legs and an upright stance. As soon as we get back to our room, Catriona starts unzipping my jeans, and no matter how much I try not to give in, I get hard anyway. "Cat, please don't," I mumble.

"Want you," she pouts and pulls me onto the bed. I know she doesn't really want me, she just wants a man, but it's hard to think straight when your body has taken matters into its own hands. She moves her hand up

and down my dick for a few seconds, just to make sure I'm ready, and then she shoves it inside her without even taking off her clothes.

If I had any willpower at all I would pull out now and walk away, but the flesh is weak. Instead, I close my eyes because I can't bear to look at her and start thrusting, trying not to think about what I'm doing. I don't know how long it takes—it feels like an eternity—but eventually she comes, and I'm free to stop. I pull out and grow flaccid pretty much immediately, feeling cheap and used and wondering vaguely whether this is what it feels like to be raped.

She's going to sleep now, but I still don't want to look at her, don't even want to be in the same room with her, so I zip up my jeans and quietly let myself out of the room and head off toward the beach.

I wake up to a marching band in my head and a dirty carpet in my mouth. I also get the distinct feeling that I may not be alone in my bed on account of something warm and soft pressing against my back. I groan, partly because the hangovers seem to get worse the older I get and partly because random bits of last night are sneaking back into my memory. I experimentally open my eyes and quickly close them again because the midday sun is causing the drums in my head to build to a crescendo.

A few minutes later I start opening my eyes again, slowly this time, and chance a glance at the other body in my bed. Then I groan again at the sudden memory of last night. She's blonde all right, but judging by the color of her eyebrows the hair color comes out of a bottle. The parts of her that aren't covered by the sheets indicate that she is also very naked. She looks too young. God, I hope she's legal.

I'm frantically trying to remember what we did last night, but my memory is fragmented from the moment I left the house; all I know with some degree of certainty about my actions afterwards is that there was a lot more alcohol involved. I suppose I should wake her, but I realize with a start that I have not woken up with a girl in my bed in years and am somewhat at a loss on how to proceed. Hesitantly, I start prodding what seem to be the least controversial parts of her body. This would be a lot easier if I could remember her name. I am such an arsehole.

Eventually she opens her eyes and grins. Then she stretches out her hand and says, "Hi, I'm Gemma. I told you last night, but I doubt you'd remember."

At least she has a sense of humor, I think. "James," I mumble shaking her hand, "but I guess you know that."

An uncomfortable silence follows now that the introductions are over. I am so bad at this whole morning-after business.

"So, who's Sally?" she eventually asks to break the silence.

I raise an eyebrow, which causes my hair to throb, "Excuse me?"

"You were calling me Sally last night," she says, biting her lip, which would look kind of cute if I weren't so damn embarrassed about the whole thing.

"Sweet Jesus!" I moan. "Shall I just go and shoot myself now to save us both the embarrassment?"

She laughs, and it somehow defuses some of the tension. "I'm not holding it against you," she giggles. "You were really rather drunk."

"I'm sorry," I reply, "I apologize for anything pratish I might have done. Not that I remember right now, but there's a reasonable chance I behaved like a complete tosser." I pause because there's something I really should ask, although I have no idea how. "Did I... I mean, did we... you know... do stuff?" I finish off lamely.

"Don't worry," she laughs again. "Some groping and some slobbery making out, but—well, it wasn't for lack of trying on your part, you understand, but I think you had just a bit too much to drink to actually perform."

I feel myself blushing as fresh memories flood back into my mind. At least she thinks my inability to perform was due to the alcohol, which is the one saving grace to this entire fiasco, I suppose. Poor girl doesn't know that I invented the concept of fucking while out of my brains and that, if anything, my inability to perform had something to do with my not liking her type. Now how to get rid of her in a polite manner so I can test whether certain appendages are fully functional again?

That's when the girl wins an award. "Well, it was nice meeting you and all, James, but I think I had better go home now," she says, and minutes later she is dressed and slipping out of the room. I bang my head against the bed frame a few times and breathe a sigh of sheer relief.

9

Parable: Of Monsters and Princesses

Patrick and the kids arrive the day before we are flying out to Split. Patrick, in an uncharacteristic moment of brilliance, figured out it would be much easier to spend the night in London and make it out to Heathrow for a leisurely afternoon flight than it would be to pile five cranky kids into a car at the crack of dawn and do several hours of driving before meeting me at Heathrow. It gives me a chance to peruse the little pests and see whether I should feign illness at the last moment, so I'm not complaining too loudly.

They get out of the car mid-afternoon and make their way past the door I'm holding wide open. Liam comes first, and there's no doubt he's Patrick's son; he's just as dark-haired and blue-eyed as my brother, and judging by the scowl on his twelve-year-old face, he's inherited the brooding gene as well. Next come the twins, Joey and Danny, who were babies when I saw them last. Their eyes and hair didn't darken when they outgrew infancy, and it's clear that they will take after the Sheahan side of the family. Two and a half now, they are blond and fair and bursting with energy. Shane, who also resembles his father, makes up the rear of their little column, nine years old with scratches and scabs all over his bare knees and elbows.

They push past me into the house, which seconds later is once again reverberating to the shouts of four Sheahan boys. The sole Sheahan girl in the immediate family is still hiding behind Patrick at this point. Patrick walks up to the door slowly, looking like he endured the seven circles of hell, or else a seven-hour car ride with five kids in the backseat.

"Afternoon, James," he says. "Don't mind them. They've been cooped up in the car half the day and are feeling a little restless. Should settle down by tea time." He looks down to the girl peeking out from behind his legs and says, "You're going to say hullo to your Uncle James then, princess?" Siobhan shakes her head but continues to peek out at me from behind her father's legs.

Siobhan is a princess all right. Ten years from now she'll break every boy's heart. In her seven-year-old face I can see the best of Irish and Slavic heritage combined. She's got her father's raven hair curling down her shoulders, the wide face, and the big blue Sheahan eyes, but I can also see my own cheekbones and nose there, the kind of features that promise great beauty in years to come. For a moment she makes me regret not having any children of my own.

Patrick's voice jolts me out of that temporary lapse of reason. "Right then, princess, run along and see what your brothers are up to. Dada needs to talk to Uncle James about grown-up stuff for a while."

The girl nods almost imperceptibly and bolts up the stairs after the boys while Patrick pulls me through the sitting room into the kitchen. He heads straight for the liquor cupboard and pulls out a bottle of Scotch. "Do you know where mother keeps the aspirin?" he asks while he fetches a couple of glasses and pours us generous doubles.

"That much of a lightweight in your old age, are you, Patrick?" I tease him.

"You just wait a few days until you've been stuck in a car with Liam for seven hours and we'll see whether you want to eat a bottle of aspirin afterwards," Patrick counters, but he's laughing. "To your health,

Seamus," he says and raises his glass.

"Don't call me that," I growl, albeit in a friendly manner, and down the shot. Actually, I've never liked whiskey much, but it remains Patrick's poison of choice, and I suppose we should bond now because the fighting will come soon enough.

"Why are you doing this, Patrick?" I ask.

"Doing what?" Patrick asks blithely, pouring another shot.

"You know what I'm talking about," I reply, "All of this."

"Sorry, still not following you," he says, and I know he's lying. He knows perfectly well what I'm talking about, but he wants me to spell it out for him.

"What brought on the great effort to save the loser, Patrick?" I ask, spitting the words out at him. "Don't give me that shite about Siobhan either, the girl hardly recognized me. Besides, Mother and I had that little chat you instigated."

Patrick sighs. "Has it occurred to you that after spending each and every day surrounded by prepubescent boys I may just want to spend some time with an adult?"

"It has, but no. If that were the case, you would have asked Micky to join you," I reply. "Let's face it, Patrick, the only times we talk these days are when we are hurling insults at each other or when I use you as a punching bag. So why don't you tell me what this is really about so I can tell you to go fuck yourself."

Patrick puts the bottle down on the breakfast bar and sinks onto one of the stools, motioning at me to have a seat. "I'm not really sure myself," he says, "All I know is that you're clearly not happy with your life such as it is. Maybe I can help you figure out what would make you happy, or at the very least give you a holiday from the tedium of everyday life."

"Why?" I ask.

"Because when all is said and done, I can't help thinking that maybe you're right and I am to blame for everything," he explains. "I know you only say it when you're angry, when you're trying to lay on the guilt, but I know I made mistakes. I know there is a chance, however negligible, that I started the chain of events that led to you being where you are today, and if I did—you were right about one thing, James, I need to be able to look at my kids and not feel guilt over how I failed you."

Crap. I may have just sent him on one guilt-trip too many this past spring. I must learn to keep my mouth shut. "Patrick, you shouldn't take it too seriously when I go off on you while I'm fuming or drunk or both. I really don't blame you for the mess I've made of my life," I sigh. I'm bending the truth just a bit though; I don't blame him much.

It's Patrick's turn to sigh now. "You only ever tell the whole truth while you are pissed as a newt, James, always have," he says. "You're too proud to actually admit that I had any influence on your life while you're sober, and there's a whole lot of could haves and should haves that run through my mind every time you treat me to one of your drunken outbursts. I could have stayed instead of running out on you boys. Later, I knew where you were for the first few months after you left home, and I could have come and dragged you kicking and screaming all the way back to London. I should have taken the boys instead of leaving them to you when you were barely more than a boy yourself. I should have made Her go away forever before she really got to you."

He's scrutinizing me, studying me, seeing if he can get a reaction other than stoicism out of me. When I don't respond, he continues, "If you're so desperate for a reason, how about because in my worst nightmares I know I could have fixed everything had I tried, but I never did, and I got everything and you got nothing?"

"You have nothing I would want, Patrick," I say, wondering whether he will believe it any more than I do.

"I have a good life, James," he says. "I have five and a half healthy children, a wife who loves me, and a nice house. Well, technically the house belongs to the bank, but you know what I mean. I have a job I quite like, and once a year Annie lets me head over to Berlin for a week to re-live my misspent youth."

"Whereas I've all the drugs I want, a nutcase brother who clings to me like a leech, a brilliant career as a writer-for-sale, and the Sheahan magic still works on any girl I care to bed," I reply sarcastically.

"Then why are you so unhappy?" Patrick asks, and there's no answer to that question, at least none I would admit to.

"If the mess I've made of my life bothers you so much, you could always claim the debt I owe you, Patrick," I say, almost too quietly for him to hear because I'm scared he may take me up on the offer.

He nods. "I could. I've thought about it."

"Why don't you?" I ask in spite of the warning sirens that are going off in my head. "I really wish you would claim it, you know. Maybe then we could go back to being how we were before. Maybe then you would stop hating me."

"I never hated you, James," Patrick says. "I hate who I became that day. I hate myself for every moral and religious law I broke, and no amount of rosaries can fix that. Most of all, I hate myself for what I allowed you to become."

"I am still me. That never changed," I say.

"Oh, but it did," Patrick snarls. "I tried to save your neck and created a martyr in the process. I never knew a boy who had as much spirit and talent as you had. I tried to give that spirit back to you, tried to recover what was salvageable by protecting you, but it was all for naught. Now, all that's left of you is a bitter, drug-ridden cretin marinating in cheap liquor and wallowing in self-pity. I dare you to look me in the eye and tell me you never changed."

Christ, he thinks he broke me. Doesn't he understand that by the time he stepped in there was nothing left to break? The boy Patrick knew, the essence of me, was long gone by the time reality forced his hand. Patrick was never to blame for that. He didn't even force me to acknowledge who and what I am. I did that all by myself with a little help from the goddess who, in the final analysis, proved to be merely mortal.

I follow his eyes, which are fixed on a spot on my shirt just above my heart. So that's what's bothering him. The fact that I went out and had that image etched into my skin a scant few days after the world came crashing in around me, the day after he thwarted my attempts to throw myself into Her grave. Did he guess its true significance? Did he somehow work out that it was never meant as a memorial?

"It's just a tattoo, Patrick," I say. "Luka has a homemade one himself. He was just a little bit less poetic about it than I was, never went in for the visual imagery."

He snorts. He clearly doesn't believe a word I'm saying. Luka's scars are an angry statement of defiance engraved upon his heart. My scars symbolize surrender; I resigned myself to who I am, who I will always be, as the needle drove the ink into my skin. Patrick had nothing to do with that. On a whim I unbutton my shirt and watch the pained look travel across his face.

"Look at it, Patrick," I order, my voice much too raw. "So I borrowed a line from Neil Young. Doesn't mean much in the end. Every junkie plunges headfirst into the darkness, we both knew that beforehand, but the point was driven home that night. You've hated me every day since because you realized that I was travelling down the same road and taking Luka along for the ride."

Patrick still won't look me in the eye. "Damn you, Patrick!" I shout because the choir of traitors in my head has started a cacophony of its own. "You didn't allow me to become what I chose to be. I did that all by myself. The only thing that changed was that you no longer could blame Her. This is who I am, this is who I was before that night, and the only way you'll ever change that is by calling in the debt."

I feel my hands trembling, and I find myself wishing, praying, that for once in his life Patrick will listen to what I cannot say. I want this to end. I want to force his hand. Maybe, if I push him hard enough, I can be whole again.

I'm an idiot for thinking that, wanting and needing and wishing for Patrick to do what can't be done, because when push comes to shove, when have I ever listened to anything Patrick had to say? He's never been able to influence me. There are only two people who ever held that kind of power over me. One of them is dead, the other one insane, so no matter how much I pray, nothing will change; there will still be a broken shell hurtling toward oblivion, with or without Patrick's interference.

He shakes his head, "I cannot claim that debt for two reasons," he says quietly. "Firstly, you are selfish to demand that I use your debt to benefit you and you alone, but more importantly, you taught me long ago that we cannot force others to change unless they want to change themselves. You have never once shown any inclination for wanting to change; you just persist in feeling sorry for yourself and blaming the rest of the world for your shortcomings. I will not waste the debt you owe me on a hopeless cause."

"Claim the debt, Patrick, please," I plead, but he just shakes his head, and it is clear that the conversation is over for now.

I don't know how long I cling to Her lifeless body. Somewhere far at the back of my mind, a voice is screaming at me, clamoring for my attention, trying to convince me to get up and move before the coppers show, because they must, sooner or later, mustn't they?

Eventually I hear the door opening—someone with a key—and quiet footsteps moving quickly through the flat. Then strong arms are pulling me up, disentangling me from the corpse. Patrick isn't fighting me, just block-

ing my random blows as he pulls me to my feet. I vaguely notice the vomit all down my shirt, and I try to remember whether it is Hers or mine.

Somehow Patrick maneuvers me into the backseat of the car that is sitting outside, the engine idling. One of Patrick's rugby mates is sitting at the wheel, and Annie is in the passenger seat. Patrick shoves some clean clothes into her arms and turns to his mate. "Take him to your place and don't let him out of your sight. Sedate him if you have to; Annie's got some Demerol from when I broke my collarbone last year. Don't let him talk to anyone. I'll try to get there as soon as I can, but I don't know how long that will be." He turns back to Annie. "I don't know if I can fix this, babe."

Then he stalks back into the house and the car takes off. The next day passes in a blur of pills and booze. Annie left soon after we got to a flat in Brentford, I suppose she had to go and relieve the babysitter, but Patrick's mate is following his instructions to extremes, keeping me doped up. I suppose I ought to be grateful for it, but all I can think about is that Patrick should have returned hours ago.

When Patrick finally arrives it is night again, and he looks like he went on a ride straight to hell and back. He throws the keys to his car to his mate and says, "There's a rubbish bag in the boot of my car. Take the car and drive out of the city, at least thirty miles from London, then find a bin to throw the bag in. Give us a few hours and then come back here."

The guy just nods and leaves, and even in my befuddled state I realize he must owe Patrick for something big to do as he asks without question. How much will I owe Patrick when this night is over?

Once we are alone, Patrick picks me up by the scruff of my neck and drags me into the bathroom, "Time to sober up, lad," he mutters as he shoves my head into the shower and turns on the cold water.

After a few minutes I start fighting him, and he takes that as confirmation that I'm clear-headed enough to absorb whatever he has to tell me. He lets me sink to the floor and throws a towel at my head, then he sits down on the side of the tub, exhausted, and lights a cigarette.

"I fixed it for you," he says after a few deep drags. "There will be an inquest, of course, but no one will come after you or Declan. Your place is a mess, but they didn't find anything incriminating once I was finished with it. I called her mother too and took care of the funeral arrangements. You won't have to worry about it. I also got this back for you."

He fishes a ring out of his pocket. The ring I put on her finger when I married her. My great-grandmother's wedding ring. He strings it onto a gold necklace. "She pawned it a few days ago. I found the receipt while I was cleaning out the flat," he says as he hands it to me. "I got the chain because I thought you might want to wear it around your neck until you can give it to someone else."

"Why? As a reminder of what I had?" I ask, aware of the note of hysteria in my voice.

"As a warning for all eternity that some women come with too high a price attached," Patrick spits out in anger.

He fastens the chain around my neck. Trust Patrick to take the concept of the memento mori to an entirely new level. When he leans back again, I quietly wish I were crying so Patrick would embrace me, but I feel too empty and too drugged to shed real tears, and the ice in Patrick's eyes tells me that sympathy would not be forthcoming.

"Now understand this, Seamus," he says, "I sold my soul to save your sorry arse last night. I betrayed everything I know to be right and broke every law imaginable in the process. I have no doubt I will pay for that one day, if not in this life, then in the next. But we are brothers, and blood sometimes demands sacrifices that wouldn't be asked of others. You owe me a blood debt, and this debt you cannot erase with money or season tickets to Upton Park. This debt will remain to the day I choose to claim it, and claim it I will. When that day comes you will pay your debt to me upon pain of damnation."

I nod. Since I ceased to believe in god the threat of damnation has become ineffective at best, but I am still a Sheahan and we Sheahans understand debts that can never be repaid.

Patrick and I are cooking tea, and it is no easy task. It would appear that Liam doesn't eat anything that hasn't been fried, Shane avoids anything that started out without a heartbeat, and Siobhan doesn't like meat all that much. At least the twins are perfectly happy to eat anything that's put in front of them so long as it's bland and drenched in ajvar. About a half hour into the process I'm asking myself aloud why anyone would choose to have children of their own free will, so Patrick sends me out of the kitchen.

I make it into the living room. Correction, the room that my mother considered her living room before the kids were let loose unsupervised. I should have known they were being too quiet, I think, as I peruse the furniture piled up in the middle of the room and topped off with blankets and sheets to create a kind of fort. Then Siobhan is tugging on my sleeve. "Uncle James, d'you wanna see the Barbie doll Daddy got for you?"

"What's that, princess? Your daddy got me a Barbie?" I ask.

She nods and pulls me out into the hallway to pick a Barbie out of her overnight bag. I grin when I see it. Patrick actually dressed up a doll to look like Buffy, probably had to get the clothes specially made, including a toothpick for a stake.

"Don't you like it?" Siobhan asks worry spreading across her face.

I pull her into a tight hug. "No, princess, she's perfect," I laugh. "I just need to say something to your Daddy and then we'll play, OK?"

She nods and starts pulling other dolls out of her bag while I run back into the kitchen. "I take back everything I said, Patrick," I laugh.

"I take it you like the doll," Patrick says dryly without looking up from the frying pan.

"It rocks, but next time, can I get evil Willow?" I shout as I run back into the hallway.

I spend the remaining time until tea playing with Siobhan and her army of Barbies, and the initial shyness is swept away and replaced with adoration. It feels nice being admired by a little girl, being a hero, and I feel that twinge of regret again when I look at her knowing that if my life had taken a different turn fifteen years ago she could be my daughter. I quickly push away those feelings because I know no matter how much Siobhan adores me, I am no hero. I will never be a hero.

During tea she monopolizes me with her chatter, making clear to anyone listening that I'm there for her benefit, not her brothers', and I'm fairly certain that the rest of my vacation too will be dominated by the princess. When it's time to go to bed, Siobhan insists that I should tell her a bedtime story, and somehow she convinces me.

That's how I find myself sitting at the side of her bed and asking, "What kind of story do you want to hear then, princess?"

"I want a story about princesses and witches and brave knights," Siobhan exclaims excitedly.

The girl wants a fairy tale, it seems, and I think for a moment before obliging her. "Very well, Siobhan," I agree. "A long, long time ago, there lived a beautiful princess in a castle in a small market town. She had long black hair, just like yours, and the most brilliant green eyes anyone in the kingdom had ever seen, eyes that sparkled like emeralds."

"This isn't Snow White, is it?" Siobhan interrupts. "Only, I know that story, and I know Cinderella too."

"No, princess, this is a brand-new story just for you," I reassure her. "Where was I?"

"You were telling me the princess had black hair and the most beautiful green eyes in the kingdom," Siobhan helpfully supplies.

"That's right, princess," I say. "She had white skin, and freckles on her nose and shoulders, and her subjects thought she was the most beautiful princess there ever was, but all her beauty didn't mean anything because she was under a spell. You see, her mother, the queen, had made a bargain with a powerful witch when the princess was only a baby. The queen wanted her daughter to be the smartest and most beautiful girl anyone in the kingdom had ever seen, and instead of waiting to see just what nature held in store for her, the queen asked a powerful witch to lay a glamour on the princess when she was just an infant."

"I know Sleeping Beauty too," Siobhan pipes up.

I sigh. "For crying out loud, Siobhan, I already told you this is a brand-new story," I mutter. "Will you just let me get on with it?"

"Sorry," Siobhan pouts.

"All right," I continue. "As I was saying, the queen asked the witch to enchant the princess. At first the witch didn't want to do it. She was a good witch and she knew that all magic came with a price. She thought that it would be best to just wait until the princess had grown up a little, and she told the queen in no uncertain terms that they could always enchant the princess later on, but the queen wouldn't listen to her. So eventually the witch agreed to perform the spell.

"The princess grew up and became the smartest and most beautiful girl in the entire kingdom, but she also became the cruelest and meanest girl in the entire kingdom, because she knew that nobody was as beautiful or smart as she was. When she was old enough to get married, she haughtily rejected every suitor as being too stupid or too ugly to be a good match. The king, her father, grew more and more worried every day, thinking that if the princess remained so heartless, no prince would ever want to marry her.

"Word got around about how impossible the princess was, and after a while, fewer and fewer princes came to ask for her hand in marriage. Then, one day, the princess was out riding in the palace grounds and she encountered the most handsome knight she had ever seen, riding a black charger. He reined in the horse and stopped a few yards away so she could get a good look at him, and the princess fell in love instantly, but before she could ask him his name, the knight turned around and rode away.

"Every day after that, the princess rode out along the same path at the same time, hoping to catch another glimpse of the knight. Sometimes she could see him in the distance, but it was weeks before he came close enough to talk again. 'Ho there,' she cried, 'What is your name, noble knight?'

"The knight laughed and spurred his horse. As he was riding away, he proclaimed, 'My name is whatever name pleases you, my princess.'

"This continued for quite some time. They would meet while out riding, and each time the princess asked a question about who the mysterious knight was or where he came from, he would answer that he was whoever the princess wanted him to be. After some weeks the princess started to grow impatient. She was in love with the handsome knight and wanted to spend more time with him, so the next time they met she decided to ride after him and find out for herself where he came from.

"She followed him out of the palace grounds and into the woods, and she hardly noticed that the sun was starting to set as she spurred on her horse in an effort to keep up with the knight on his black charger. Eventually, as daylight was fading, they came at last to a clearing deep in the woods where an old castle stood. There the knight dismounted and his horse trod a few paces away and started to graze.

"'Why do you follow me, princess?' the knight asked when the princess' horse finally caught up with him.

"'Because you are the most handsome knight in all the kingdom and I love you and wish to marry you,' the princess said a little breathlessly. She wasn't very used to being nice to other people.

"The knight helped her dismount from her horse, drew her into his arms, and kissed her passionately. Then he looked her in the eyes and said, 'You do not know who I am or whence I came, yet you wish to marry me?'

"'Yes!' the princess swooned, still beside herself from the passionate kiss she had received.

"'Be careful what you wish for,' the knight said seriously, before taking her in his arms again.

Then they kissed again, and the princess felt like she was dying a little with the joy of being kissed by the knight, and then she must have fainted, because when she opened her eyes she was alone, stretched out on top of a bale of hay in a dark room.

"She didn't know where she was, but truly she didn't care either, because all she wanted was to be kissed again by her knight. Meanwhile, the king and queen had noticed that their daughter hadn't returned from her afternoon ride and grew more and more worried, thinking that some evil might have befallen the princess. So the king summoned the most powerful wizards of his kingdom, beseeching them to work all their magic to find the princess.

"They looked for many days, casting all sorts of spells, but however hard they tried, they could find no trace of her. One by one they gave up and returned to their own homes. The princess, meanwhile, was back at the castle in the woods, not noticing the passage of days while she was entranced by her knight. He would kiss her and she would forget every other concern in the world. She didn't even notice that she was growing thinner and wasting away while she was in the knight's arms. At long last, weakened by the days without food or daylight, she fell into a deep trance and didn't wake up again.

"At her father's castle, only one wizard remained. He summoned his most powerful magic to cast a spell older and more potent than any the kingdom had seen before, and with this spell he finally pinpointed the princess' location. The king sent out his personal guard at once to rescue the princess, but when they arrived at the clearing in the forest, they found her weakened in a deep, dark sleep amongst the ruins of an ancient castle.

"They carried her back to her father's castle and all the finest doctors in the kingdom were summoned at once to examine her. They could find no obvious reason for her sleep. She was emaciated and sickly after her many days without food, but there was no reason why she shouldn't be awake, and they concluded at last that it was magic that was keeping the princess unconscious.

"The king then summoned the wizard who had found her in the first place. The wizard cast many spells to determine what was wrong. He found that the princess had been enchanted, but he also found that he couldn't lift the new enchantment without undoing the spell that had made the princess the smartest and most beautiful girl in the kingdom. When he told the king and queen about this, they didn't know what to do, because nobody had any idea what the princess would look like without the enchantment, and nobody knew whether she was really smart or not. The king was even more worried that the princess wouldn't be able to make a good match. She was already notorious throughout the kingdom for her bad temper and sharp tongue, and he feared that were she no longer the most beautiful girl in all the kingdom, absolutely no prince would want to marry her.

"The king thought long and hard about what to do and eventually decided that he couldn't take the risk of the princess being ugly and dumb on top of being unpleasant, so he thanked the wizard for his troubles and declined his offer to lift the enchantments. The king then proclaimed that the prince who could wake the princess from her unnatural sleep would earn her hand in marriage.

"A few princes answered the challenge and tried to rouse the princess from her sleep by various means. Some of them brought their own wizards and warlocks to work all sorts of magic, but to no avail. There weren't that many princes to start with, since many had been put off by the princess' generally bad behavior, and there were even some rumblings in the kingdom that the royal castle had never been as pleasant before, so the few remaining princes soon lost interest in lifting the enchantment.

"The king, desperate to save his daughter, then proclaimed that any man in the kingdom who would rouse the princess from her sleep could marry her and become a prince. First the knights and other men of noble birth tried to save the princess, but they all failed.

"Eventually, after all of the high-born men of the kingdom had given up, a humble boy from the king's own stables stepped forward and claimed he could wake the princess with the wizard's help. He was the same boy who tended to the princess' favorite horse, and although she never so much as looked at him, he was in love with her. Everyone laughed of course, because they couldn't believe that a stable boy would succeed where all the knights and princes and gentlemen in the kingdom had failed, but the king was desperate.

"The stable boy and the wizard went into the chamber where the princess was laid out on a bed, looking like an angel with her black hair and freckled skin. The stable boy then did the bravest thing imaginable: he persuaded the wizard to lift both enchantments, determined that he would love the princess for herself, even if she were ugly or stupid or both. You see, the humble stable boy had realized that true love meant loving the person inside, no matter how abrasive or mean, rather than the face that person wore."

"That isn't a very happy ending, Uncle James," Siobhan interjects. "Doesn't that mean that now the stable boy will have to marry an ugly and mean princess who's in love with someone else?"

Smart girl, that one. I shake my head. "No, Siobhan, because by being so utterly selfless and showing that he was willing to do anything in order to make the princess happy, the stable boy proved to the princess that he loved her for herself, rather than for how she looked or how smart she was. After the enchantments were lifted, it turned out that while the princess was no longer the most beautiful or the smartest girl in the kingdom, she was still quite pretty and fairly smart. She still had quite a temper on her, but the princess learned her lesson and tried to be nicer to everyone. Thankfully, she couldn't remember the knight that had enchanted her all that much, so she soon fell in love with the stable boy who had woken her. The king lived up to his word as well and made the stable boy a prince and gave him the princess' hand in marriage, and they lived happily ever after."

I take in the satisfied look on Siobhan's face for a moment, before soft clapping prompts me to turn around to where Patrick is leaning against the door. "That was a beautiful fairy tale, James," he says. "And now it is definitely time for bed, Siobhan."

Siobhan nods and snuggles up underneath the blanket, closing her eyes. I turn off the bedside lamp and slowly get up and walk out of the room. At the door I turn around and say, "Good night, princess."

"Good night, Uncle James," she replies drowsily.

I shut the door and look at Patrick who's staring at me with an unreadable expression on his face. "How long were you listening?" I ask.

"Long enough to recognize the metaphors," he says. "Dying a little when the dark knight kissed her? For crying out loud, James, she's seven years old. Do you think you could perhaps go easy on the Elizabethan sex imagery?"

I grin. "Writer, remember? Besides, she'll never get it—well, at least not for a few years yet."

Patrick scowls at me. "I trust you'll never tell her the true conclusion of the story?"

I shrug. "Why would I want to do that? Life will teach her soon enough that happy endings are the stuff of fairy tales."

"There are happy endings in real life too, if you want them badly enough," Patrick says.

I look at him, eyebrow raised, with what I know is cockiness. "Grow up, Patrick. There are no happy endings in this life," I say. "You and I both know that the dark knight drove the princess to an early grave because the humble stable boy never got his head out of his arse long enough to save her. We were there, or had you forgotten?"

"The princess chose the dark knight over the stable boy," Patrick replies.

"So the morale of the story is that in real life the monster always wins," I snap at him.

He looks at me quizzically for a moment and turns away. "The monster only wins when you choose to let it win, James," he mutters as he retreats back down the stairs.

10

History: Into the Old Country

On the drive from the airport to the village of our mother's ancestors, I unostentatiously scan the countryside for signs of fighting. Logically, I know that we're too far away from points where armies tried to break through to the coast, too far away from where the fighting took place, but I'm still looking for the bullet holes that will make it all real.

I know Patrick comes down here at least once or twice a year to take care of family business. At the height of the war, when commercial flights were halted, he flew to Italy and made the long drive down the coastal highway to tend to the few remaining relatives of my grandparents' generation. I never came with him, partly because I had my hands full with Micky and Luka, and partly because coming here would have meant acknowledging the reality of a merciless conflict that swept through the mountains I associated with some of my happiest childhood moments. I have not been here since my grandmother died.

Once, driving through Sinj, it seems I can glimpse the ruins of a burnt house in the distance, but it could be natural decay. We're too far away to tell the difference. Then we're driving into the mountains again, getting closer to the newly re-drawn border with Hercegovina, and just before the border, the village my mother comes from. Patrick and I park the cars at the bottom of the hill, just off the winding mountain road. The last half-mile will have to be completed on foot; the road up to the village wasn't designed with modern vehicles in mind.

"All right, boys, princess, everyone carry as much as you can. We'll come back for the rest later," Patrick instructs us. "Don't get off the path either; there are snakes up here."

Siobhan squeals, and I lean down to her ear and whisper, "Don't worry, princess. In thirty years, I haven't yet seen a snake. I think Daddy makes it all up."

She looks at me gratefully and grasps my hand in hers as we start walking up the hill together.

The house is much as I remember it, built with rough-hewn thick gray stone carved out of the mountainside at least a century ago. Over the years, amenities were added, electricity and a kitchen with running water, but it remains essentially the tiny three-roomed structure my mother was born in, a house without indoor plumbing in which my grandparents raised half a dozen children. There is an old cistern that still collects rainwater for irrigation, but over the past twenty years our cousins have added water and sewage tanks to bring the design up to the twentieth century. Still, the toilet is outside, set a good fifty yards from the house.

Behind the house I can hear the clucking of hens, which have been kept alive by cousins who drive up from modern condominiums in Split once or twice a week, arriving in large German cars, to tend to the house. Patrick unlocks the door with a key that is hidden underneath a planter box on the front porch. I doubt it is really necessary; nobody would come in here unless they had a right to do so and even if they did, there is nothing to steal here save poverty, and there is plenty of that for those who want it.

He shoos the kids inside and fumbles for the light switch. A bare 60-watt bulb hanging from the ceiling lights up the room, a cross between a sitting room and a kitchen, with a couch and some armchairs at the front of the room, a large 60s-style Formica table with some folding chairs scattered around it at the center of the room, and a large porcelain sink and a wood-burning stove in the back. No refrigerator—what little electricity made it up the mountain is not enough to sustain such modern contraptions. I know from the fading memories of my childhood that there is a kind of cooler though, carved into the foot-deep stone of the wall, that will keep food reasonably fresh for at least a day or so even in the heat of summer.

The two other rooms are the master bedroom and the children's room respectively, and even that is luxury for a house such as this. The master bedroom is filled almost completely with a large, cast-iron double bed, a bed in which my mother and all her siblings were conceived and born. The other room has two ramshackle twin beds in it and two loose mattresses leaning against the wall, mattresses which were added much later to accommodate my brothers and me when we were visiting. When mother was growing up, the children simply doubled up in the beds.

While the twins are happy enough to sleep anywhere, and Siobhan and Shane are young enough to see all of this as a big adventure, Liam is scowling. Well, he does little else even in England, but he is scowling a trifle more now. "You brought us here, and that's supposed to be a holiday," he looks accusingly to his father. "There's not even a telly."

Patrick laughs. "Not enough electricity, Liam," he replies, "And even if there were, I doubt you'd be able to pick up a signal, mountains in the way and all that."

"Some holiday!" Liam whines.

"Liam, your grandmother was born in this house," I try to reason with him. "Spent seventeen years of her life living here together with five brothers and sisters. I'm sure you'll survive for a couple of weeks."

"Yes, and I'm sure she had to walk five miles to school, in the snow, uphill, both ways," Liam says sarcastically.

Patrick remains unfazed. "More like seven miles, all the way down the mountain and back up again," he grins. "And you should see the winters up here, something fierce."

"I hate you!" Liam shouts and runs out of the house banging the door behind him.

"Do you think we should go after him?" I ask Patrick.

Patrick shakes his head. "No. Nothing up here except stones for miles and he isn't wearing the right shoes for it. Anyway, it's tea time soon, and he'll come back when he's hungry. Let's get settled, and then we can get ready to pick up Tetka Jela and go for dinner. I'm sure she's expecting us, and when Liam sees her house, he'll be glad of the home comforts this one offers."

It's a hot summer afternoon, and Declan, Micky, and I are running up the terraced hill looking for trouble. Our knees are scabbed from countless encounters with stone walls, and our ankles are scratched from the underbrush. Down the hill in front of the house, I can see the glow of the massive stone grill above which a lamb is roasting. Patrick is down there somewhere. He decided to join us for a few weeks, sans the girlfriend, because in these parts you just don't sleep with girls you aren't married to.

Patrick and Dida moved the kitchen table outside this morning. Baka is peeling potatoes, and Dida is sitting there with a bottle of plum brandy, occasionally rising and waving his walking stick at us. Right now he is hollering in his most menacing bark, "If you don't get out of my potato field double-quick, I'll tan your hides the minute you get back down here!"

We giggle, because Dida is more bark than bite and more likely he'll shower us with kisses when we finally make it back to the house. By then he will probably be gone to pick up his crazy spinster sister, although he wouldn't thank us for calling her that. He's explained at least ten times already that she is a little "touched," something that happened during the great war while he was off in the mountains fighting with General Tito against the Germans, something that left her changed, but that is only ever hinted at, never explained, in front of us children.

Nevertheless we oblige him and hurry out of the field, up to the stonewalled pasture where the donkeys are grazing. Last summer Micky was still terrified of the animals, wouldn't come within yards of them, but this summer he's taken a liking to the docile beasts and spends long hours riding them around the field. We chase them around for a few hours, hop onto and off their backs, all the time squealing with pleasure. This is heaven on earth for us: the home where once a year for three long, glorious months we get to be children.

When the sun begins to set behind the mountain, Patrick makes his way up the hill to fetch us for dinner, entertaining us with tales of poisonous snakes all the way back to the house. It's a typical Saturday evening. There will be roast lamb and fried potatoes, raw onions on ajvar, and pickled cabbage. There will be sweet homemade wine, diluted with water for us children, and plum brandy for the adults. Eventually they will chase us to our beds, only to wake us at the crack of dawn on Sunday to get us dressed in our church clothes. Down the hill where the road starts, Dida will load us into an ancient automobile and drive us the five miles to church to hear mass. There is a graveyard there, with row upon row of our mother's ancestors, the older tombstones almost too faded to make out the family name, but our great-aunt will be there, ready and willing to tell us who is buried where and what relation they are to us.

There will be cold, carved lamb for lunch, and then we will run up the hill again, shouting all the way, until Patrick comes to fetch us for supper. This must be paradise.

At tea time we set off to collect our ancient great-aunt. She still lives in the house she was born in almost eighty years ago, a few more miles up the mountain. We drive further up the winding road until we get to the path that leads up to her house. Again we park the cars by the side of the road and complete the last part of the journey on foot.

She is expecting us. I assume the last cousin who came up here to check on her let her know that we were coming to visit, because she comes running out of the house excitedly to peruse Patrick's brood. I elbow Liam to stop scowling, and once the initial greetings are over and Patrick tells her that we are going to take her to dinner, she runs back into the house to get her scarf. Patrick follows her inside, no doubt in order to slip her an envelope of cash. Independence to her meant the cessation of the paltry war pension she had received under the old system, her sole source of income.

I take Siobhan's hand and lead her up to the house: a square of the same rough-hewn stone as my grandparent's house, but barely larger than six yards on each side. There is a single small window into the one and only room. Underneath the house is the stable with a solitary cow in it, which provides central heating to the room above, as long as one doesn't mind the smell. This house has no running water and no electricity. There is a wood-burning stove in a corner of the room that serves as bedroom, kitchen, and living quarters, and water must be gotten from the well in the village square.

Of course it isn't much of a village anymore, hasn't been since 1941, when half the houses were burned down in a single night, never to be touched again. The only villagers that returned were those that had nowhere else to go. Now there are just three houses still habitable. One is Tetka Jela's, the other two have weekend-residents only.

When Patrick and Tetka Jela come out of the house again, Tetka Jela is talking to Patrick, whose facial expression is grim. I have trouble following the conversation, but the gist of it seems to be that the local government is trying to convince Tetka Jela to sign over the deeds to the land in exchange for a government pension. Patrick is telling her not to do anything of the kind. This mountain belongs to our family, no matter how worthless. Besides, we take care of our own, always have.

Suddenly, Patrick shouts, "Shane, Siobhan, get away from there at once!"

I turn around to see them at the threshold of the ruins of a house that none of us will ever enter, and Tetka Jela is crossing herself. Siobhan, startled by Patrick's urgency and probably tired from all the travelling, bursts into tears. I run up to her and pick her up from where she is dissolving into a crying mess. I don't know where it comes from, but it seems natural to hold her and pat her back while she sobs into my shirt.

"Shh, princess," I murmur. "Daddy didn't mean to shout at you like that."

A few yards away Patrick is loudly scolding Shane, which probably doesn't reassure Siobhan any.

"I didn't do anything wrong," Siobhan sobs.

"No you didn't, princess," I say. "You didn't know that we never go into that house."

"Why?" she sniffles.

I look at Patrick, the question written all over my face. She's his daughter, and it's up to him to decide whether or not I can tell her the truth. He shrugs, then nods almost imperceptibly, his eyes pleading with me to tell her the most child-friendly version I can come up with under the circumstances.

I carry Siobhan over to a low stone wall that long ago probably surrounded a vegetable patch and sit her down on my lap. Patrick pushes Liam and Shane in my direction. It's clear that he only wants to cover this story once and he's relieved that he won't have to do the telling.

I think for a moment before I begin. "A long time ago, when your grandmother was only a baby, there was a great war. This country was controlled by the Ustashe, who collaborated with the Nazis. Your great-grandfather and some of his brothers and cousins were off in the mountains, fighting with the rebels against the occupation. One day, a German soldier was killed by the rebels, so their commander said that unless the villagers gave up the rebel that had killed his man, he would have ten village men shot for each soldier that had been killed by the rebels.

"The villagers wouldn't give up their own sons and brothers, so the commander got mad and ordered every man over the age of fourteen to be killed. That house we don't go into was the house where Tetka Jela's father and four of her uncles were executed. Then the soldiers set fire to all the houses of the people they shot. Tetka Jela and her sisters and mother ran up into the mountains and hid for three days, until the soldiers left, before they came back down here to bury their men.

"Something really bad happened in that house, Siobhan. The ghosts of the people who died are still there. So we don't touch it, and we don't go in there, ever. We leave it there as a reminder of what happened, a kind of memorial and a kind of warning to the generations to come, but we never touch it. You must never go in there."

I look up at Patrick, and he seems satisfied with my explanation. Probably thanking his lucky stars that I didn't delve into details about the SS and the fact that they made the women watch as they shot their fathers and brothers. Didn't tell her that the real reason the men were left unburied for three days was that the women weren't allowed to bury their dead. Didn't tell her what three days in the summer heat will do to a corpse. Didn't tell her about the question that haunts me, the question that has never been asked aloud and never answered: after they'd shot all the men, what did they do to the women?

I'm helping Declan study for his English Lit A-level because I have been deemed an appropriate English tutor. God knows why, because I never got around to finishing my own A-levels; I was too busy running around Europe for that. Nevertheless, here I am on my day off, slugging through "King Henry IV, Part One" with Declan, vaguely wondering whether they'll ever kick that one off the syllabus in favor of one of the more bloodthirsty historical plays and thanking my lucky stars that Declan has judged me too much of an idiot to study A-level Latin or Ancient Greek with him. At least Micky had the decency to pick Physics, Chemistry,

Maths, and Further Maths for his subjects, so there's no chance in hell I'll be asked to do any helping whatsoever.

I'm more than grateful when the phone starts ringing and interrupts our painstaking memorization of quotes that might be of use in the exam. "Sexgods Incorporated," I answer. It has become something of a running joke over the past few months. Last week I startled at least three callers by answering 'city morgue.'

"I thought your household was better known for its nymphomaniacs. I mean, its one nymphomaniac," Patrick remarks dryly.

"Fuck off, Patrick," I reply. "Is there any reason why I shouldn't hang up on you now?"

"Yeah, actually there is," Patrick says. "What are you up to?"

"A-level English, and I'm not entirely happy about it," I grumble. "Did you have anything better in mind? A couple of pints maybe?"

Patrick sighs. "This isn't a social call, James. Switch on your telly, BBC News."

I grapple with the remote for a few seconds before the picture comes up. I look at the view of the town being shelled for a few moments before bursting out laughing.

"It's not funny," Patrick says angrily.

"I'm sorry mate, it's the irony of it all," I gasp, "We were just reading 'Henry IV, Part One.'"

"Not following you there and would you stop laughing!" Patrick snaps.

I roll my eyes, "Honestly, you're such an uneducated pillock, Patrick. Act 2, scene 3: 'in thy faint slumbers I by thee have watch'd, and heard thee murmur tales of iron wars.'"

"Fascinating. I'm glad that Shakespeare can amuse you so. I always found the historical plays intolerably boring, but then again I didn't call you to discuss the finer points of English literature," Patrick says exasperated. "Now can we get back to the reason I'm calling, which is that at this very moment Vukovar is being bombed into oblivion. The war's started."

"I can see that, Patrick," I reply. "All of them get out?"

"Yes, as a matter of fact they did, thanks so much for asking, you coldhearted bastard. What's more, we're starting to move the women and children over here for the duration. Not only the ones from Vukovar but all of them. It's only a matter of time until the shells reach the coast."

"Yeah, well, I've got to go right now, Patrick," I say, trying to suppress the panic that is threatening to engulf me. "Nice talking to you, let's do it

144

again real soon, goodbye." Then I slam down the phone.

Declan looks up from his notebooks in surprise as I crank up the volume of the television. I wordlessly wave him into silence as I watch the scene unfolding on the screen. This is war, up close and personal. Those are the cities of my ancestors being shelled to smithereens. These are my people at each other's throats.

That makes it real. Realer than a conflict over oil in the Middle East that was over before it even started, thanks to NATO muscle. There won't be any NATO muscle this time: there's no oil to be had. There's nothing to be had there except poverty, and NATO isn't interested in that. So who would care that a backwater country created artificially by allied treaties eighty years ago is tearing itself apart? After all, it's far away and foreign and why should we care who shoots whom? We only create the countries, never stick around long enough to mop up the mess because it doesn't really affect us one way or another. Except this time it does. This time there's a personal stake, for my family at least.

My mind is spinning with words that Declan will claim as his own in years to come: this isn't real, this can't be real, if I refuse to believe this is real it will go away.

I think I've lost the last of my innocence this evening.

Patrick and I are sitting on a low stone wall behind the house, passing back and forth an old water bottle that has been filled with sweet, homemade wine. Appropriately enough, the wall we are sitting on in the cool night breeze surrounds a patch of vines that are bearing this year's crop. The kids were too tired to argue much about going to bed and have been asleep for an hour or so, all except Liam who is probably still reading quietly in his bed. Danny, who was too scared by the new surroundings to sleep on his own, is curled up asleep in a blanket on Patrick's lap.

Patrick hands me the bottle and nods at the ground in front of me. "Go on," he says, "I know you want to. I won't hold it against you."

I hesitate for a moment before hopping off the stone wall and moving a few steps away. Then I tilt the bottle and let a liberal amount of wine splash to the ground. "For friends forsaken, lovers lost, I offer you libations in praise; accept them on behalf of the souls whom we remember today," I whisper breathlessly before sitting down again.

"*Absolve Domine animas omnium fidelium defunctorum ab omno vin-*

culo delictorum," Patrick adds and I want to punch him, but I control myself.

"No sin greater than being omnipotent and letting the world come to this, Patrick," I say acerbically, handing the bottle back to him. "Your God had better get down on his knees and beg forgiveness for the sorry state of creation before judging any of us."

Patrick takes the bottle and doesn't say a word, just drinks for a while. Eventually, when I'm half-thinking that he's decided to stop talking to me altogether, he says, "You handled the house story very well."

"Yeah, well, it's my job, you know. I make up stories for people who cannot deal with reality. That's all romances are really," I grin. "An escape for those that are too scared or too fucked up to make their own sex lives, complete with love handles, groin sweat and undignified struggles with the condom wrapper. Rather than dealing with the messes and hooplas of real sex, they choose instead to live precariously through stories of perfect encounters that can only happen in smut. It all boils down to anatomically unlikely women begging 'fuck me, please' and unreasonably endowed men moaning 'you're so tight, baby.'"

Patrick laughs, "For someone who makes a living writing this shit, you are very dismissive of it."

"Believe you me, Patrick, writing toaster user manuals and dime-store pulp was not my idea of a grand career as a writer," I say. Because I can't resist the look on Patrick's face that is sure to follow, I add, "But I'll gladly slip some of my better pieces to Liam. He's at that age where he might just start appreciating it."

"I'll thank you to do no such thing," Patrick growls. "Anything Liam needs to know about sex he'll hear from me, thank you very much."

I laugh and pass the bottle to him, enjoying a moment of comfortable silence. Except for the short interlude offered by our grandmother's funeral, this is the first time in fifteen years that the two of us are sitting together in the Dalmatian night passing a bottle of homemade wine between us, and it feels so very right.

"I meant it though," Patrick says passing the bottle back to me, "you're good with kids, always have been. Don't you ever think about having your own?"

"That's a can of worms you don't want to open, Patrick, because you almost certainly wouldn't like the truth if I were to answer that question."

Patrick takes a long pull from the bottle and sighs. "James, I've spent twenty years controlling the damage in your wake. Don't you think I'm prepared to handle any truth you'd care to throw at me at this point?"

I don't know what possesses me, but I feel the sudden urge to give Patrick exactly what he's asking for, the unvarnished truth, no matter the consequences. The reason Patrick only ever got the highly edited accounts of my life wasn't so much that I feared him unable to handle reality. Rather it was that I was afraid that a day would come when even Patrick would write me off as a hopeless cause, a being not worth the effort he poured into maintaining our fractured relationship.

Maybe it's because we are sitting here together for the first time in god knows how many years and we aren't hurling insults at each other or trading punches, or perhaps it is because this seems to be the year of confessions if the last few months are anything to go by, but I think that if I were to take the chance and tell him about events that haunt me, maybe, just maybe, I could get them off my chest for good. My real motivation may very well be that I realized a few months ago that I am thirty years old and I have spent half of my life caught in a web of half-truths and lies, arriving at a point where I can no longer remember the difference between the two. So maybe it is time that I take the plunge and spill the truth, such as I remember.

"I almost had a kid once, Patrick, but then I screwed up so royally it all went south," I say beneath my breath. "I was terrified. That was one of the details I edited out of the tale of the grand disappearing act. I was sixteen, I was scared shitless, and I could barely take care of myself. How the hell was I supposed to take care of another human being? I couldn't call you, or Dad for that matter, because that would have meant explaining where I'd been, and I wasn't up to that. Besides, what would you have done except kick the shit out of me for being such an idiot and getting Her up the duff in the first place."

"I never would have—" Patrick protests before I cut him off.

"I said some terrible things, Patrick, acted in ways I never thought I was capable of, drove Her to do things She didn't want to do," I say, avoiding his eyes.

Patrick reaches out and grabs my chin, forcing my head to turn until our eyes lock, and it seems to me that he is looking straight through me. "Whatever you did, James, you couldn't have driven Her to anything She wasn't already contemplating Herself."

There's no escape now. "I slept with Her sister, Patrick," I blurt out.

He didn't expect that. "You slept with Etain? If you were sixteen, then she was—" he doesn't finish the sentence. I'm sure he's frantically trying to remember another sister. There isn't one.

"Thirteen, Patrick. She was thirteen and as innocent as they come," I admit. "If I had an ounce of belief left in me, I know I would burn in hell for that alone."

Patrick doesn't say anything. I think this is getting a little bit too close to home for him. I know he's thinking about Siobhan now, thinking about what she'll be like at thirteen, not so many years from now. If he doesn't hate me already, there's a fair chance he will in the morning. He insisted he wanted to hear the truth though, so that's what he'll get tonight.

"I am the coldest bastard I know, and I've known a few pieces of work in my time," I say.

"Oh yeah, you're tough as old boots, you are," Patrick replies. "That's why you start bawling like an infant every time one of us mentions the name of Catriona Finley." I reel back at the verbal slap in the face. "Face it, James, all the self-flagellation in the world isn't going to solve your problems unless you face a few truths of your own and bury the ghosts."

His voice hardly registers as more words are trying to force their way past my lips. "She just snapped. She screamed and cried and shouted some, and once She had collected Herself, She said She would teach me what misery was really about. She went and got rid of it the next morning, to spite me more than anything else, I think. The worst thing was, the only thing I could feel was sheer, bloody relief that I had angered Her enough to make the problem go away."

"Oh, James," Patrick sighs and it looks to me as if he's drawing Danny closer to his chest.

"That was the beginning of the end you know," I continue, because now that I've started talking I don't seem to be able to stop again. "I don't know whether it was the guilt or whether She really wanted that baby, but She just kind of gave up after that. Started using needles. Don't get me wrong, She had a healthy taste for heroin even before I met Her and a fair liking of cocaine. Well, we all did; it was the eighties after all."

Patrick snorts derisively. "Oh, don't look at me like that, Patrick," I laugh, "You know I'm not entirely clueless as to what you got up to in Berlin. You've done your fair share of fat lines."

Patrick nods slightly in quiet acknowledgement, which surprises me. I don't think I can recall another time when he has admitted indulging in what he considers my weaknesses.

"The point is, it was always recreational," I explain. "She smoked it, chucked Her guts up afterward and the next morning we'd be back to normal, or as normal as we got in those days. It all changed after She got rid of the kid. We never got back to normal in the morning."

"You never forced a drug on her, James," Patrick maintains quietly.

I shake my head. "No. But all I can remember now is that She'd ram those needles into Her arms until She passed out or ran out of veins and then She'd go out and fuck anything with a prick. She always came back to me when it was time to go to sleep though. Probably thought that was the ultimate punishment."

Patrick doesn't say anything. I expected mocking, or at least a few snide remarks about watching Her extracurricular activities for all those years, god knows he was quick enough to point them out at the time, but the only expression that flits across his face is pity.

So Patrick feels sorry for the poor, cuckolded fool, the idiot who didn't have the courage to walk out when given half a chance and instead settled for a few rounds as a neutered puppy. I never wanted his pity; it hurts more than ridicule would. I know I really should shut up now. I've already said much more than I ever intended to, but once the gates are open, it's hard to stop the flood.

"She was good at turning your own weapons against you," I say. "She was much better at playing head games than I ever was, realized that the real torture would be to insert the knife and keep on twisting it without ever striking a vital organ. She never slept with any of you, because that would have meant we were even, but She blatantly fucked anyone else, sometimes in front of me, and I had no right to object. A thousand lashes for one deathblow—does that sound fair to you?"

I don't really expect an answer. Patrick should know to leave rhetorical questions alone. Being his infuriating self though, he laughs humorlessly and snaps, "You're a fool, James, always have been when it came to women. Relationships aren't about getting even—leastways successful relationships don't include punishing each other for each indiscretion. The sooner you realize that, the sooner you'll be able to actually behave like an adult around some chit of a girl."

"And what would you know about it, Patrick?" I ask, my voice raw.

"I've been with the same woman for over twenty years now, not all of them made in heaven," Patrick says. "There were lapses in judgement, on both our parts, but we worked through them, dealt with them, decided to stay together, because that was ultimately what we both wanted. Real relationships are a lot of hard work, James. Sometimes they're worth it, sometimes they're not, but no relationship solely based on the premise that what's good for the goose is good for the gander stands a chance in hell of surviving."

"Admirable sentiment, Patrick, but you never slept with your girlfriend's kid sister," I say.

"Annie doesn't have any sisters, not that it matters, and no, I never went as far as to sleep with anyone else. I never got much beyond kissing a few other women." He pauses for a moment, probably trying to make up his mind about how much ammunition he wants to furnish me with. "Annie did, though, way back during the Berlin days. I think she was terrified that she was missing out on something, having been with me for all those years. We were so young when we got together, I suppose we both struggled with the idea that maybe there were other people we should be experimenting with, playing the field so to speak.

"You're probably going to throw this back in my face at some point, but you realize that she is the only woman I've ever been with? I sometimes wondered, still do occasionally, what other women were like, but I never even got close to sleeping with anyone else. I never felt the urge. Annie, well, there was someone else before me and then there was that punk in Berlin. When she told me, I think she expected me to be angry, to break things, to display that notorious Sheahan temper. You know what I did instead?"

I shake my head, feeling uncomfortable at this sudden surge in intimacy. For someone who keeps his emotions as closely guarded as Patrick does, someone who has spent twenty years honing the image of tough masculinity, never daring to display any emotion that could be interpreted as a sign of weakness on his part, this admission must be harder than anything else he has ever deigned to tell me.

"I bawled my eyes out, James," he states simply. "I've only cried twice since, once when Liam was born and once when we buried Baka, and I don't think Liam's birth counts because I'm pretty sure Annie broke a couple of bones in my hand that day, which caused my eyes to water. The day Annie told me she'd been sleeping with someone else I cried properly though, and it floored her. I've never exactly been known for my public displays of emotion. I wasn't even angry because I was hurting so much. I think that was the first time she realized how much I love her. By the end of it, she was crying too, asking me whether I wanted her to leave. I begged her to stay, James. I love her even if I've never been any good at saying it."

How am I supposed to respond to that, I wonder? Patrick has just demolished my entire concept of who he is. He is merely human after all.

Patrick looks at me and says quietly, "One of the definitions of love is that no matter how much the other person hurts you, you don't do anything to hurt them back. Being in love means never doing anything that would cause the other pain, but I guess you never learned that." He sighs. "The real tragedy is that it didn't stop with the two of you torturing each other senseless in a futile attempt to get even. You're still paying back every woman you meet for your perceived wrongs at Her hand."

"I did love Her, Patrick, more than I have ever loved anyone else," I say through gritted teeth. "I spent years after that trying to make up for one ill-conceived and foolish mistake."

"Trouble is, she never loved you as much as she loved—"

"One time she cleaned up," I interrupt to keep Patrick from finishing the sentence. "I asked her whether She wanted to try having a child. She turned me down flat, said we had missed our chance and that people like us didn't deserve any children. I doubt She could have conceived anyway. Heroin does something to girls, stops them ovulating after a while.

"Of course, once they quit they get three years' worth of periods wrapped into one, but they're never regular again. You know, Luka and I have both kicked, and it's unpleasant all right, for a few days at least, but we never had to put up with a month of bleeding like a pig. If only they put that into the 'just say no' campaigns, they might be a lot more successful at convincing girls not to do it." I pause, because I realize I'm only talking to fill the void at this point and add, "Sorry, Patrick."

Patrick laughs, "Strangely enough, after witnessing five births, a little blood no longer disturbs me."

"Yeah, well, She probably had a point. Junkies really shouldn't go around making babies," I say to convince myself more than anything else. "I just stopped thinking about it those last couple of years. I knew where She was headed, just couldn't think of anything I could do to stop Her."

"There are people that get off on playing Russian roulette; Luka is one of them, Catriona was another," Patrick says. "I've spent the past decade living in perpetual fear of the day that Luka finally self-destructs and we don't stop him in time. Catriona would have taken that joyride to hell even if you hadn't been in the picture. It was her nature."

I shrug. Patrick has been beating that particular dead horse for years. He knows I don't believe him, knows that no matter how often he tells me, I will still know, as I've always known, that I bear considerable responsibility for her decline and demise, if not through my actions then through my inability to act.

"Look, I don't quite know how to put this in terms you will understand," Patrick says impatiently, "but I'll try anyway: Catriona was always Mrs. Rochester, never Jane Eyre."

"Bravo, Patrick," I sneer, "and there I was thinking you illiterate for all those years."

Patrick doesn't dignify this obvious attempt to goad him with a response. So I sit there for a few moments, drinking from the bottle that is almost empty now before I add quietly, "A thousand lashes for one deathblow. It didn't sound right even then."

11

Drown: Swimming Against the Current

It's early when Patrick shakes me awake, holding a chipped cup of sweet and pungent coffee under my nose. "Grounds haven't settled yet," he warns me as he shoves the cup into my unresisting hands.

I nod groggily and blearily try to work out what's wrong with this scene of early-morning domesticity. Then it hits me. "So you're still talking to me then?" I mumble, more a question than a statement.

"Why wouldn't I?" Patrick asks, startled. Then the gears in his head click into place and understanding sweeps across his face. "Oh, for God's sake, James!" he exclaims. "It may come as a surprise to you, but you weren't the only sixteen-year-old in the history of humanity who couldn't keep his hormones in check. Happens quite a bit, and it isn't the end of the world, so get over yourself, why don't you?"

He hurries off into the kitchen area, and seconds later I hear him holler, "Danny, get out of the chicken pen at once!"

When he returns to the front of the room, where I have been sleeping on the couch, he's holding his own cup of coffee in one hand and a hairbrush and pink bathing suit in the other. "We're going to the beach," he informs me. I'm still staring at him blankly, so he sighs and sits down on the armrest of an overstuffed chair. "Look, James, I really don't have time for it this morning, but Etain is fine too, got a brilliant career with RTÉ."

I'm not a natural morning person. Actually, that's not quite correct. It would be more accurate to say that I'm not a natural sleeper, never have been, but when I do sleep it does take a while for my mind to wake up afterwards. By the time I get my head around that statement, Patrick is already hurrying off into the other room, to fix Siobhan's hair, no doubt. I experimentally swing my legs to the floor and try getting up. Not too bad of a hangover, I decide after swirling some of the coffee around my mouth to get rid of the morning-after taste.

"How the hell do you know what Etain's up to?" I yell after Patrick.

"This is really not a good time, James," Patrick shouts as he hurries after Joey, who is running around the house butt-naked. "I'm kind of up to my armpits in kids right now."

"Patrick!" I whine at least as petulantly as any of the under-tens in the house would.

Patrick mumbles something I can't quite catch as he passes me with Joey under his arm on his way back into the bedroom.

"What was that, Patrick? Sorry, couldn't quite catch it," I say insistently as he pulls a shirt over Joey's head.

"I said," Patrick says enunciating every word slowly, "that she is shacked up with Micky in Dublin."

It takes me about thirty seconds to remember to close my mouth. When the power of speech finally returns to me, Joey is fully dressed and Patrick is tying up his shoelaces. "You mean they're flatmates, right?"

Patrick rolls his eyes. "I wish," he says. "I have never seen anything as nauseatingly saccharine as those two."

So Micky finally got laid, I think to myself. Well, it was about bloody time. Although why anyone would choose to live with a pillock like

Micky is beyond me. It's not as if she were ugly. Maybe she's gotten fat since I saw her last.

Patrick cracks up. "The look on your face is priceless," he gasps between peals of laughter. "Jealous, are you, James?"

"Hell, no!" I reply. "Surprised that Micky managed to score is all."

"Not half as surprised as I was," Patrick says. "I mean what is it with you lads and those damned Finley women, anyway? I don't pay attention for one frigging minute and another one of them has got her claws into one of my brothers!" He takes a breath to calm himself. "Now would you kindly go and get dressed so we can go to the beach before the boys manage to tear the house down."

I look down and realize for the first time that I'm standing there in a cut-off pair of sweats and not much else, while Patrick leans out the window and shouts, "Shane, put that chick down and step away from the hen!"

I laugh and start whistling as I walk out of the room in pursuit of my trousers. Before we'll finally set off for the beach, there will be another few rounds of changing the twins' clothes, there is Siobhan's hair to be fixed, and there is the issue of tracking down Liam, whom I saw skulking up the mountain out of the corner of my eye as I was talking to Patrick. We will play our roles quite well, Patrick his as the exasperated father of a brood almost too large to handle and I mine of the bemused bystander. It worries me a little that I'm enjoying this simulacrum of domestic bliss so much, and I'm starting to think that maybe this vacation wasn't such a bad idea after all.

Won't you at least try to come into the water, kitten?" I shout from my perch atop a rock in the middle of the bay.

She's sitting there on the small, concrete pier, dangling her feet in the water. She's wearing what can only be described as a granny-style burgundy bathing suit, which only makes her skin look so much paler than it already is, with a large flowery wrap tied around her waist to keep her legs modestly covered, and a large straw hat which is keeping the sun's rays from her freckled face. She shakes her head almost imperceptibly as I slip off the rock back into the ocean and start to swim toward her.

We've been playing this game for several days now, making our way to this secluded stretch of black sand, only accessible by either boat or climb-

ing across the large hill of craggy, volcanic rock that surrounds the small beach and protects the calm waters of the bay. While I head straight into the shallow water, barely taking the time to strip off my clothes into an untidy pile on the beach, she sits on the boating dock watching me. She's graduated to dangling her feet in the water now, which I suppose is progress after three days of not getting wet at all, but she steadfastly refuses to leave the safety of dry land behind her.

It's comical really, considering that she spent the last few months harping on about how she wanted to spend the summer somewhere warm, somewhere with beaches and oceans and lots of sunshine, but she seems almost afraid of the water. I was raised in it, can't remember now what came first, walking or swimming. I've always known how to swim, as far back as I can remember. I'm the strongest swimmer in my family, better even than Patrick, who usually has me beat at anything whiffing of athleticism. I guess swimming doesn't come naturally to boys whose grandfather once walked three days across mountains to reach the water's edge.

I wade the last fifty yards or so across rough igneous pebbles until I reach her and pull myself up onto the slab of concrete next to her. I'm nude, having dispensed with the need for bathing suits days ago when I realized no one else would be reckless enough to scramble across the cliff face to get to this little stretch of paradise.

Cat glances at me, and her look is composed of lust and disapproval in equal measures. This is the woman who taught me everything I thought I knew about sex and quite a few things I never even suspected, the woman who whispers words into my ear that make me blush scarlet even as she clenches her muscles around me, the woman who rejected Catholicism in favor of depravities I had never dreamed of before I met her, and the woman who apparently remains just Catholic enough to deplore my wanton display of public nudity.

Considering the things she asks me to do to her on a nightly basis, the things that make her scream, the unmentionable things I have allowed her to do to me, the things that make me gasp and moan, she's shy about exposing her body in public. Which is a shame really, because I've spent the better part of the last few days fantasizing about taking her there on the beach and again in the warm salt water of the bay, waves crashing around us even as the ecstasy washes over her face. Of course, that would require getting her into the bloody water to start with.

"Cat, kitten," I purr, "can you tell me exactly why you were so adamant about spending the summer by the beach if you refuse to get into the water?"

"I like the beach. It's the water I have a problem with," she says curtly.

I roll my eyes in mock despair and try the humorous approach. "Admit it, kitten, it's all a conspiracy, isn't it? You women have all banded together, decided to become the most frustratingly incomprehensible creatures on God's green earth, with the ultimate goal of driving us men from power by simply confusing us until we give up." I stop my diatribe when I see the look on her face and quickly add, "Come on, that was supposed to be funny."

"Well, it wasn't," she mumbles, staring at the sparkling green water.

"It's not cold," I say.

She laughs. "I know, I've got my feet in it."

"Then why won't you come in there with me?" I whine petulantly.

"Don't want to," she replies.

"I can tell when you're lying, kitten," I keep on prodding.

I can feel her body tensing next to mine. "I can't swim, Seamus," she almost shouts. "Happy now?"

She looks like she's about to bolt, so I quickly grab her wrist and turn her toward me, talking straight into her eyes. "Let me teach you."

She struggles a bit, but her body relaxes, and I interpret that as agreement. I lead her off the concrete onto the beach, reverently undo the knot that is keeping her wrap from sliding past her hips and let it fall to the sand. Then I take her firmly by the hand and lead her into the water. She follows me, slowly, reluctantly. When we are just past the knee-deep stage, I pause briefly, giving her time to get used to the small waves lapping up against her thighs, then I tug her hand to draw her further into the ocean. I don't stop again until she is waist-deep in the water, even though Cat's nails are starting to dig into my palm painfully.

I realize she is really afraid. That in itself surprises me because I have never known Cat to show fear, but she's truly terrified now. After long minutes of just standing there amid the gentle waves, she starts to relax her grip on my hand. Then she looks down at me and starts to giggle. I follow her eyes and have to laugh myself. I'm quite a bit taller than she is, and in my case the waves come just high enough to cause certain parts of my body to float atop the water in a most undignified manner.

"Right, kitten, now that you've had your laugh at my expense, it's time to learn to swim," I say, trying to sound much more confident than I actually feel. "Remember the water only comes up to your waist, so you can always stand up. Nothing can happen to you. Now, lie down on the water and slowly raise your legs off the ground. I'll hold you."

I place my hands underneath her body as she slowly sinks into the water. Then, very, very slowly, she lifts her feet up from the ground. I smile. "Now start pushing the water away with your arms," I say, and she complies. After a few minutes, I tell her to do the same with her legs. I have long since taken my feet off the ground, keeping myself afloat while treading water, my hands still firmly holding her up by her waist. Slowly, hesitantly, she starts moving her legs. I don't think she expected surging forward like that because she shrieks a little, but I'm quite aware of the muscle power in her thighs, have felt it wrapped around my back often enough to anticipate her powerful thrust through the water, and I never relax my hold on her waist.

We are moving adjacent to the beach now and she is gaining confidence. Her swimming strokes are getting calmer and stronger, propelling us through the water. Without thinking, I let go of her hips to swim alongside her, unable to keep up with her tempo with the use of my legs alone. That's when she panics, loses her rhythm and starts fighting the water.

"I'm going to drown," she shrieks and throws herself at my chest with all her weight. I'm not prepared and topple over, painfully slamming my foot into a rock on the ocean floor.

I howl. "You silly cow, you can't drown in water that's only waist-deep," I shout.

She's standing now, feet firmly planted on the ground, and looking at me sheepishly. I raise my foot up to examine the damage and flinch when I see the black quills sticking out of my foot. There are sea urchins on those rocks. Cat is completely unfazed, looking at me quizzically now that the panic has passed.

I clench my teeth trying to ignore the pain. "Are you just going to stand there and watch, or are you going to help me pull those quills out of my foot?" I ask through gritted teeth.

She laughs and carefully starts pulling out the offending quills while I try not to scream. Luckily, it was only the side of my foot that struck the sea urchin, and the few quills that stuck didn't get driven in too deeply. It still hurts. A lot.

"You're still going to teach me to swim, aren't you?" she asks as she pulls out the last quill.

I sigh. "Kitten, you were swimming before you panicked there," I point out. "All you need to do now is practice."

She pouts at me a little and then nods. "Will you swim with me then, Seamus?"

I wrap one arm around her waist and pull her back to my chest, kicking off the ocean bed and starting to move along through the water with slow, confident strokes of my free arm and my legs. After a few lengths she finds my rhythm and joins in with her own languid swimming strokes. A few minutes later, as I watch the beach recede into the distance a little, I think that maybe my erection pressing into the small of her back is not answer enough for her.

"I will swim with you to the ends of the earth if that is what it takes, Catriona," I say quietly.

She seems satisfied with that answer for a few seconds. Then she dislodges my arm from her waist and turns to me. Treading water, she asks, "Will you always catch me when I'm drowning, Seamus?"

Maybe it's because I'm in love. More likely it's because I'm a fool. "Always," I say, knowing full well that this is a promise I might not be able to keep.

I notice too late that I have just driven past Patrick's parked car. Cursing, I do a sweeping three-point turn and drive back a few hundred yards, parking my car next to his on the mountainside. Really I shouldn't have driven at all considering the state I'm in, but I've already been gone for more than a day, and I don't much fancy feeling the extent of Patrick's wrath if I stay away another night.

I stumble out of the car and start heading up the hill, feeling elated that my legs are at least marginally under my control again. For a time during the drive up the winding mountain road, I actually feared that I might have to make my way up the hill on my knees like a worshiper coming in supplication. Of course, praying might not be such a bad idea right now, because Patrick will be seriously pissed and I don't have the strength for a real fight. I've been chasing dreams I thought long lost for the past thirty hours.

When I finally get up to the house, all the windows are dark. I think briefly about sneaking into the living room and going to sleep, pretending tomorrow morning that nothing ever happened, that I never just disappeared for a whole day, but I quickly dismiss the thought. Luka might be able to get away with a stunt like that, but I won't. Besides, I see the solitary kerosene lamps sitting on a stone wall about thirty yards away, and I know that even though I can't see him in the darkness, Patrick has undoubtedly watched my approach.

I sigh and start walking toward the light. Patrick wordlessly hands me a bottle of wine and sits there for at least five minutes before losing his cool. "Where the fuck have you been?" he yells.

"Do you know the greatest lie I've ever told you?" I ask, ignoring his question for the moment.

"That you were only going to be gone for a summer?" Patrick replies sarcastically. "Or how about the one about Her just dabbling? Because that one was a real stinker."

"I'm serious, Patrick."

Patrick rises abruptly and shouts, "Well, fuck you, so am I." He grabs the bottle of wine and gulps down several mouthfuls before saying, "Enlighten me then."

I shrug. "It's that all I need to do in order to kick is to leave town, go somewhere far away, where nobody knows me, where I have no connections."

Patrick is mulling this over, it seems, trying to determine whether I'm just having an existential crisis or there's actually a point to my statement.

"Every decent-sized town, especially every decent port, has its junkie row, Patrick," I say. "Dump me in any mid-sized town, and in a few hours tops I'll have found where to score, because dope attracts me like shit attracts flies."

I don't know why, it could be the climate and the people, so reminiscent of those lost years of my youth, but from the day I arrived here, I have been hearing the siren call of heroin. I haven't craved heroin in years. I never liked it much to begin with; stimulants were always my drug of choice. I only ever did heroin because it was something She and I did together. I never developed enough of a death wish for it to indulge when left to my own devices.

Being here though stirred up old memories, brought ghosts back to haunt me, illusions to torment me, sent me scrambling for an elusive dream I couldn't quite catch even then. The flesh is weak, they say. I held out for five long days before I answered the call, rushed off in search of junkie row, mumbling something about going to buy cigarettes. I found junkie row all right, shoved needles into my arm, but I didn't find the dream I was chasing. That remains lost to me.

I absentmindedly scratch the tracks. The syringes down here are alien, old-fashioned, much larger than the insulin syringes I have become accustomed to. I think I might have missed a little. Not much though, because the rush still coursed through my blood and straight to my brain. Patrick doesn't say anything. He doesn't need to; I know he's disappointed at my failure to keep a clear head while I'm with his family. I suspect that being aware of what I do when I'm a continent away is quite different from having his nose rubbed in it in person.

The wine is making me light-headed much quicker than it ought to, but I'm not in top physical condition right now. I'm starting to feel nauseated again. I heave a little but suppress the urge to throw up. Still, there is nothing but silence from Patrick. After sitting there for god knows how long, I turn to him slowly, meeting his eyes for the first time this evening. There is desperation in my voice when I ask, "Would you break my arms if I asked you to, Patrick?"

"Because that worked so well on Luka, as demonstrated by your shining example?" Patrick snorts.

"It was a promise, Patrick, not punishment. Luka knows that," I say quietly. This is a topic I would rather not talk about. Being reminded of what transpired in Portland has a tendency to remind me of the events that brought us to Portland in the first place, and those are memories I'm not willing to face.

"But it's punishment you're looking for," Patrick sighs. "James, I stopped beating you because you enjoyed it too much. It's another thing you have in common with Luka. I am not going to break your arms, or any other part of your body for that matter. I am not your father, and I refuse to be your judge and executioner. If you're really that keen to be punished, I suggest that for your next whore you pick someone who has got a full compliment of whips and chains rather than the usual basketcase."

"You're a pillock," I say.

"Probably," Patrick concedes, "but I worked out a while ago that beating you to a bloody pulp doesn't solve any of your problems. It just puts them off for a while."

I laugh. "How very considerate of you, Patrick."

He shrugs. "I used to worry about both you and Luka," he says. "I still worry about Luka, because I know he's always one step away from self-destructing. I stopped worrying about you when I realized that you were too afraid of dying to take any real risks."

"I'm touched," I say.

"This whole vacation was a bad idea, wasn't it?" Patrick asks. "I was deluding myself thinking that you were capable of change."

"Patrick—"

"I think I've finally sussed you out," Patrick interrupts me. "If you die an untimely death it'll only be at the age of sixty or so when your kidneys and liver finally give out after years of trying to process every chemical known to man. You're never going to be reckless enough for anything else because no matter how much you deny it, you still believe in heaven and hell and purgatory and that St. Peter will meet you at the gates."

"That record is getting old, Patrick," I say. "I'd sooner believe that Luka is a god."

"Yes, he's rationalized it quite well, hasn't he? Mad as a hatter of course, but you've got to give the boy credit for solving a moral dilemma," Patrick nods. "He no longer needs to fear dying, partly because he thinks he's a god and as such is immortal and partly because being a god absolves him of any qualms he may have. The kind of gods Luka believes in, and the kind of god he would make himself, aren't moral beings to begin with."

"Gods are immoral and unethical by definition, Patrick. It's not as if anyone will actually call them on it," I point out.

"By definition they're also immortal," Patrick shrugs. "The trouble is it's an easy step from imagining you're a god to imagining you're immortal, and Luka isn't going to survive that fallacy any more than She did."

"Patrick, don't," I grind out.

He holds up his hands. "Right, sorry, because we should be singing Luka's praises instead, *gloria in excelsis deo* and *te deum laudamus*. As it was in the beginning, is now, and ever shall be, world without end and our brother declares himself a fucking god and you don't see anything wrong with that because you're too busy living in denial," he says, shoving the bottle into my hands.

I grab it and get up, stepping a few feet away from the wall in order to perform the ritual of pouring a libation. I stumble and something inside me snaps, even as I struggle to keep my balance. I hurl the bottle across the wall into the vines and scream, "Why can't you get it through your thick heads? I can't think about Her. I can't allow myself to think about Her, because if I do—" I don't finish the sentence. There are things Patrick doesn't need to know. I kick the wall in frustration.

"You'll do what, James?" Patrick asks dryly. "Actually deal with your issues instead of ignoring them in the hopes they'll disappear?"

I start smashing my fists into the trunk of an olive tree. It's either that or throwing them at Patrick's face, and that never achieved much. "She took everything, Patrick! She took everything I was or could have been and twisted and distorted it until... There was nothing left after Her."

My knuckles are bleeding, but I don't care. I don't feel the pain. There is something to be said for opiates besides the cheap high: I can give a tree a good thrashing if need be. "I wanted out, Patrick. I wanted out so bad it hurt. The one time I tried She damn near stuck a knife through my chest. I couldn't get away."

I'm panting. Getting into a fistfight with a completely immobile object isn't a good idea even when you haven't just spent thirty hours beating your own body into submission. I let my arms drop to my sides and immediately realize my mistake. When the rage dies down, what else is there? I can feel my shoulders slumping and the tightness in my throat. I send up a silent prayer to any gods that might be listening to strike me unconscious where I stand before I crack up in front of Patrick. The bastards never listen.

I stare at my bleeding hands for a while, stubbornly willing my tear ducts to dry up. It's really quite pretty, that crimson torrent. Makes me wonder whether Luka provokes fights he cannot win simply to see his own blood flow. We pay for our sins, the two of us, in sweat and tears and blood.

"I'm done."

Patrick's calm assertion jerks me back to reality, and I wave my arms wildly for a moment to keep myself from falling.

"I'm done," he repeats stoically. "I won't come after you again, won't try to fix things again, won't care what you get up to from here on out, because I'm through with you. I'm through with the drama and I'm through with the self-pity and I'm through with the insane accusations and the assignment of blame. You're thirty years old, James. You no longer have a right to blame anyone but yourself for the messes you make. You're thirty years old, and it's not my place to interfere anymore, so I won't."

"Patrick, please," I whimper. "I don't know how to—"

"No," he interrupts, shaking his head. "No more. If you're wanting for penance and redemption, you'll have to consult with the priests; they are much more adept at assigning rosaries and forgiving transgressions. I'm washing my hands of you."

"You can't," I say angrily. "No more than I can abandon Luka."

Patrick laughs and stands, the lamp swinging from his hand. "I can. I will." He turns to walk toward the house.

"Patrick!" I shout at the top of my lungs. "You never changed. You're still as big of a coward as you were twenty years ago."

He turns on the porch just before entering the house and replies, "I've never been a coward, James, but I've never martyred myself to a lost cause either."

12

Limbo: Ghosts Across the River Acheron

The flight back to London is hell on earth, thanks in large part to Liam's incessant whining, and by the time we arrive back at Mother's house, I'm in a foul mood. The fact that the door is opened by a smirking Micky doesn't help my temper any. "What the hell are you doing here?" I ask.

Micky bares his teeth in a parody of a smile. "Had business to take care of in London and decided to visit my mother," he says calmly. "How about you? Have they run out of dope in the colonies?"

"No, but your presence here indicates that they might have run out of potatoes in Ireland," I counter.

"Believe me, I had much rather be a mick than be as sorry an excuse for a yank as you are," Micky replies grimly.

Patrick's iron grip on my shoulder prevents me from lashing out at Micky before he retreats back into the living room. Even then, Patrick doesn't let go, just loosens his hold on my shoulder a little. "You better behave yourself or else you'll have to answer to me," he says quietly before he lets go.

I skulk into the living room after Micky, determined to at least needle him until he starts a fight all on his own, but I'm stopped in my tracks in the doorway. Etain. I suppose I should have expected her to be here as well; after all, Patrick told me that she and Micky were an item. What I'm not prepared for is that contrary to my earlier fantasies she hasn't been hit with an ugly-stick, and she isn't fat either. Far from it.

She never looked much like her sister, never was fragile and elfin. Even I can see that she's beautiful, though. Wholesome in a stereotypically Irish way, much more Irish than her sister ever was. A natural redhead, at least as tall as I am, maybe taller, and those curves! I think I'm in lust. Her demeanor exudes the kind of confidence I always longed for in Her. How did Micky manage to bag that one?

"Seamus," she says, old country lilt in her voice.

"Etain," I nod and head off into the kitchen.

As I hit the liquor cabinet, I mull over my chances of stealing her from Micky. I'm not looking for an entanglement, but I'd like to feel those thighs wrapped around my back for a while, show her how much better than Micky I can be.

Patrick enters the kitchen behind me. "Don't even think about it," he says as though he has been reading my mind. "She's Micky's. At any rate, we'll be heading up to Durham in the morning; all I ask is that you behave yourself until then."

I nod, but I already know that I won't be going with him. I'll stay in London and take my chances with her.

"I still don't see why we have to go and stay with Patrick," Micky whines. "It's not as if you can't run away while we're in London."

"I'm not running away, Micky," I explain for the hundredth time. "I'm taking a short vacation, and since it's unlikely that Mother would allow it, we're pretending to visit Patrick. You and Declan will stay with him, while Catriona and I are going to Greece. Afterwards, we'll meet up again and pretend that I was with you in Berlin the entire time."

"You're just saying that," Micky replies. "You're not going to come back."

I sigh; he's being needlessly tenacious. "What makes you think that?" I ask.

Micky gives me a long, calculating look. No nine-year-old should be capable of such intensity. "Patrick never returned," he says finally with ice in his voice.

"I am not Patrick," I say testily. "I don't run away from my responsibilities."

"You will if she has her way," Micky shouts, pointing at Catriona, before he runs out of the room leaving me to wonder just when he turned into such a tough little bastard.

I turn to Catriona and grin apologetically. "Sorry about that, kitten," I say. "He doesn't mean it, he's... I've never been away from them before."

She smiles at me and asks, "If you had to choose, Seamus, who would it be, them or me?"

I can't believe she just asked that. They're my brothers, for crying out loud. "That will never happen, Catriona," I grind out at last.

"Let's just assume for a moment that it does, in a purely hypothetical sense, who would you choose?" Catriona insists.

Is she fishing for a declaration of love? An assertion of loyalty? A testament to devotion? Does she require proof as to my intentions toward her?

I know the answer of course, have known it for months now, but I've never admitted it to myself, much less to her. I close my eyes and inhale sharply. "If I had to choose, I would choose you, Catriona."

Patrick and the kids leave at the crack of dawn. Just prior to his departure, Patrick has me promise that I will follow them to Durham within the next week or so. I doubt it will take me as long as that to seduce Etain. Micky leaves about an hour later, barely acknowledging my presence, presumably to go and take care of whatever business he has in London. I spend the next few hours skulking about the house, doing a very worthwhile impression of Liam without the scowling, while waiting for Etain to get up.

I'm in the kitchen frying a pound of bacon when she finally comes downstairs. "Are you planning on cooking any eggs with that?" she asks sleepily.

I turn up the charm a notch. "Anything for a beautiful woman," I say as I walk to the refrigerator to get the eggs.

"You're not looking so bad yourself," she smiles. "Sobriety suits you."

I smile grimly as I start cracking the eggs into the frying pan. She's flirting with me and apparently not quite as bright as I had given her credit for, if she mistakes the current lull in intoxication for sobriety. This should be even easier than I thought it'd be.

I hum quietly to myself as I watch the eggs sizzling in the pan. I'm elated. Etain was mine before she ever became anybody else's, and she'll be mine forever; girls never forget their first screw.

I'm piling the bacon and eggs onto a plate, and I start to whistle, desperately trying to drown out the voice at the back of my mind which is clamoring for attention. You idiot, she's your brother's woman, the voice is screaming at me. Micky disowned me long ago though, doesn't even have the decency to hate me anymore; besides, being my woman never stopped Her. There are rules! The traitor shrieks to combat the whistling.

I place the laden plate in front of Etain and lean in closer than is absolutely necessary, almost touching my face to her hair, murmuring, "Micky is a fool to leave you unguarded for just one second."

She laughs and it could be my mind playing tricks, but it seems to me that she is pushing her hair a fraction of an inch closer to my face. "Micky trusts me," she giggles playfully.

"Then he's even more of an imbecile than I thought," I mutter as I run my fingertips along her jaw. She shivers slightly and then presses her cheek into my hand. Score.

The plate of bacon and eggs sits forgotten as my mind and my body go on autopilot. Without quite knowing how it happened, I find Etain's legs wrapped around my waist and we are stumbling through to the couch in the living room, our tongues battling in a primal dance for domination.

How I missed that taste of Finley women! All darkness and unrefined sugar, chaos and ecstasy in equal measures, Mary Magdalenes in an ocean of Marthas. Babylon fell with a single kiss from their lips. Etain's flavor is that of faraway spices, cinnamon and cloves, sweetmeats and caramel, life's salt upon my tongue. Her body is Eden, the Garden at Gethsemane and the last temptation of Christ. She'll be my resurrection as her sister was my crucifixion.

My hands stray to the buttons of her jeans. I thirst for the everlasting life promised by her womb. Just as readily as she invited me in, she is pushing me away. "Not inside this house," she sighs.

I suppress the urge to take her right there on my mother's couch. She is pulling me up from the seat and leading me toward the door. I follow her unthinking. My brain shut down long ago, leaving my cock in charge of my body, and my cock is quite prepared to follow Etain all the way back to Dublin if that's what it takes for her to part her thighs.

Before I know it, we are sitting in my mother's car, Etain behind the wheel. She smirks wickedly and throws me a black scarf. "Put that over your eyes," she says.

"Jesus Christ, woman!" I groan. "You practically fucked me in my mother's sitting room. Don't you think it's a little late for games?"

"My game, my rules," she grins. "Put on the blindfold or get out of the car."

I shrug and start tying the scarf around my eyes. "This had better lead to some genuinely mind-blowing action, Etain," I warn her. "I don't like playing games."

"Liar!" Etain laughs. "Your entire life is a game, the mental equivalent of Russian roulette with a fully loaded gun."

"And what do you think you are doing, Seamus?" Catriona asks, an indignant look on her face.

"Packing," I reply simply as I continue to shove clothes into my duffel bag.

"I can see that," she snaps. "I thought we decided we were going to stay here for the rest of the winter."

I try to focus on the task at hand, try to focus on not losing my cool. "You can stay here for the rest of the winter for all I care, but I'm done. I'm leaving," I say.

I duck just in time to avoid the pint glass hurtling past my head and watch it as it smashes into the wall. I pick up another glass from the bedside table and hand it to her impassively. "You can break them all if you like," I say quietly. "It won't change the fact that I've had as much as I can take of your extra-curricular activities."

"I wasn't the one who started sleeping around," she yells.

I sigh. "Once, Catriona. I slept with another woman once, a temporary lapse in judgement. How many men have you slept with since?"

"You slept with my baby sister!" she shouts, and the glass flies past my head, smashing into the lamp on the bedside table, which tumbles to the floor. I barely glance at it as my eyes adjust to the loss of light in the room. I spent long years living in my mother's house; the novelty of broken crystal wore off long ago. I scan the furniture around me. We appear to be all out of glasses for the moment, so I pick up an abandoned plate from the bedside table and hand it to her.

"You love me," she says, staring at the plate in her hands.

There she stands, my queen of stating the bloody obvious. Yes, I love her, more than I ever thought possible, more than I have ever loved another human being, which makes it paramount that I leave now while there's still time. Love can turn into hatred all too readily, and I'm not prepared to hate her just yet. I need to leave. Now.

"More than my own blood. I've proven that, haven't I?" I say before turning back to my duffel bag.

I can sense her exiting the bedroom, and I sigh with relief. She's making this much easier than I anticipated. I throw the last few shirts on top of the bulging bag and sit down on the bed to lace up my boots. *Sometimes a Sheahan needs to know when to walk. I just wish it wouldn't hurt so fucking much.* My boots all laced up, I pick up my leather jacket and my duffel bag and take one last look around the room. *Here ends a chapter of your life, James,* I think bitterly.

I throw my set of keys down on the bed and get ready to leave. My path is blocked by Catriona wielding a butcher's knife. *Fuck, I should have known that was too easy.* She's hovering somewhere between hysteria and catatonia, with a look of quiet determination in her eyes. After a few seconds she makes up her mind and lunges.

I have the presence of mind to sidestep her sweeping arm, but I still feel the sensation of ice-cold steel against my ribcage. *She cut me. The bitch actually cut me.* Before I can stop myself, I grab her knife-wielding arm and twist her wrist until the knife drops from her hand. She's howling in pain, but I'm beyond caring. Still holding firmly on to her arm, I swing my other arm around in a wide arc until the edge of my hand somehow connects with her face. Catriona screams, and then there's blood, so much blood.

I let go of her wrist and drop my other hand, shaking. I've never hit a woman before. I'm dimly aware that there's still a knife floating around somewhere in the room and that Catriona might try to finish what she started, but I don't have the nerve to start looking for it. I lean heavily against the wall and then my knees give out and my body slides to the floor. Catriona is mewling quietly, curled up in a fetal position on the bed with blood running down her face. Shit. I won't be able to leave now, not like this.

I take off my shirt with shaking hands, try to block out the noises Catriona is making, and examine my chest. There's an angry, long laceration running diagonally across my chest from my abs to within an inch of my left armpit. It's large, and it's bleeding, but it looks superficial. I should probably get stitches, but I don't know that I can be bothered to go to the hospital; it'll scar either way. I ball up my shirt and press it against my chest for a few minutes to stop the bleeding.

While waiting for the blood in the wound to clot, I close my eyes and softly bang my head against the wall a few times. How exactly did I turn an act as simple as leaving into a bloodbath? I throw my shirt into the corner in frustration and get up from the floor to tend to Catriona.

"Shh, kitten," I murmur turning her toward me. "Let me look at your face."

She's unresponsive, shaking with quiet sobs. I grab one of the shirts that fell off the top of my duffel bag and gently start wiping at her face. Most of the blood seems to be coming from her nose, but she's also sporting a split lip. I clean the blood away as best I can and pull her into my arms, rocking her much like I rocked Declan all those years ago, whispering endearments in her ear.

After what seems like forever the sobbing stops and the shaking subsides. "I am so sorry, kitten," I say, and it's likely she'll never know just how sorry I am.

She's whimpering now, an almost incomprehensible litany of 'don't leaves,' or words to that effect, words that are redundant at any rate, because I won't be leaving, not now, not after what I did.

Regardless of what Etain may think, I really don't enjoy this game. The only reason I haven't ripped off the blindfold after twenty minutes in the car is Etain's hand, which has been stroking my rock-hard dick through the fabric of my jeans. Even so, I'm starting to lose patience. I'm about to shrug off the scarf when Etain slams the car into reverse with the customary lack of grace of a woman driving stick and proceeds to park.

"Don't even think about taking that blindfold off," she says, as though she were reading my mind.

The car door on the driver's side slams shut, and then the door on the passenger side opens, and Etain leads me out of the car and across the pavement onto a gravel path. I wonder where we are. Must be a park or something. I feel a right prat being led around in public wearing a blindfold and would like nothing better than to rip the damn thing off, but my cock is sending contradictory instructions to my brain.

After a few minutes we leave the path to walk across grass. Then she stops suddenly and pulls me closer. She's standing behind me now, pressing her breasts into my back, with one arm firmly holding onto my elbow. She leans in to nuzzle my ear and whispers, "Close your eyes and don't open them 'til I tell you to."

I'm such a horny idiot, I actually do what she tells me. She loosens the blindfold and lets it drop from my face. Then she wraps both arms around my chest, pinning my arms to my sides, and clasps her hands tightly in front of my sternum. I suppose it occurs to me for a moment that this is a vulnerable position to be in; unfortunately, my brain is still under the tyrant rule of my dick, and I shrug off my doubts seconds before opening my eyes.

The bitch. The cum-guzzling, motherfucking bitch. The bastard-spawn, clap-ridden, whoring cunt. The sorry-ass, no-good, cheap piece of trash. The bitch.

I can't believe her audacity. She brought me here, and for only the second time in my thirty years of existence I feel the urge to hit a woman. She's still got my arms pinned down though, is holding me in place, giving me no choice but to look at the marker in front of me, which I somehow read through the red rage boiling in front of my irises. "Catriona Finley Sheahan. 1968-1993." No epitaph. Patrick couldn't think of anything worthwhile to say, it seems.

"Let go of me. Now!" I grind out.

She's laughing, the clear cadence of mocking laughter that ran through tales of Faerie and the Sidhe in my grandfather's house. "Did you really think I would betray the only good man out of the lot of you?" she says coldly. "Are you that much of an idiot, Seamus?"

She's not letting go of me, and I see no way of extricating myself from her grasp without hurting at least one of us. "Let the fuck go of me!" I repeat.

If anything her hold on me tightens. "No, Seamus, I don't reckon I'll let go of you any time soon," she says. "This ends today, for both of us. You will banish the ghosts, even if it is the last thing you'll ever do."

I start cursing her in the old tongue and realize by about word five that I've made a tactical error. Never give an opponent an unfair advantage by taking the battle onto the field of his native language. The bitch laughs even harder. "You know, for someone who answers to the name Seamus Sheahan, you've got one hell of a thick accent," she chuckles. "Even Micky is starting to speak Irish better than that. Of course he had a pretty good grasp of the cursing before, after all those years of listening to the two of you hurling insults at each other."

"It's been a while," I say through gritted teeth. "So sue me, bitch. Let the fuck go of me."

"I already told you, today is the day you stop running," Etain says quietly. "No more games, Seamus."

With all routes of escape temporarily blocked, the only option left to me is to close my eyes, a futile effort considering the view is forever burned into my retina. "The trouble with ghosts," she continues, "is that they always come back to haunt you. What is it they say? *Coimhéad fearg bhean na foighde*? Well, today this patient woman teaches you to face your demons."

"I'm not listening, bitch!" I scream, although truthfully my voice is just a little bit too raw for it to count as anything other than a barely suppressed sob.

"I couldn't care less whether you are listening or not, so long as you hear," Etain laughs with just a touch of cruelty in her voice. "And you are long overdue to hear what I have to say. You owe me a debt, Seamus."

Fuck the lot of them. Is there anyone who doesn't think I owe them for one reason or another? "I do not recall being indebted to you," I say.

"You owe me for everything I had to be after Her," she spits out. "You owe me for years of sitting at home while my friends went to the pub, you owe me for going to Cork, not Trinity, or Oxford, or Cambridge, because after Her, Mammy would not let me leave. Most of all you owe me for having to be good."

"You've done all right for yourself," I say half-heartedly.

"I had no choice!" she shouts. "I had no choice but to be Miss Goody-

Two-Shoes because of Her. There were no parties for me, no boyfriends, and no fun. All there was for me was school and mass, and I hated Her for it."

"You're alive," my voice is barely audible in stark contrast to hers.

"That I am," she acknowledges, "and She's dead and good riddance to Her."

"You callous bitch!" I scream. "She was my wife, your sister."

"It's hard to lose your gods, isn't it, Seamus?" she says. "After all, there isn't much left once your Goddess deserts you. I suspect you know that already though; Micky tells me Declan still worships you."

"Leave my brother out of this. He's no concern of yours," I hiss.

"As you wish," she says. "Are you a betting man, Seamus?"

I don't favor her with an answer. Any idiot could tell that a man such as myself has a fair liking of the ponies. There is no higher stake could be placed than that which is risked every time I push a needle into my arm.

"She wagered She was immortal, and She lost the bet, Seamus. She had the impertinence to tempt fate. Death was really too kind a punishment for that."

"Have you completely lost your marbles, kitten?"

She bares her teeth in the most radiant of smiles. "Not at all, Seamus," she says, laughter in her voice. "I believe a man should know to play chess. It's the pinnacle of masculinity."

"You're mad," I respond. "Pool is a man's game. So is snooker, and possibly even darts after sufficient whiskey has been consumed, but chess?"

She laughs, "There's nothing to pool or snooker except some elementary physics and a bit of luck, you should know that. Chess, on the other hand, is a game of strategy and skill. More than that though, chess is a game of ruthlessness."

"Chess is what the prefects played when they weren't piously chasing down the smokers," I sneer.

"Oh, grow up, Seamus," Catriona replies. "You're not in school anymore. A good game of chess is about balls. It's about whether you are prepared to sacrifice the queen to take your opponent's king. It's endgame."

Endgame. The realization suddenly hits me that she really isn't talking about chess; she's talking about an entirely different game, and I don't know that I have the nerve for it. She smiles again, a radiantly wicked smile, "Do you have the balls to risk everything?"

My throat is drying up. "What are the stakes?"

"Same as in any game: the loser forfeits all, the winner takes the queen," she says coldly.

Of course. To the victor go the spoils, and I can't help wondering, my queen, whether I should prefer to be the runner-up, can't help wondering what kind of darkness lies ahead. The girl always comes with a price attached, and I have no desire to be Achilles when Patrokles is the sacrifice demanded in return. Not that it should matter what I wish, because errant knight that I am, I always do my regent's bidding. My dark queen requires me to duel to the death, and what knight would deny his lady's request?

I roll up the sleeve of my shirt, and because I cannot resist the inherent melodrama of the offering, I say, "I am entrusting you with my life, Catriona. Be careful of it; it's the last of what is mine that I haven't given you already."

I watch her impassively as she traces a few prominent veins with her fingertips. Then there is the short, sharp prick of the needle, and then nothing, for a few seconds at least. After that comes the wave of nausea; the balance must be maintained after all. For anything that is ingested into the body something else must be ejected. I wish I could say I were graceful about it, but there is no romance to be found in projectile vomiting in the middle of the room. My eyes roll back in their sockets as the blood rushes to my head, and then I'm resting in her lap and she's cooing words of endearment, her fingers locked in my hair. We are equals again. The knight has won the lady's hand, if not her heart.

"That's where you're wrong," I hear myself saying. "Her wager was never with God. It was with me. She wagered I'd always be there to catch her when she was falling, and I—"

"You are human," Etain interrupts. "It was entirely unreasonable to expect omnipotence from you. Only a fool would do so."

I laugh hoarsely. "Then maybe I'm the fool?"

"Perhaps," Etain concedes, "but only because you insist on believing that you are at fault."

"If I had been there, I could—"

"No you couldn't have," Etain replies entirely without malice. "She wouldn't have allowed it. She wanted to go."

I would protest now, should be protesting now, but how can I deny the truth delivered by an avenging angel? I realize with a sudden start that Etain no longer holds me in place. The urge to run is gone though; the fire consumed itself. Etain is kneeling on the grass, randomly pulling weeds out of the grave. It strikes me that somehow the lack of epitaph is fitting, because there is nothing left to say.

"Do you still hate Her?" I ask, an edge to my voice.

Etain looks up to me, green eyes sparkling with life. "Memory is a tricky thing, Seamus. It fades all too readily. I still love Her, miss Her at times, but truthfully, I haven't hated Her in years."

"Do you think I'm a bad man for hating Her as much as I loved Her?"

She stands up in one fluid movement and extends her hand to brush the back of her palm along my cheek, "You're not a bad man, Seamus. Flawed perhaps, but not bad."

"Thank you," I say underneath my breath. "For what it's worth, you've grown into one hell of a woman."

She laughs and offers me her hand. "Friends?"

I hesitate only for a moment before gripping onto her hand as if my life depended on it. "Friends," I reply. "Although if things between you and Micky don't work out—"

"Shut your trap before I shut it for you," she interrupts, but she doesn't let go of my hand, keeps holding it in fact as we start walking out of the graveyard and back to the car.

It feels like I'm doing something more than walking away from a grave I no longer am terrified to visit. It takes me a while to notice, but I suddenly realize what's missing: the dull pain that etched itself into my every waking moment for more than a decade is gone somehow, replaced by the ghost of a memory, not of pain but of love.

When we arrive back at Mother's house, Micky is waiting for us. "Where have you been?" he asks, his question directed at Etain more than myself.

"Seamus and I went for a little trip down memory lane," she replies cheerfully.

Micky looks at me for the first time since we entered the house. Some things just don't change over the course of an afternoon, and I'm still irritated beyond reason by the self-righteous git. I can't help myself; I smirk and waggle my eyebrows in an unmistakably lewd gesture. That's all it takes. Etain might as well be out of the room already as far as Micky is concerned. "You bastard, you touched my woman!" he hollers as he launches himself at me.

"She was mine long before she was yours," I grin as he slams me against the wall. Then fists are flying, Micky's for the most part. I'm not really fighting back; I'm too busy laughing my arse off.

My laughter seems to rile him even more, because he isn't pulling his punches as he slams his balled fists into my face. The first punch rattles my jaw, the second splits the skin above my left eyebrow, the third nearly breaks my nose; still, I'm not fighting back, and I don't know why. Micky, with his body pinning me against the wall, grabs me by the shirt and moves his face so close to mine, our noses are almost touching, forcing me to look straight into his too-near eyes. Suddenly, I am intensely uncomfortable with the situation.

"Nobody touches my wife," Micky hisses.

I'm laughing again, but this time the laughter is fueled by anger. What makes the idiot think that anyone would ever stoop to marry him? I raise my arms, place two palms on his chest and push him away forcefully, shoving him so hard he stumbles into the opposite wall. I can feel the blood trickling down my face, some of it obscuring the vision in my left eye and burning a little as it slips beneath the lid. The blood only serves to fuel my anger. Time to teach the insolent boy a lesson he won't forget in a hurry. He should know that only Patrick can beat me in a fight; such is the lot of younger brothers.

I slap him hard across the face, an action that brings another howl of anger from Micky, who is clearly distraught that I don't even consider it worthwhile to use my fists. "The lady may show a certain lack of good judgement by shagging you, but I doubt she'd ever marry you," I laugh before slamming my right fist into his stomach. He topples forward, the wind knocked out of him, and I'm about to follow up with a fist to his jaw, when I'm pulled off balance by Etain, who jumps onto my back, locking her arms in a stranglehold around my neck and her legs around my waist.

"The lady already followed up on her initial lack of judgement and married him," Etain shouts. "I swear to God, Seamus, if you try to harm one hair on his head, I will kill you with my bare hands."

Laying into Micky again is the farthest thing from my mind following that revelation. He's still panting, trying to draw air back into his lungs at any rate. "You did what?" I ask.

"I married him last month in Dublin," Etain replies.

I slowly retreat away from Micky, Etain still clinging to my back. "Marvelous. The two of you really deserve each other," I say.

Micky looks up at me still holding his belly. "And I suppose that's why you were so determined to screw her," he pants.

"Give it a rest, Micky," Etain sighs as she slides down my back. "No need rubbing it in."

I almost start laughing again when he gives in without another word. The boy is so pussy-whipped it isn't even funny. It's a dominant character trait of those Finley women, my traitor snickers. They have a tendency to wrap you lot around their little fingers; her sister did the same to you. For once, I don't fight the treacherous voice; there's no point to it. Instead I lean heavily against the wall across the hallway from Micky and try to collect myself.

Etain sinks down to the floor in front of Micky and takes hold of his face. "You're a pillock sometimes," she murmurs. "There's no way I would have made those vows had I not meant them. Marriage is for good where I come from."

"Then what were you doing with him?" Micky asks quietly.

Etain sighs. "I took him to my sister's grave, if you must know."

Micky lowers his eyes and mumbles, "Tell me again how much of a pillock I am?"

Then she's talking Irish, so quietly I can't make out what she's saying. The expression on Micky's face when he looks up again gives me a pretty good idea though. The look in his eyes is straight out of Jane Austen, the best word to describe it, "smoldering." Christ, he really is in love. He runs his hand down her face and along her hairline until it reaches the nape of her neck, and then he pulls her into the most graphic kiss I have ever had the misfortune to witness. Is that what Catriona and I looked like to him, I wonder. Probably not; she never reciprocated quite the way Etain does, I think bitterly.

There's nothing sweet about that kiss; there's lust and passion and a thousand other primal forces at work in front of my eyes, but I would be hard-pressed to identify anything I could liken to romance. They might as well be fucking right in front of me. I have a feeling in a few minutes they will be, regardless of whether or not I'm still there, and I don't think I'm ready to observe my baby brother in the act of copulating quite yet.

As his hands travel from the nape of her neck down to her breasts and latch on to nipples that I can see are rock-hard even through the cotton of her shirt, I quietly detach myself from the wall I'm leaning against and flee to the kitchen as fast as I can while not disturbing the coupling in progress.

I head straight for the liquor cabinet and pull out a bottle of bourbon, since Mother doesn't appear to have replaced the vodka I finished off my first night under her roof. At the rate I'm going I may well turn into a drunk before this vacation is over. I don't bother with a glass and start downing the liquor in long gulps, trying to block out the unequivocal sounds of fornication issuing from the corridor. God, is that what Luka heard every time one of my whores came to visit? How could he stand it?

I slump onto a stool at the breakfast bar and stare gloomily at the bottle while patting my pockets down for my cigarettes. I don't particularly care whether Mother will give me grief for smoking inside the house, considering everything that has transpired today. I whimper quietly at the thought that pushes itself into my consciousness and send up a fervent prayer to any gods that might be listening that Mother doesn't return home while Micky and Etain are fucking in her hallway.

13

Purgatory: Cast into the Fire

Patrick meets me at the end of the platform after I get off the train in Durham. "Didn't take you long to change your mind, did it?" he smirks.

"Yeah, well, what can I say except that I got a front-row seat in a floor-show Micky and the missus put on," I shudder involuntarily, the memory still fresh in my mind. "You could've told me they got hitched."

Patrick stops dead in his tracks and spins around. "They did what?"

"Ah, so he didn't invite you either. Well, that makes all the difference," I shrug.

Patrick isn't listening though. "He married her?" he roars. "Would it be too much to ask that at least one of my brothers doesn't settle for your rejects?"

I back off slightly to give him some space. "Hey now, don't kill the messenger," I say.

For a moment it looks like Patrick is about to ram his fists into my gut, but then he shrugs and starts striding out of the train station mumbling obscenities to himself. I grab my bag and follow him. He doesn't say another word all the way to the car and only grunts as he unlocks the passenger door for me.

His continued silence as we drive through Durham is making me acutely uncomfortable. I have never taken Patrick's brand of brooding well; it riled me when I was a boy, and it riles me still. Finally, because I can't take the silence any longer, I say, "She's not that bad, you know. Got her head screwed on right if nothing else."

Patrick grunts noncommittally.

"She's not Catriona," I venture.

Patrick slams on the brakes so hard I almost hit the dashboard. I can feel the seat belt cutting into my chest through the shirt, and I know I'll be sporting bruises come tomorrow morning. I moan quietly.

"What did you just say?" he sputters.

"I said that Etain isn't Catriona, far from it," I reply, enunciating each word with exaggerated care.

Patrick pulls the car over to the side of the road before turning to me slowly. "What on God's green earth happened in London, James?"

"I don't know what you mean," I say, avoiding his eyes. I know damn well what he means. How do you explain the careless use of a name that hasn't crossed your lips in eight years? How can you possibly rationalize that it ceased hurting within the space of twenty-four hours?

"Bullshit," Patrick responds, mirroring my thoughts.

"Etain and I, we—" my voice trails off, because I'm unable to formulate the vocabulary necessary to finish that sentence in a somewhat understandable manner. *Etain and you almost fucked*, the traitor shouts, enraged. *How about you tell Patrick that you almost fucked your brother's wife?* I push the offending voice far back into my mind, struggling to think of words that will convey to Patrick that which I haven't comprehended myself yet. "Look, Etain and I—it's complicated. Can we just leave it at that?"

Patrick looks at me strangely, but decides to drop the subject. He shifts the car back into drive and starts heading toward his house again, the only outward sign of his inner turmoil being the sound of his fingers drumming on the steering wheel.

"James, are we out of jaffa cakes again?" Declan drawls. He's been awake for so long, he has trouble forming coherent sentences.

"I think you finished the last box yesterday," I reply. "What do you want all that sugar for anyway? Don't you think it's about time you went to sleep?"

Declan giggles maniacally. "I want sugar and caffeine to keep me awake. Sleep is for nancies, James. Who needs it?"

I sigh. I refuse to let myself be drawn into that conversation again: we've been having it daily for over a week. Declan decided, out of the blue it seems, that all his troubles were due to sleeping, so now he's experimenting with never sleeping again and today is day nine of his endeavor. I try my damndest to remember whether I was as pig-headed as that at seventeen, but I can't. It seems so very long ago.

"Well, I'm knackered, so I'll be turning in," I say. "Try to keep the rubbish you play on that stereo at a sociable volume, would you?"

I head straight into the bedroom, not bothering with the bathroom. I will probably regret it later, but right now I'm too tired to take my clothes off, never mind brush my teeth. As I collapse on the bed it occurs to me that Catriona should be here by now, but then, she hasn't exactly been keeping predictable hours recently. She's tail-spinning fast, and I'm too tired to give it any consideration. How did it come to this? I wonder briefly before slipping into unconsciousness.

I'm woken hours later by the sluggish signals my bladder is sending to my brain. I need a piss, badly. Noting that Catriona is still missing, I stagger into the bathroom. After nature's call has been heeded, I shrug off my shirt and splash cold water over my face and shoulders. I look at the face in the mirror in front of me. Truthfully, I have been avoiding that reflection of late. My face has always been hard angles, much more so than Patrick's, but recently it's gotten much harder than I ever thought possible. Something has gone missing from those eyes looking back at me, and I'm not quite sure what, but I suspect it might be empathy, that last bastion of morality and the social contract. "What kind of parody of humanity have you become, James?" I ask my reflection.

Reflections don't answer back as a rule, but they also don't lie much either. What I see in the mirror these days is a petty criminal, and not for the kind of anarchy I could revel in in years gone past. What I see is an incompetent father figure and a failed husband, a man who can't keep his charges sane or his wife out of the arms of others. I don't like what I see.

I tear my eyes away from the traitor staring at me through the looking glass and peruse the bathroom. There are discarded clothes all over the floor; apparently, neither my brothers nor my wife are capable of picking up after themselves. I bend down to a pair of jeans, ready to throw them into the hamper, when a small plastic bag slips out of the back pocket. I hesitate only for a moment before picking it up, cursing Catriona in my mind. She's being careless again.

Except, these jeans are too large to be Catriona's, and looking closely at the bag, I realize it doesn't look like heroin either. I carefully open the bag and dip a moistened finger into it. A taste is all it takes to be sure. The acrid bitterness washes across my tongue. Oh, I know that taste, though it's low-quality, dirty shit, cut with rubbish if I'm any judge; this isn't Catriona's style. Never mind that Catriona doesn't do stimulants, she would never buy shite like this: too street-smart for that. That leaves the usual suspect.

A brief glance in the mirror reveals a face much paler than the one I saw mere minutes ago. The muscle underneath my left eye is twitching of its own accord, my teeth are clenched and my jaw is set so rigidly, even I can see that I'm seconds away from the paroxysm of the decade. Except I don't have time to lose my temper right now, I remind myself. Instead I must go out there and control the damage before things get out of hand. I carefully close up the bag again and slip it into my pocket. Time to have a serious chat with sleepless boy, seeing as I have just discovered the likely culprit for his insomnia.

I stride into the sitting room driven by a determination I didn't know I was capable of. I can do this, I think. I can have another drug talk with Declan, tell him exactly why staying up for nine days straight with the help of amphetamines is a bad idea. I can even do it with a straight face, no matter how much of a hypocrite I feel inside.

I never get the chance. Declan is sitting at the small Formica kitchen table in a puddle of his own blood, carving into his fingers with a switchblade. Business as usual then.

"Declan, what the fuck do you think you're doing?" I shout.

Declan looks up at me, frenzy in his eyes, and mutters, "My hands. I realized I have webbed fingers. Have to cut out the webbing—"

I grab the switchblade from his hand while throwing the bag on the table in one fluid movement. "You left your stash lying in the bathroom," I note calmly. "It's cut with something. Judging by your actions, probably *a hallucinogen.*"

"*I haven't had any of that in a couple of days,*" Declan stammers, blindly batting at my arms in an effort to retrieve the switchblade. "*Wanted to see how long I could stay up without any help. Give back my knife. I hafta cut out the webbing.*"

I find myself wondering how long the average human being can stay awake before starting to hallucinate even without the aid of mind-altering drugs. Nine days seems as good a guess as any. My gaze shifts down to the damage Declan did to his fingers. He must have been working at it for quite a while before I interrupted him; the injuries are extensive, even to my unschooled eyes. I pick up a couple of reasonably clean tea towels and wrap them around Declan's bleeding hands.

"*Declan, we have to go to the hospital,*" *I say in a clipped tone of voice, trying not to alarm the boy too much.*

"*Will they remove the webbing?*" Declan slurs, his eyes unfocused.

"*Yeah,*" *I say, unwilling to reason with someone the other side of sanity just now.* "*Yeah, they'll remove it and stitch you back up again.*" *I don't mention the likelihood of skin grafts as I herd him out of the flat toward the car.*

Lounging in an overstuffed armchair while carefully balancing a tumbler of malt whiskey in my hand, I look at the scene of domestic bliss in front of me. Patrick is sitting on the couch with Annie's head in his lap and an arm loosely flung around her waist. She is sleeping now, a rare occurrence these days if Patrick's word can be trusted.

In my fragmented memory, there are only two versions of Annie I can remember. There is Annie with purple hair and black lipstick, Annie BC, before children, as I think of her, and then there is this: Annie AC, the honey-haired creature with the painfully swollen belly. Logically, I know that this is only her fifth pregnancy in thirteen years, yet in my mind I cannot conceive of an adult Annie who isn't with child. It is becoming increasingly difficult to recall Annie BC.

Patrick has had twenty years of this, I can't help reminding myself. Patrick has had twenty years of unconditional love, twenty years of Annie. Twenty years. I am seething with envy. Patrick has had twenty years of happiness, or as close to it as a man is able to get, while I have had twenty years of Luka.

Ah, but that never mattered until Luka stopped adoring you, did it? My mind whispers to me. You gladly sacrificed all just so long as Luka worshiped the ground you walked on, and all was a very small price to pay for deity. But even if that were true, it no longer holds, not since Luka decided to become a god in his own right, does it? The traitor laughs, whispering that all children grow and leave, and sons of gods will surpass their own fathers in time, have done so since time immemorial. Unlike Patrick, I've never had the luxury to create more children, more worshipers, more life. I can feel unequaled rage building within myself.

Soft chuckling from Annie jolts me out of my thoughts. I realize I have been staring at her midsection for longer than is polite even amongst family. Patrick is grinning. "Go on, James," he says, "I know you want to cop a feel. It's all right by me as long as you keep your hands below her chest."

Annie slaps him playfully. "Oi, don't I get a say?" she laughs. "Go on then, James, meet footie player number six."

"No!" I say, much more violently than I intended to and get up abruptly. Out of the corner of my eye I can see Annie throwing a questioning look at Patrick. I try my best to stalk out of the room nonchalantly.

"Don't look at me," I hear Patrick saying. "I don't know what gets up his arse half the time."

Once in the kitchen I start searching for something to drink, anything that doesn't entail whiskey, that is. Through the open door I can hear subdued arguing in the sitting room. Annie, bless her, is trying to convince Patrick to go after me. Of course, Patrick had his fill of that while we were down in the old country.

Finally, Annie, looking rather disheveled, appears in the doorway. She struts, or rather, waddles, past me and leans down to the cupboard underneath the sink. After some rummaging she pulls out a half-full bottle of vodka and hands it to me. "Want to tell me what that was about?" she asks.

I shake my head, staring at the bottle. I know I'm being silly now. I'm not even sure I could explain my jealousy, my complete and utter envy of Patrick's life, because it has never been what I wanted. I never wanted safe and boring and nine to five. I never wanted an army of children; I didn't even want the ones thrust upon me so long ago. I've no reason to be jealous of Patrick, but I am, and I might be jealous of Micky too. How long until he starts breeding?

I look down and notice the sticker somebody stuck to the bottle for the first time. A child's drawing with "James" written in large, irregular block letters. So there you have it, James, I think bitterly. You're so seriously fucked up that even one of Patrick's brood can identify your bottle of booze without too much trouble. I don't even notice the petulant tears running down my face. I do notice Annie gingerly removing the vodka from my hands and pulling me into her arms, followed by the soft kicks of an in utero child against my belly. That's when something snaps.

It would be comical if it weren't so utterly, pathetically tragic, because in the grand scheme of things, I was never the one whose mind just gave. Luka is broken all right, has been for a decade or more, but that's what we've learned to expect of him. Catriona broke, and I played no little part in her destruction, but I? I was never the one to break, I hadn't the luxury; too busy putting the broken beings back together—until now. I am breaking at long last.

I've got to get out of this house and I have to do it quickly; I won't be a pretty sight before too long. So I push Annie away none-too-gently and start running. Don't know where to; I just run. Out of the house and down the street, trying to get some distance between me and the house before I start howling. I have to get away. I have to disappear again; for good this time.

"I have to get away from here," Luka drawls. *Oh joy. He's been gone a week, arrived in Philly less than four days ago and he's already wanting to leave.*

"Why? What happened?" I ask unadvisedly.

"Nothing happened," he replies. "I just remembered that I hate Philly. I'm getting a ride to the freeway tomorrow morning, heading out your way. I'll be there in a week or two."

"Luka you've spent the past few months telling me how much you hate California," I sigh.

"I do," he says after a short pause, "but I've just remembered that I hate Philly more."

"You've only just realized that?"

He doesn't say anything for a while and I start to wonder whether he's gone and stepped away from the phone: it wouldn't be the first time. "I can't stay here, James," he explains eventually. "I can't stay here and pre-

tend that everything's normal and that I'm just some 18-year-old kid with nothing better to do than sit around and steal the beer out of the fridge when nobody's looking. I just can't. Nothing will ever be normal again."

"Because of me?" I ask knowing full well that the answer more likely than not will be in the affirmative.

"No, not because of you. Well, mostly not because of you," he says. "Because of Portland, because of Barstow, because of London, because nothing's ever going to be the same again. Everything's changed."

Give the boy a cigar for saying the bloody obvious. Nothing is right, and everything is wrong, has been for nearly a year now, has been for longer than either of us has been in this godforsaken country. "Coming back out to California won't change that, Luka," I say quietly.

"I know," he replies. "Ain't no cure for what's wrong with us except for dying, and you'll never let us do that because there would be hell to pay. You'd rather live in purgatory."

I think he might be drunk again. "Don't believe in heaven and hell or angels and devils anymore, Luka. Stopped believing in them a while ago."

He laughs quite humorlessly at that. "You've still got the schoolboy in you, James. You might not be going to mass and you might be denying the ancestors, but there's no way you'll ever change who you are, no matter how hard you try. In our world there's always heaven and hell and purgatory. In our world there's God and his sweet angels watching and devils all around. In our world there's only fool's gold and never any riches at the end of the rainbow, because that's who we are, who our fathers were. Go stick your head in the sand if you will. Deny your name all you like. Run to the ends of the earth if you think it'd help; we both know that at the end of it all there'll be last rites and a wake and the obligatory spilling of whiskey. It's in the blood, James. It's always been in the blood."

"It's you that's talking of running," I say harshly.

"So I am," he chuckles. "You taught me well, James, taught me above all else how to run, forever if I have to."

This isn't getting us anywhere. He may be drunk or delusional but either way there's no reasoning with him. There never is. He's set his mind on leaving Philly, and I have no doubt he will, regardless of what I have to say on the matter, so I do what I always do where Luka is concerned: I cave. "Fine, have it your way," I say. "Sure you don't want to take the bus? I could send you the money."

"Don't reckon you'd be able to get it here by tomorrow morning, though," he responds. "I'm leaving tomorrow, one way or another. I'll be fine hitching a lift. I really will."

"You'll be careful, won't you?" I ask despite my misgivings. He'll be truly reckless now, just because he knows I'll be worried sick.

"I always am," he says. "I'll call you along the way when I can, but I'm planning on going fast. Should make it out there before the end of the month."

"I'll be expecting you."

"You always do," he sighs and hangs up the phone.

It's pissing down with rain, so this must be Manchester.

That's quite a logical conclusion considering my state of mind: the rain makes it Manchester, just as clouds would make it London and fog would make it San Francisco.

It doesn't feel like Manchester though. I think it might be because I came into the city the wrong way this time, came from up north somewhere, and I'm used to coming up from London, passing Stockport where the rain usually starts. Still, it's Manchester all right, and it's dark and I'm cold. Not that I care much about that; I'm surprised I'm even aware of where I am. I've been steadily slackening my hold on reality ever since running out of Patrick's kitchen without so much as a coat and no more money than was in my pocket at the time. When was it now? Two, three days ago?

Can't remember. Can't even remember making my way down here. I had no intention of coming here, never liked the place very much to begin with. It must be ten years gone since the last time I've been, but the parts of Manchester I know, the parts the likes of me frequent, never change much. I still have an unerring instinct for finding my way to where I belong, because by god, this part of town is still as piss-poor and desperate as ever. There are still lunatics and whores and junkies and ghosts of wasted lives, and this is where I belong, where I've always belonged.

And Patrick won't come for me this time; that I am sure of.

I'm drenched and shivering, as much from the cold as from other, less wholesome causes, wandering aimlessly around the alleys looking for something, anything, I'm not sure what. Don't know much anymore really, nothing much besides the siren call of heroin and the beckoning arms of insanity, and I wish, not for the first time, that I were Luka because I'd have no qualms about losing my mind if I were.

Every once in a while I hear the sounds of screeching brakes as a car pulls up to the curb to negotiate with one of the girls or boys on the corner. I wonder silently when it was that they started looking so very young, and then I ask myself when I became so very, very old. It can't be more than ten years since it was Her on a corner very much like this one, but memory fades all too readily.

The johns don't bother me much, they never did. I'm getting much too old for a market dedicated to fresh meat, and I don't look the part; even at my worst, I never looked to be the type who would get desperate enough or addicted enough to play that game. There are a few things I have never—will never—do, and bending over for some dirty old man with a wife and kids at home is one of them.

Luka. If I were Luka that might be a different story altogether. Not that I'm sure; I've never dared to ask directly, but there must be reasons he can cross a continent the size of North America in eight days. Contrary to what he might believe I am not an imbecile, for the most part. No matter how much my brothers choose to avoid the topic, I knew for every excruciating second where the money came from, knew full well She was on the game. I only learned to ignore it very quickly. Luka's skill at traversing vast distances in the blink of an eye made me wonder long ago whether he had picked up any skills from Her, besides the fine art of finding his veins, that is.

And I am so very cold.

Maybe I could bring myself to—the thought alone makes me gag, and I can feel the bile rising in my throat. There are always other ways of achieving warmth and nourishment, ways other than begging or selling my body, and at one time or another I've tried them all. There's petty theft, of course, and then there's getting yourself detained by the right honorable constabulary on purpose, because the cell usually comes with a meal and a cot out of the rain.

I am so very tired.

My fingers find the ring still strung from the necklace about my neck as it has been these eight years or more. If I were desperate enough I could sell it, I suppose, or at least pawn it, but I'm not that desperate. I doubt I ever will be. Delicate, precious metal that chain may be, but Patrick ensured it was wrought harder than steel when he fastened it around my neck like a noose. It has been strangling me ever since. Not that I could bear to be freed from my collar; it's one of the few reminders of what was, what is, and what the stakes are, and I'm a gambling man at heart. Always a gambling man.

Still there are needs that must be met, a craving to be satisfied, a sickness to be fought. I remember too late why I've stuck with the stimulants for so long: opiates cause havoc in my mind and body. There's the exquisite sickness to contend with, followed in short order by a craving for more of the same. I'm a masochist as much as I'm a gambling man, and I rejoice in the chance to chuck my guts up at every opportune moment.

It's thoughts like these that convince me that apparently my nascent talent for cynicism didn't desert me when my mind snapped like a brittle twig in Durham, but my will broke.

And still I crave.

Maybe just a quick one off the wrist. How bad could it be? I'm reasonably certain Luka has done so countless times and much more besides. It rankles me a little that there is something, no matter how vile and repulsive it may seem to me, that Luka does better than I do. In everything else, he could never beat me at my own games, could never defeat me in a fist fight, could never be any more wild and reckless than I had been in my time.

Just a quick one off the wrist, because I know Luka could do it to serve his purposes, and I will not be bested by a madman. I wouldn't have to look at what I'm doing, could close off my mind enough to imagine that it was myself I was touching... I'm reasonably certain I could hold the sickness at bay, reasonably certain I could go through with it, because Luka can and has and I am by far the stronger of the two of us.

A quick one off the wrist would pay for a dime bag at least. Enough to tide me over until I can get back down to London where I can fend for myself because I've done so countless times in the past. Enough to make me forget that Patrick won't be coming for me this time. Enough to make me forget that nobody will be coming for me this time because there's no one left to give a damn.

And I throw up.

"Do you know how you can tell you're in the boondocks, James?" Luka cackles over the phone line.

"I'm sure I will in a moment," I reply testily. It's one in the morning on a weeknight.

"People around here drive until their cars break down, and then they build a hovel right next to it. It's redneck country," he drawls.

"Where are you?"

There's a pause while he thinks. "Nebraska, I think."

Christ, he only left Philly three days ago. How can he make time like that? "How the hell did you get there so fast?" I ask, my mind spinning, trying to wrap itself around the possibilities, none of them palatable in the least.

"There's this guy," he explains. "He picked me up in Kentucky, was going to give me a ride as far as St. Louis, except he kept on driving. I think he—"

"Don't go around playing strangers, Luka," I say much too fast and much too roughly. "It's dangerous."

"I know what I'm doing," he replies flippantly. "I told him I was only along for the ride and he kept on driving anyways. It's no skin off my nose. A ride is all I'm looking for."

"It's not what he's looking for," I say, can't really help myself. For all his street smarts, and his knowledge has been increasing exponentially, Luka is still a kid, more worldly and jaded than most eighteen-year-olds but a kid nonetheless. He hasn't quite realized yet what human beings are capable of, though he's had a steep learning curve recently.

"I can take care of myself," he replies. He's got an eighteen-year-old's arrogance too, the belief that he's immortal, invulnerable.

"I don't doubt that you can. Still..." I can't say what I really want to say. Can't tell him that I'm sick with worry; he'd only take greater risks.

"You wanna know why I had to leave?" he suddenly blurts out apropos of nothing. I wonder, not for the first time, whether he's drunk or high; I don't think he would have offered to tell me while sober.

"Why?"

"I kissed someone," he says.

"Kissing isn't bad, Luka," I coax him. Not sure that he's ever gone all that far with anyone. I'm not blind. I knew he was in love with Her, just as I knew She never paid him any mind because he wouldn't have—Luka may be a madman, but he's no Judas, never was that fond of transactions in silver, and at any rate, wasn't it Christ who was tempted by Magdalene? As far as I'm aware, there never was anyone else he was even remotely *interested in, but there is still Portland. I've never asked about that, never asked where the money came from because I'm afraid of the answer. I should know better than most; there's only so many ways you can feed an addiction.*

"I kissed Niamh's boyfriend," he says, stumbling a little over the words.

I sit down reflexively. I wasn't really expecting that, and I know I had better say something pretty damn quickly, otherwise he'll mistake my silence for condemnation. "Did you like it?"

I could kick myself. That was, with one or two exceptions, quite possibly the most inane response I could have thought of. What am I supposed to say in a situation like this? They never cover those in the parenting books. In fact, it's pretty safe to assume at this point that anything Luka has ever bothered to throw my way wasn't covered in Parenting 101.

"Yeah. A lot," he says.

"Are you gay?" I ask before I can stop myself. Shit. Didn't mean to put it that bluntly.

"No," he says vehemently. "I just—I don't even know why I did it really. He had a nice mouth. I never expected him to kiss me back, but he did and it was nice and—"

"There's nothing wrong with kissing anyone, Luka," I interrupt. "It's supposed to be nice."

"I'm not gay though," he whines. "I'm really not. I've thought about it and just the thought of—I can't imagine being with another man in that way, James. The thought repulses me. I don't want to be with anyone like that..."

"Then don't," I say. "It was just a kiss, Luka. You don't have to do it ever again."

"You don't understand," he snarls. "I don't want to like it, but I did. It was good. It was really good and I got hard and I would have gone on, I would have... if Niamh hadn't come in, I think I would have..."

Poor sod. I can't remember ever being that insecure about anything; I always knew whom I wanted. "Yeah, but you didn't Luka. That's all that matters," I try to reassure him. "It's normal to get hard when somebody kisses you, especially if they do it well. I've gotten hard from kisses myself. Hell, I've gotten hard just looking at some people. It's just a physical reaction. It doesn't have to mean anything."

"Yeah, but you never kissed a bloke," he says. He's right, of course. The opportunity never arose. I've never wanted to kiss another man, ever, but

right now I wish I had, if only to reassure him that it doesn't matter. He's waiting for it too, I think. He pauses just long enough to allow me to contradict him, and I briefly consider lying but dismiss the idea as being unhelpful; he'd call me on it sooner or later.

"I've never felt like that when I've kissed a girl, James," he stammers. "Not that I've kissed that many, but it never felt that good, never made me want more, never made me want to touch and move and... I don't want to be gay, James."

I'm starting to think the real reason he's flustered is something else entirely; it's not kissing a boy that's upset him. "What happened when Niamh walked in on you, Luka?"

He snorts. "Well, she wasn't too happy, let me tell you. Called me a pervert and a lot of other names and then went complaining to Uncle Diarmuid, and next thing I knew I was being dragged to confession. Only they didn't actually trust me to go and confess my sins, as it were, so before standing guard outside the confessional to make sure I'd receive my ear-bashing, Uncle Diarmuid had a good long chat with the Father."

I don't even notice the pain when my fist slams into the wall, but it leaves a nice dent in the plaster. I have to physically restrain myself from following up with a few more punches, and it takes me a few seconds to unclench my teeth enough to ask, "What did the bastards say, Luka?"

"Nothing that Niamh and Uncle Diarmuid hadn't said already." His laughter is bordering on hysterical. "Said I was a pervert, that I was sick, that I'd most likely burn in hell for my sins. Said that all I could hope for was that if I led a blameless life from now on and prayed for forgiveness and said God knows how many rosaries, then maybe the Lord would see fit to forgive me in time because He is a merciful God, after all."

This time the skin around my knuckles bursts. "Bastards!" I yell. "Goddamn fucking bastards with their goddamn fucking god and their holier-than-thou rhetoric!"

"You'll still take me in, won't you?" Luka asks hesitantly.

I try desperately to pull myself together. I'm beside myself he even has to ask. "They've got it wrong, Luka," I grind out. "It's them that are going to burn in hell for being mindless automatons spewing doctrine. Screw them and a curse on the church and a curse on its henchmen. This is your home. You are my brother, always will be, and I don't give a damn what those bastards say. I don't care if you're gay."

"I'm not though. I've told you," he replies.

"I believe you. I'm just saying I wouldn't care either way," I say quietly trying to stem the flow of blood from my hand with a discarded shirt. *"You'll always be my brother."*

"Even if—"

"Yeah, even if," I assure him. *"Come on home, Luka."*

I can't quite remember how I made it back to London, but I did and somehow ended up here in Camden. It was Soho, Piccadilly and Leicester Square a very long time ago, but the coppers put a stop to that on account of the tourists. Soho's been thoroughly sanitized, and in exchange Camden's gone to the dogs, because they can shift us around all they like, but we'll always be there, lurking in the shadows. I almost don't notice that it's 'we' and 'us' now, when it has always been 'She' and 'them.' Fifteen years on, and I've become one of them, except they won't have me now any more than they would have me fifteen years ago.

This is my city though. The boys and girls on the corners may have been replaced by younger, fresher faces over time, but here, in my city, I can instinctively tell who's selling bodies and who's selling pills; nothing much at all has changed. I know where there's food to be had, I know where there's petty theft to be committed, and I can tell which girls are likely to share given certain... incentives. I might have been exiled for a decade, but London is still my whore and I her willing servant.

I suppose were I to get really desperate, I could go to my mother's house, though I'm not certain she'd let me in. I suppose I really should have given my body a break from the dope a few days ago; I'm wedged precariously on the edge of physical dependency as it is. I suppose it would help if I actually gave a damn, but the only benefit to insanity I've been able to determine is my utter inability to care.

That's a falsehood too. Isn't the working definition of a madman somebody who is incapable of reasoning? I'm still quite capable of reason, I think, I've just chosen to disregard all reason. It was either that or lose my mind. So here I am, as mad as I'm likely to get, older than I ever expected, still playing a game I was never any good at in the grand scheme of things, though I'm a damn sight better at it than any of the kids playing not thirty yards away; it's the reason I'm old and they'll die young.

I scan the corner and settle on a likely girl. She's young, too young, and lost-looking and running scared, but judging by the way she's scratching her arms, she's also doped up to the gills quite recently. It takes one to know one and all that rot.

I'm not much to look at any longer, having been out and about in the same clothes I left Patrick's house in—how long ago? A week? Two? Haven't kept track of time properly. I think I must have spewed up all over my shoes at some point, or maybe someone else did, but it all adds up the same: I'm nothing to write home about at the moment. That suits me well. She'd be less likely to respond if I appeared a john looking for a free ride, and there's practically no way I'll be mistaken for that with the state I'm in. I run my hands over my face, noticing the stubble in passing. My hands are shaking slightly; give it another hour or two, and I'll be as sick as a dog unless I score beforehand.

I amble up to her and melt into the shadows behind her. I've no intention of disturbing her business, should there be any, and remain silent whenever a car drives up. I know that even if she got into one of the cars, chances are she'd be back within half an hour or less and it would be extremely bad form to interfere with her livelihood. I can wait out a blowjob if I have to. When there aren't any cars, I talk.

She's much more jaded than any girl her age has a right to be. Eventually she warms to me a little, tells me her name, or a name at any rate. So I tell her mine. Oh not the real one, not the one granddaddy Sheahan gave me while her own mother was likely still playing in a sandbox, and she knows it too; there's too much power in a name. We're negotiating, not like she'd negotiate with the old men in the cars, there's nothing subtle about that, but we are caught up in a dance of sorts. She's sizing me up, determining if there are benefits to my company, and I turn up the charm a notch.

Just when I think I'm about to get somewhere with her, someone says, "She's half your age if she's a day, James."

Now that's a voice I wasn't expecting to hear again for a good long while. "I'm younger than I look," I smirk.

"She's still too young for you."

I shrug. "How did you find me?"

"Habit," he says sarcastically. "Ten years on, and you still head for the same places when you're running. You've no imagination at all, James."

Never mind that he's right, I still don't appreciate being told that. "Why are you here, Micky?"

He steps out of the shadows but keeps a respectful distance. Either that or I'm smelling worse than I thought, which is possible, of course. "I've come to fetch you," he says. "Patrick won't come for you this time."

"I know," I reply quietly. "Why?"

He sighs. "Because Luka needs you."

I've heard that one before. Heard it put in fairly similar terms a lifetime ago in an alley very much like this one. I was as much of a mess then as I am today, my mind soaked in cheap liquor, and I still knew it was only a half-truth. "Luka needs a keeper, Micky. It has naught to do with me; anyone could do it. Why did you come for me?"

He looks at me for long moments before he replies. "You came for me. You always came for me when it mattered, even when I wouldn't give you the time of day. Is that a good enough reason for you?"

"So you're wanting to pay up then?" I ask.

He shakes his head minutely. "Patrick plays those games. Patrick may go on about debts and such, but Patrick's a little bit more old-fashioned than either of us, wouldn't you say? Though there's one or two ways I'd pay up if I had to. I could lock you in a wardrobe for a few days if it were needed." He pauses, the question evident in his eyes, and it's my turn to shake my head. "No, I didn't think so," he says quietly. "You're too afraid of dying. You'll probably be sick as a dog for a few hours but no more. Very well then, let's go."

I can't quite believe his audacity, the assumption that I will just come along because he's told me so. "What if I won't go with you?"

He's wearing that predatory smile he perfected at some point between the time he moved in with me and the time he left for university, another feature I'm at least partially responsible for, I suppose. "I'm bigger than you are now, James," he says.

"And I still fight dirtier than you," I reply with a grin.

He's edging closer. "I don't want to fight you, but I will if I have to," he says.

I will my body to relax. We're on my home turf here, and I'm at an advantage. "You will have to," I say calmly, the challenge clear in my voice.

I must have been running on dope and not much else for too long because my reflexes are shot. His balled fist hits me square in the jaw before I've so much as a chance to take up a defensive stance. What's more, I find myself not wanting to repay him in kind. I feel my jaw gingerly. Nothing broken so far as I can tell. "You'll have to do better than that, Micky," I grin.

So he does, cursing, with flailing fists, laying into me for all he's worth. I'm still not fighting back though, and I've no idea why. He's got a mean right hook too, has me backed up against the wall behind me within ten seconds flat and doesn't let up, even though my knees are starting to give. "That what you want, James?" he shouts between punches.

I'm a little surprised I do. I can hear myself hissing, "more" and "make me" and "harder" as the pain spreads from impact points all over my body like fractals. It's what Patrick refused to give me all summer: pain and more pain and possibly redemption at the end of it, though thinking that probably makes me a much bigger fool than I've been all my life. There's no redemption to be had around here and not much solace to be found in raining fists, but there is some, which is all that matters. I don't know that Micky truly understands. More likely he's just lost his temper, but I don't care either way. I'm getting what I want.

Another punch to the kidneys and my knees really give out from under me, and then I'm sinking to the wet street with a strange sense of déjà vu. I've been on the ground in an alley once before, and it feels like I've come full-circle. There was a big, broad-shouldered Irish bastard who looked a lot like this one laying into me then, and god help me, eight years was too long to go without punishment.

Unlike Patrick, Micky doesn't stop when I'm down on the ground. He keeps on punching and kicking, cursing all the way. I want more. Steel-capped boots to my shins and my stomach and I want more, beg him for more. Beg him to give it to me good. Then I'm beyond speaking, and there's only the pain, mind-numbing, liberating pain.

"That what you want, James?" he pants with a few more random kicks to my body.

I can't answer him. I'm beyond talking, curled up there in the street reveling in the pain, no words, just glorious pain. I still want him to hurt me. I want him to hurt me, mark me, bruise me, make me feel. Make me know blood and punishment and solace, all rolled up in one.

He stops and leans back against the wall breathing hard. "God almighty, James, is that what it takes to make you whole?"

The wake and the funeral took more out of Patrick than he let on. Not that I remember the wake. I don't really remember anything much except my thwarted attempt to throw myself into Her grave immediately followed by my spewing up all over Patrick, but we're Catholic; there's always a wake.

The next day he finally takes his eyes off of me long enough to allow for my strategic escape. Perhaps it isn't so much because Patrick is any less vigilant than he has been but instead because I'm within reasonable proximity of sober for the first time since we started this little charade, and not by choice either. I'm reasonably sober because Patrick has finally started running out of hard liquor and he's made no effort to replace that which I've drunk. I've a feeling that the sudden cessation in alcohol purchases may be due to my chucking my guts up all over his best suit. Either that or he's noticed that I've started shaking a wee bit whenever I wake up from my alcohol-induced stupor—until I have the next drink that is. At any rate, there's no more alcohol.

So I do a runner. Quite literally. I'm still far from being in my right mind, but I just know that I have to get out of there. Away from Patrick and his pregnant wife and the kids, away from everything that reminds me that there can be happily ever after if you want it badly enough, because it has become quite apparent that happily ever after won't happen to me. I bolt out of the flat, more or less, when Patrick isn't paying attention, and I take off for God only knows where. Except, I have to remind myself, I no longer believe in God, do I? Not since last week, not since... I need another drink. Soon.

Without quite knowing it, I'm drawn to a house I haven't been to for a while now, though I'm certain that She was there within the week. I'm not sure what I'm doing there, know only that there is a reason I must go and ring the bell. I step up to the door hesitantly; I'm not sure that Lizzie will be glad to see me, not sure she'll see me at all really. There were others beside myself that got a healthy dose of reality last week.

It takes her so long to answer, I'm about to give up and walk off to find a handy ditch to crawl into when the door swings open. Lizzie is squinting at me through pinpoint pupils, pupils that are unnaturally small for twilight. "Seamus?"

"Lizzie, can I come in?" I ask.

She shrugs and glances up and down the street furtively a few times, probably to make sure I came on my own; we're all a little skittish of late. Then she pushes open the door to let me in. I walk past her into the dimly lit room and shrug off my coat, quite aware of the interruption I present.

She motions for me to sit down and says, "Mind what you touch. I was in the middle of preparing for a clandestine drop-off at casualty on Saturday night."

She flops down on the sleeper sofa and takes up a black felt-tip pen before proceeding to mark the flat top of the plunger of each syringe carefully.

I haven't seen markings like those in a while, but I've been around, recognize the code: Lizzie's an old-school type of girl. "Why?" I ask.

"Obvious, innit?"

"Didn't mean the code. I recognize that," I reply. "I mean, why drop them off on Saturday night?"

"Saturday night's the busiest night," she shrugs. "There's drunks and idiots, and casualty tends to be understaffed. They're less likely to take notice of someone dropping off a box full of used works."

She continues marking syringes for a while, methodically and carefully. Then she turns to me and says, "Is there a reason you came here, Seamus? Short of sympathy, I mean, because I haven't got much of that to spare."

"I'm not looking for sympathy," I reply.

"It weren't me," she says bluntly.

"Didn't think it was," I say. "You're a little too street-wise for that, you wouldn't... I've a favor to ask of you, though."

She puts down the pen and studies me closely for a few moments. "I'll not help you do anything monumentally stupid," she finally says. "If you're looking for an easy way out, you won't find it here."

I shudder slightly. I must be much the worse for wear if that is what she thinks. "I want—if I describe an image to you, can you draw it and tattoo it tonight?"

She looks at me incredulously for a second, her mouth slightly open, before pulling herself together and laughing humorlessly. "Fuck, Seamus, are you certain you know what those marks mean?"

It's one of the things I like about her; she's straightforward like that. I pick up one of the syringes and make a show of studying it carefully, just to put her mind at ease. "Yes, I do, and I am sorry for what it's worth," I say quietly. "I need to get this tattoo, and I need to get it now. There's no reputable shop that's going to do it the state I'm in, so I'm willing to take the risk. Will you do it?"

She nods. "What do you want?"

"An exploding star," I say without hesitation.

"Where?" she asks.

I have to think about that even less. My hand clenches into a fist almost of its own accord and bashes into my chest just above my heart.

Lizzie laughs properly this time. "Christ, Seamus," she cackles, "has anyone ever told you you've got a cheap sense of cliché?"

"Will you do it?" I ask, ignoring the laughter.

"It'll hurt," she replies. "That's just above your breastbone, not much underneath except nerves and skin."

"Good," I say. "I could do with a little bit of pain right about now."

She gives me another one of those long, calculating looks before she nods. "You realize it won't stop the other pain, don't you? Nothing but time will stop that."

"Time's highly overrated in the healing department, I've always thought," I say. "Let me have a few moments of real pain before I settle in for the torture that's to come after."

"If you know it won't achieve anything, why do it?" Lizzie asks.

I shrug. I have my reasons of course. I want to feel pain as bright and blinding as the pain I felt a week ago. I want to feel pain so intense I can forget that other pain, if only for a few moments. I want to feel anything but that dull aching pain that hasn't left me since the moment I... I want to feel pain. I have a feeling I'll always want to feel pain from now on. I doubt Lizzie would understand that, though.

I reach into my shirt, fish out the chain Patrick gave me that still bears the ring he retrieved. She recognizes it of course, it's quite distinctive, probably even understands what I'm trying to say, because she smiles slightly and gets up from the sofa.

Before I know it, I'm reclining shirtless in the chair and the needle is driving the ink into my skin above my heart. Lizzie's got a steady hand. I can't help thinking, as I impassively watch the drops of blood appearing on my chest, that with one slip of the needle there could be more than just my blood there. More than just a tattoo. So much more. She was right about one thing: not one of our so-called friends is likely to aide me in any stupidity I might contemplate, but neither are they going to stop me from playing with fire. If the needle slips, just once—it won't slip no matter how much I might pray to a god I no longer believe in. For all her faults, Lizzie has one of the steadiest hands in England.

I watch as the needle marks me, sending tendrils of fire through my nerves, the same tendrils of fire that ran through my veins not so very long ago. The soft light from a side lamp catches on the chain around my neck, causes me to tear my eyes away from the star that is appearing on my breast and contemplate the ring for a moment. I remember Patrick's words when he handed it to me a few nights ago, remember just what he said it was to signify.

This is more real. As real as it is likely to get. Jewelry may be lost or mislaid, but some marks last forever. While Lizzie traces the outlines of the farthest corners of the dying sun on my breast, I look up at her, a pained smile on my face. "It achieves something, Lizzie. It doesn't soothe the pain, but it does achieve something."

"And what would that be, Seamus?" *she asks quietly.*

"When Patrick returned the ring to me, I asked whether it was intended as punishment, testament to what I'd lost. He said it was a warning, a warning for all eternity that some women come with too high a price attached."

She nods. "Gold doesn't last forever, does it? Leastways it don't last forever around the likes of us, too easy to pawn... the ink is forever though, keeps the pain alive even if memory should fade. She'll always own you now, in death as she did in life."

She understands. There is mercy to be found after all.

The pain is surging and subsiding in waves like the tide. I make no effort to get up from the ground though, not even when I'm reasonably certain I could stand on my own two feet again. I lie there, I don't know how long, shivering and nauseated, as much from the beating my body took as from the onset of withdrawal.

Eventually, after I've finally made up my mind he is gone, Micky enters my field of vision and offers me his hand. "I'm sorry," he says. "Not for the whooping you took, you were asking for that one, but I am sorry you got stuck with the lot of us, and I'm sorry we never stopped long enough to thank you for it."

I run my tongue over dry lips caked with blood. "It's not you that ought to be apologizing," I mumble through my swelling jaw.

"No, but it's I who ought to tell you that it wasn't your fault," he says quietly. "None of it was ever your fault, James. You did the best you could, always."

"It was never good enough," I grind out with difficulty.

"Maybe not for Luka, maybe not for Catriona, but it was good enough for me," he says. "You raised me right. God knows how, but you did, and I'll always be grateful for that, even if I don't tell you nearly often enough."

I can barely keep my eyes open. "Thought you despised me."

"I despised Her," he corrects me. "I despised Her for taking you from us in the first place, I despised Her for turning you into the man you became, and I despised Her for humiliating you."

"You left, like a bat out of hell, couldn't get out of the house quickly enough, couldn't get away from me quickly enough."

"It wasn't you I was trying to get away from, James," he replies. "I'm here now, offering to take you home, if only you'll let me. For once in your life, swallow that goddamn pride of yours and let one of us help you."

14

Hell: Upon This Rock I Will Build My Church

"How sick are you going to get?" Micky asks after fifteen minutes with the only sounds being the hum of the engine and the rhythmic drumming of his fingers on the steering wheel.

I shrug. "How long's it been? Two weeks?"

Out of the corner of my eye I can see Micky wince slightly before his face looks as if it were cut from stone once again. "Three and a half since you left Patrick's."

I lean back against the headrest, close my eyes and concentrate on breathing. "I didn't think you'd still—"

"I wasn't. I caught the ferry over to Hollyhead this morning," he interrupts me. "How sick, Seamus?"

More than three weeks. I was certain it wasn't as long as all that. "Sick."

"Can you make it to Dublin if I drive all night?" he asks.

This is not the time to lie. "Won't make it as far as Bristol," I reply.

Micky drives on in silence for what seems like hours but is probably only minutes; my sense of time is askew.

"Mother's?" I ask hesitantly.

Micky shakes his head. "I'd prefer her to keep some of her illusions if it's all the same to you. She never—" he pauses to negotiate the roundabout to the A40. "I'm not entirely sure she ever fully understood."

I don't argue the point. Micky pulls off the A40 at White City and drives down a side street before parking the car. "How much to get you to Dublin?"

I have to pinch myself to make sure I'm awake, and even then I can't quite believe I heard what he said. "I beg your pardon?"

He shrugs. "I want you lucid and able to walk of your own accord, that's all. How much?"

I hesitate. "Ten pound if we drive back to where we came from, a little bit more out here."

Micky laughs quite humorlessly. "It was never a question of money, James. Ten pound and the last shreds of human decency; anyone but us would think that too high a price for a calm crossing to Dublin."

"You're a conceited, arrogant prick," I reply.

Micky shrugs and starts the engine. "I learnt it all from you. Where to?"

An hour later gold has crossed palms in exchange for poppy dreams, and whether that makes Micky Judas or Caiaphas I no longer know, but we're back on the road to Wales, and time has come out of joint.

Pounding drums beat in sync with the pounding of my heart and the throbbing in my groin. Catriona is pressing her body closer to mine, her eyes tightly shut, rubbing her exposed belly against the insistent hard-on I'm sporting. I wrap my arms tighter around her shoulders, close my eyes, just for a little while, and give myself over to memories of summer.

A packed bar on the far side of Kefalari Park and oppressive heat: only foreigners, expats and tourists are stupid enough to stay in Athens during August. Beyond the wall of the bar lies the park, dark but still steaming from the day. There's a cement pond that never held water as far as anyone remembers, and then, on the very far side of the park, there's the church, and behind the church, screened by bushes and undergrowth, is a piece of cardboard leaning against the stone wall.

Catriona is smiling at me, downing the last of her pint of Heineken, and then she's grabbing my hand and dragging me out into the hot night air. We barely make it down the stairs to the street before her tongue is assaulting me. She's stumbling backwards into the park, her lips never leaving my mouth, struggling to unzip my jeans while we're moving. There's no way in hell we'll make it to the cardboard mattress by the church wall today.

I'm moving blindly. She's finally undone my jeans and is stroking me with nimble fingers, her other hand sneaking up my shirt to pinch my nipples. My own hands, without my noticing, have traveled to her waist and are untucking her shirt. We bump into the railing of the wooden walk bridge that spans the empty cement pond, and with strength I didn't know I had in me, I take hold of Catriona's thighs and hoist until they are wrapped firmly around my waist, pressing her back into the railing for leverage.

I have one hand on her buttocks, trying to hold her up, and another hand sneaking underneath her skirt. Thank Christ she's not wearing any knickers. She's ready and mewling into my mouth when I touch her. We are in the middle of the fucking park, in the most exposed location possible, but none of that matters to Catriona. Her hand pulls me closer. Screw the cardboard leaning against the church wall; this'll have to do for the duration.

With a sigh I sink into her warmth. Hot and wet and so fucking tight it never ceases to amaze me. Then I'm thrusting none too gentle, and I know her back is pounding hard against the wooden railing, so hard she'll likely have bruises in the morning. I can feel the reverb of the bass far away, see the lights of the bars in the distance, hear far-away laughter of late-night revelers, but none of it matters while I'm inside Catriona.

She's throwing her head back, moaning loudly, one hand letting go of my shoulder and pushing her shirt up to expose hard, pointy nipples, and without another thought my mouth latches on to one of them, my thrusts matching the beating of drums in the distance.

Then the music ceases. I open my eyes, the ghost of Catriona still pressed to my body. There are club lights and dancers milling around us and I remember: this isn't Athens in the summer, this is England in November.

I come to screaming and shaking. There are streams of cold sweat pouring down me like glaciers and the hesitant touch of a cloth to my brow. Struggling against the waves of nausea that are trying to overcome me, I open my eyes and make out the soft outline of a woman in the dim light from the doorway. "Catriona," I breathe through vocal chords raw as freshly ground meat.

"Etain, Seamus," a voice answers softly. "My sister's been dead eight years come All Souls' Day."

There's no air in my lungs to scream again. Instead, the bile is rising in my throat. The glaciers are steadily working their way down my back, and I try to will my muscles into working, all for naught. I start choking on my own spew before strong arms grab my shoulders and wrestle me to my side.

I pass out again minutes later, my face buried in my own vomit.

Catriona, all dressed in black, is swaying to the music in front of me. There might be a hundred other people in the union bar this evening, but none of them register except for Catriona, all pale skin and raven hair and bright red lipstick. Her eyes are closed as she rolls her hips closer to mine, and I'm glad of it; her pupils are unnaturally dilated this evening. We almost fought over that before coming here, but she just laughed off my protests with a few careless words: "Just live a little, Seamus. There's time enough for sobriety come morning."

So now she's pressing into me, her eyes firmly closed, undulating to the slow beat of the music. She's running her hands up and down my spine, pressing her hips to mine with very little consideration for our public situation. My brain's gone on holiday at any rate. My entire being controlled by the knowledge that there are only a few thin layers of fabric separating our bodies. I'm starting to think I may be possessed somehow.

Suddenly her hands stray further down past my back and come to rest on my hips for a moment before stealing around front and squeezing themselves between our glued-together bodies. I startle when her fingers start unbuttoning my trousers. I rapidly step away from her, mortified. "What in God's name do you think you're doing, Catriona? We're in public."

She laughs. "It's dark, nobody will notice," she smiles seductively.

"I'll notice," I say, still slightly flummoxed.

She laughs again and wraps her arms around my neck to nibble on my ear. "You're new to this game, aren't you, Seamus?" she whispers. "It's all right, nobody will mind if we're discreet about it."

I don't say anything, temporarily speechless, but I don't walk away from her like I would if I had any sense at all in that head of mine. Unfortunately, the brain's still on holiday.

She takes my hand and pulls me to a free table in the corner, pushing me down in a chair and sitting on my lap facing me. As she starts kissing me in earnest, I feel her fingers struggling with the buttons of my trousers again, but this time I don't shirk away.

Then it all becomes unhinged somehow. There's a cold draft of air and a warm hand and then—oh Jesus suffering fuck, woman! Christ, that feels good. I think I've died and gone to heaven, and I can't help myself. She starts rocking her hips and I dig my fingernails into her shoulders and it's all gone sideways somehow.

Not quite how I ever imagined losing my virginity, but it'll do.

I continue rocking against the body next to me even as the music and the buzz of the union bar fade into night sweats, and I realize I am sick and feverish and laid up in bed, decidedly not smelling of roses. All that hardly matters to my dick, which has been feeling neglected as of late. I didn't know you could get hard feeling as rotten as this.

"Catriona," I sigh and pull the other body closer to mine.

"She's been dead and buried and left to the worms these eight years past, James," Micky's voice answers.

I freeze, stop my hips moving in mid-rock amid the waves of panic enveloping me. He moves away some, sits up and gives me a calculating look. "Are you well enough so we can change the sheets?"

I nod mutely and stagger to my feet, only to collapse in a miserable heap on the floor again seconds later. Micky pays me no mind, but starts stripping the bed expertly. "Etain!" he calls before turning to me. "Can you make it to the bath? I think you pissed yourself."

My face crimson, I nod, though truthfully I have no idea how to get up on my own two feet even. Micky comes to the rescue and pulls me up by my shoulders, half carries me the few short steps down the corridor.

"How long... what time is it?" I say with difficulty.

"About one in the morning," he replies. "Wednesday morning."

"Shit," I grunt.

"That too," he sighs, "and plenty of vomit, and it's only been... it'll get harder tomorrow. Christ, James, you idiot, you're strung out worse than a marionette."

I collapse on the bathroom floor, too sick to say anything in turn, and Micky leans down to start the water running and then begins to strip my soiled clothes without so much as a twitch.

As he heaves me into the tub, I note, quite detachedly, that my dick's still at half-mast, and I feel the heat spreading across my face once more. Micky ignores it.

"I'm not—" I stutter. "It's nothing—I can't—"

"I know," he says. "Don't worry about it."

"But I'm not—"

"James, for chrissakes, stop panicking. I'm quite capable of telling you and Luka apart," he snaps, emptying a pitcher of bath water over my head.

"You know about—" I ask, the question trailing off into bewilderment.

"I've always known about Luka," he says.

"But—" another pitcher of water unceremoniously dumped over my head forces my mouth shut. When I open my eyes again, Micky is crouching there on the bathroom floor, his eyes level with mine, and scrutinizing me closely.

"He's never told you, has he?" he finally says, and I'm not sure whether it is a question or a statement of fact.

"Never told me what?" I ask, stunned.

"Why he turned up on your doorstep the way he did," Micky says slowly. "He's never told you."

"He... you all wanted to get away from Mother," I protest.

Micky shrugs and starts soaping my chest. I watch the washcloth impassively for a few moments, trying to keep myself from getting sick again.

I even manage to bite down on my tongue for a full minute before the question forces itself to the surface. "Why did Luka leave home, Micky?"

"You'll have to ask him that question," Micky mutters. "It isn't my secret to tell."

I gather all my reserves of strength, such as they are, and hiss, "Tell me, Micky, or so help me god I will give you a thrashing you won't forget for the rest of your life."

Micky laughs in my face. "You can't even stand up by yourself, James. How the hell do you expect to make good on that promise?"

"Give me a few days, and I'll be standing and beating you within an inch of your life," I reply. "Now tell me!"

"No," he shakes his head. "But I give you my word I've always known. Ever since we were boys."

"But he was in love with—"

"The only woman he knew for certain he could never have," Micky interrupts. "Whatever else Luka is, he isn't an idiot. He knew, just as well as I did."

"I don't believe you," I grind out through clenched teeth.

Micky stoops to pull out the plug, then grabs the showerhead to hose me down. "Then don't. What difference is it to me whether you believe me or not?"

"You haven't even talked to each other since... well, in years, really," I mumble.

"No, James. Luka hasn't talked to me in almost ten years. I never stopped talking to him," Micky sighs.

"But—"

He waves me into silence. "Tell me, how did you find out? Did he tell you?"

I shake my head mutely.

"And I imagine he's still fucking your rejects when you throw them his way, just to prove he can?" Micky continues.

I feel sick again—well, sicker. Micky's on a roll though; he won't let up now. "And if I were to hazard a guess, I'd say you are blindly agreeing with his assertions that he's as straight as they come, if only to keep the peace," he says coldly.

"I don't want to force—"

"No, you wouldn't," Micky interrupts. "Much easier to keep pretending, for your sake as much as his. He knew that. He was hitting puberty full-force and experiencing feelings he'd been told all his life would result in eternal damnation, and it was only a matter of time before Mother, for all her faults, would notice. So he made the choice to go to you, because he knew you were too absorbed in your own drama, too busy trying to keep a roof over everyone's head, to really make an effort to see what was there in plain sight. And because you never forced the issue, he adored you. I never allowed him that luxury, and he hates me for it, the same way you hate me for not letting sleeping dogs lie."

"Micky..."

"Too many lies, James," he says. "Too many goddamn fucking lies that I refused to play along with."

He pulls me up out of the tub and throws a towel across my shoulders before dragging me back to the bedroom. There are new sheets on the bed, and Micky struggles to get my legs into fresh pants and a t-shirt over my head. "You're not doing him any favors, you know," he mutters as he pushes me back down on the bed. "He's got to face his demons one of these days. You both do, and the sooner you get it over with the better, because Patrick's through with the lot of you and there's only so much bloodletting I'm capable of. I never had your patience."

I nod miserably, too exhausted to answer. The last thing I hear is Micky standing by the door and saying, "If you have to be sick again, try and aim for the bucket this time."

Catriona's elbow nudges me in the side, and I follow her eyes as she looks pointedly at Father Mitchell, who exits the confessional and starts walking up the nave toward the altar. She grabs my hand and pulls me up from the pew. Out of the corner of my eye, I can see Father Mitchell kneeling and crossing himself in front of the larger-than-life effigy before rising and shuffling off to the back of the church.

Catriona half-drags me to the confessional, totally oblivious to the few worshipers that are still strewn across the pews of the church. She's a woman on a mission, is Catriona. Got it into her head a couple of weeks ago that she wanted—no, needed—to break every sodomy law, and on consecrated ground too. Won't even consider the graveyard, or sneaking into the church after dark. No, instead she drags me to mass and then sits patiently after until the worshipers leave and the priests abandon the confessionals. That's where she wants to accomplish the task: in the confessional.

Catriona's bloody-minded. She's got a skull thick as anything, and who am I to argue with her? It's not as if there aren't perks to her plan. I still feel guilty though; I was brought up to respect the church. On the other hand, the things she does—oh, the things she does!—and the thrill of knowing that we could be discovered, it's almost too much to bear.

Stealthily as a prowling feline, she opens the confessional and with a quick look over her shoulder pushes me in and against the back wall. She quietly closes the door and molds her body into mine. I can smell traces of wine on her breath, feel her nipples pressing into my back, and any thoughts I might have entertained about the sin of blasphemy flee from my mind as the blood flees my brain for more southerly regions.

The part of my body that has taken over all thinking is dimly wondering what she has in mind this time. We're fast running out of laws we haven't violated yet. I can't see her face, but I can sense her Cheshire cat grin. Christ, I can't believe the things that woman makes me feel. I can't believe the things she makes me do either, but that's a minor point right now.

A hot, rough tongue is nibbling my neck, and slim, white fingers are quickly creeping around my waist and to my belt-buckle. She's anything but shy when the mood is upon her. She makes short work of the belt and the buttons, and before I know it, my trousers are pushed down my thighs. She's laughing softly now. Her accent thicker than usual—I think she does it on purpose—she asks, "And how shall we earn our Hail Maries today, Seamus?"

My dick jumps at the question but I find myself incapable of answering. So sue me. I'm male. A male teenager, no less. It doesn't take much to transform me into a whimpering mess of testosterone. She's laughing again; the confines of the confessional make her laughter sound much louder than it really is.

Then one hand is stroking my arse while another is sneaking up my shirt to pinch my nipples. "I think we shall try sodomy good and proper this time around," she breathes into my ear.

I moan loudly, ancient curses falling from my lips. Oh well, add another item to the list of things that will send me to hell instead of the pearly gates of St. Peter. Except I hardly have time to think about my transgression before Catriona's hand moves where no woman has gone before.

I tense slightly, but she purrs and nibbles on my ear and moves her other hand down to my straining dick to stroke it with sure, easy movements. I'm prepared to forget any reservations I might have, so long as she doesn't stop what she's doing. Yeah, I'm a pushover.

I barely notice questing fingertips stroking against a part of my body I've never considered sexual in the least before; my mind is too focused on that other hand, the one that is squeezing and rubbing and generally causing much happiness in my groin. I do notice a slim finger slipping inside me, but it's coupled with a thumb-stroke across the slit of my dick, and once again, that hand wins out in the attention department.

She twists her finger about somewhat, clearly searching for something, but never once slows down her other hand. "Holy Mother of God," I yelp, when she finds what she's been looking for. Suns explode in front of my eyes, my knees turn to pudding, and I whimper at the sensation. "Don't stop whatever you're doing," I groan, making an effort to stay upright.

She plants one thigh between my legs for support, pushes my shoulders to lean heavily against the wall of the confessional, and starts working in earnest, slim finger sliding across that spot over and over again while her other hand is pulling me off harder than she's ever done before.

I don't last long. Didn't expect to, really, after that first implosion of white light in front of my eyelids. I can't be sure, but I think I yell when I climax. She quickly wipes both her hands on my shirt and pulls my trousers up. Just as quickly, she turns me around and plants a chaste kiss on my lips as she buckles my belt. "We had better be moving, Seamus. You were none too quiet there," she says with a twinkle in her eye.

I follow her out of the confessional and then the church on unsure legs with, no doubt, the most inane grin of my short life plastered across my face. "Can we do that one again at home, Catriona?" I ask as we walk up the high street.

She turns around with a brilliant smile on her face and says, "If we hurry, we can just about make it for the last ten minutes of mass at St. Catherine's."

Then she's running up the street and I after her, and there are only two thoughts on my mind: I really want to do that again, frequently, and I really pity the poor soul who goes to confession next.

I wake screaming Declan's name in the half-light from the drawn curtains, drenched in cold sweat, my voice much hoarser than it would be if this were the first time I'd screamed this day. Something shatters to the ground in another room of the flat, and then Micky pushes open the door looking decidedly disheveled, his black mop spiked up in a way reminiscent of Patrick's hair twenty years and some change ago.

"Declan's gone, James," he says tiredly, stepping into the room.

"Luka—"

"Luka's no more Declan than you are Ciaran," he replies harshly.

I shudder, feel the cold shivers running down my spine like a ghost crossing the room. "I never changed my name," I protest.

Micky favors me with a glare and says, "You haven't been Ciaran in fifteen years or more, and Declan's been gone half as long."

"Do you really believe that?" I ask.

He shrugs. "Luka does. Says Declan died in a bathtub in Barstow eight years ago, and who am I to doubt his word?"

I struggle to my feet, my knees as soft and malleable as jellied eels, and favor him with what I hope is an icy stare. "I have always been Ciaran James Sheahan. I never denied my name nor my ancestors, and maybe it were time I should use my name again."

"That won't bring him back," Micky replies unmoved. "Nothing will ever bring him back the way you want him, no matter how much you pray and you hope and you keep on trying. He's gone, James. The question now is why you persist in trying to raise the dead." Micky's eyes are nailing my skull to the wall. "This is another one of those things between you and Patrick, isn't it?" he finally asks. "Another one of those obligations that is never mentioned and never explained but still defines each breath you take."

"Something like that," I shrug, unwilling or perhaps incapable of ever explaining things that Micky would never in a lifetime understand.

"And if I were to say that you are free to live your life, that Patrick has released you from any and all debts you owe?" he asks.

I sigh. "Then I would reply that there are some debts that can never be repaid, can never be undone, not by deeds, not by blood, not by your will, and then there are promises that can never be broken."

Micky sits down on the bed and buries his face in his palms. He's looking younger now and more tired than I've ever seen him. Then his tightly-clenched fist bounces off the mattress and he's yelling, "Damn Patrick and his fucking demands, and damn your misplaced sense of loyalty. It's over, James, because ghosts can't be owed. The Declan you raised is gone, as good as dead. He won't be back."

"And what am I to do with that knowledge?" I ask sarcastically.

Micky gets up from the bed and starts walking out of the room. He turns just inside the doorway and says, "Get on with your life because I've given you your freedom."

15

Requiem: I Am That I Am

I wake one autumn day in Dublin, and I'm fifteen pounds lighter and twenty years older, with one brother gained amidst the shakes and the puke and the shit, another one lost, perhaps forever, and Luka still AWOL. Business as usual then. That's when I remember that there are mundane matters at hand. There are bills to be paid and money to be earned, and zealots are crashing airplanes into buildings and I am in Ireland, land of my fathers, shirking obligations that run deeper than blood, more urgent than any need I've ever known, no matter what Micky says, and freedom can't be granted.

More words are exchanged and Patrick is cursed, but in the end none of that matters, and Micky grudgingly agrees to let me go—on one condition. He extracts a promise, sworn on our grandmother's grave, that I will neither indulge in nor allow Luka to partake of any poppy dreams again, and because I know there's a fair chance I now owe him my life and possibly more, I agree. I'm back in California by Michaelmas.

Luka turns up on my doorstep a scant two weeks later, harder and leaner and more of a grown man than I've ever seen. He's tanned three shades darker, his hair buzzed short and its natural color, and the first words out of his mouth are, "I don't remember, James."

"What don't you remember, Luka?" I ask.

He stumbles through the open door into the living room and sinks down on the floor. "I... I woke up in Iowa three weeks ago and I had no recollection of ever going there. I remember—I'm not sure what I remember."

"I'm not in the mood for your brand of mindfuck, Luka," I say testily. "Had a bit of a rough summer, all told."

"You look like shit," he observes, biting his lip. "You're not—are you sick?"

I shake my head. "Not anymore. I went off the deep end and things came apart, but Micky decided to lock me up for a while—"

"Since when are the two of you talking again?" Luka interrupts.

"Since Patrick stopped talking to me," I reply.

Luka is staring at me in disbelief. "Can we try that from the beginning, James?"

I sigh. "During the summer you left a message on my machine when you were out of your brains, something I wasn't supposed to—I don't think you ever intended for me—"

Luka's entire body shudders and he blanches, then he's blushing fiercely. "What did I say?"

"That you were buying when it all went to hell," I reply much more steadily than I thought I would.

For a moment there, just before Luka gets a grip on himself and winces, I can see the relief wash over his face, and it makes me wonder what other—worse—secrets he's been keeping. "I'm sorry," he finally says rather subdued. "I'm sorry you had to find out like that."

I nod my head, accepting the apology for what it is; it's not an admission of guilt, of complicity in Catriona's death, but simply an expression of regret for having kept the truth from me for all these years.

"It all finally made sense," I continue. "Some things that were said at the time and some of the details, and I knew Patrick knew, and I chewed him out over it. Called him a lot of names and a brought up a few home truths that were long overdue. So he did some quick thinking on short order and invited me on holiday with him and the kids. You know how he is when you catch him off-guard."

Luka's laughing now, throwing his head back and chuckling with glee. "And I missed this?" he gasps. "How did it go?"

"Terrible, if you must know," I sigh. "Might be a good idea if you didn't try to call him for a while, because I think he's a little fed up with the both of us. At any rate, I snapped and went some places I haven't been in years, and then Micky turned up out of the blue, and well, things got a little strange for a while."

Luka's grinning now, his earlier discomfort forgotten, as he says, "This I have to hear."

"Nothing much to it, really," I say. "He gave me a right good kicking, beat me up better than Patrick's ever managed, and then he took me back to Dublin with him and locked me up in his flat, while I—" I make an expansive gesture that probably doesn't say all that much, but I'd rather not go into the details if I can avoid it.

"No shit!" Luka laughs. "Did he break your wrist too?"

I cringe inwardly. With hindsight, that was quite possibly up in the top ten of the most asinine things I've ever done. "Sorry about that," I have the decency to blush.

"'S all right, I survived, didn't I?" Luka says dismissively. "I'm almost disappointed I missed the party though. I just... I'm drawing a blank. I sort of remember leaving here and then there's almost nothing—just flashes—until I woke up behind a Wal-Mart in Davenport a few weeks ago. How can I just... I've had blackouts before, James, but I've never... how can I be missing several months of my life?" He's sounding almost desperate now, his eyes searching mine.

"If you're messing with me—"

"I'm not messing with your head, James," he interrupts. "I truly cannot remember anything past leaving in the spring."

"Luka—"

He waves me into silence. "No, James. I'm fine, better than I've been in years, I think. I... I woke up in Iowa and everything had slid into place somehow. I know who I am now."

I just look at him for a full five minutes or so; his eyes never waver, meet mine full on, blue and clear and determined, and I'm almost given to thinking that Micky was wrong and Luka's toying with sanity at long last. I sigh and walk into the kitchen. I fetch a couple of bottles of beer and hand one to him when he follows me. We're drinking in silence for a few minutes, studiously surveying the walls and the floor, before I turn to him and ask, "Who are you then?"

"I am not you. I will never be you. I will never be a father. I will never be a husband. I will never be a womanizer. I will never be a fraud. I will never be a coward. My life will never be a sacrifice to others because I am too afraid of choosing my own path. I will never be any of the things you are."

Each of his words feels like a slap to the face, even if they are true, or perhaps because they are true. "I didn't ask you who you weren't," I snap. "Who are you?"

Luka laughs. "What do you want me to say, James? That I'm a madman? That I'm a loser and a freak?"

"How about the truth, Luka?" I ask quietly. "You say you've finally worked it all out, and after all these years, I reckon I deserve some answers."

Luka finishes his beer and smiles crookedly before turning and stepping into the living room, hips swaying, humming the melody to that thrice-damned Suzanne Vega number under his breath. So that's it then, just another mind game that allows him to throw some insults my way while he's at it.

"Well, fuck you too," I holler after him.

I open the kitchen door and am about to step out onto the patio for a smoke when Luka clears his throat in the living room and says, "I was Declan Kelly Sheahan. If I had lived, I would have been twenty-five years old, though I doubt I can prove that any longer."

"Go on," I say, not daring to turn around.

"I was born on April 16th, 1976, in the administrative district of Sinj in Yugoslavia," he says more confidently.

I sigh. "You are reciting facts, Luka. Who are you?"

"I am."

He stops, and I slowly start counting to ten, my lips moving silently. Maybe Patrick isn't the only one of us who ran out of patience.

"I was Declan Kelly Sheahan. Now I am Luka Antic, and I have been lost for a very long time," he says haltingly. "I denied my name because I didn't want to—didn't know how to—be Declan, and I invented Luka Antic in a bathtub in Barstow eight years ago. I didn't know then—was too young to understand—that sometimes you lose more than the name you deny, gain less than the name you invent for yourself. I was wavering, lost, couldn't find Declan again. The harder I tried the further he went away. You know better than any of us that you can never reclaim the past you left behind."

I finally dare to turn from the kitchen door and walk slowly back into the living room. Luka's leaning against the wall, breathing hard and pale as a ghost, but he's there and he's meeting my eyes. "What changed?" I ask hoarsely.

"Everything," he replies, "and nothing. I think I finally stopped running long enough, allowed the voices in my mind to grow calm enough, that I could hear myself think again, and I knew how to reach Luka and became him. Everything slid into place. I am Luka Antic, and I can never go back. Declan is gone."

If he weren't so deadly serious I should think this was an elaborate hoax, orchestrated by Micky and Luka to convince me that my life is finally my own again; but he is serious and he is calm and he is entirely sure of himself, which is more than I can say for myself, so maybe I should give him the benefit of the doubt.

If this were a fairy tale it would end here, but life is not a fairy tale. There's no instant forgiveness for all that occurred. There never can be. I'm enough of a realist to know that absolution is the stuff of legends, and I'm enough of a realist to know that there were only ever two ways our journey would end. Until today I was prepared, expecting even, that there would be death and redemption at the end of it all when I finally reclaimed the body of my brother and buried Declan Kelly Sheahan. I'm beginning to think that I missed my chance to bury him when first he died. Micky was right; there is only Luka now and no chance of salvation.

He's looking at me almost pleadingly, so making the best of the situation, I ask, "I've been invited to this party. Do you want to come?"

He nods, relief washing all over his face.

He accompanies me to a warehouse in West Oakland, where the party is already in full swing, fueled by just the right mix of freaks and geeks. The geeks have outdone themselves and rigged up the videogames console through a projector pointed at the whitewashed wall of the building across the street; they're racing larger-than-life cars on the makeshift screen.

The minute we arrive, Luka zeroes in on a little skank named Kerry and starts working hard while I find myself a bottle of beer and join a few guys in a corner discussing music. I'm only half-listening to the conversation because I'm trying to keep an eye on Luka, who has Kerry on his lap on the other side of the room and is chewing on her ear, probably trying to charm his way into her pants; god knows, he's already charmed his way under her shirt.

I know better than most that Luka can be a manipulative little bastard when the mood is upon him, and he's really giving it all he's got. I wonder whether I should enlighten him as to some of the changes that have transpired since he came to visit me last before I decide to let him work a little bit longer.

About twenty minutes later, when it starts to look like Kerry's top is about to come off permanently, I slowly walk over to where they're sitting.

"What's up, James?" Luka smirks, not taking his mouth off of her neck.

"Not too much," I say nonchalantly. "Just thought I'd clue you in that Kerry here went straight-edge about four months ago."

His smile fades fast. With one quick movement, Luka grabs Kerry by the waist and lifts her off his lap to dump her unceremoniously on the couch beside him. "Well, fuck you, James," he says. "You could've told me that before I wasted half an hour playing nice with the *cailleach*."

Before I can utter so much as a word that he had better watch his mouth around Kerry, she's planted a deceptively hard fist somewhere around his left eye and is storming off in a barrage of Irish curses.

I wince. "Well done, Luka," I say. "You had to go and say that in front of the only other person in the room with a passing knowledge of Irish."

Luka is gingerly touching his fingers to his cheekbone. "Fuck, that hurt," he pouts. "Who would've thought a girl that size had it in her?"

I know he's milking it for all it's worth. Trying to score high on the sympathy meter to see whether I'll crack and hand over contacts. I can't do it; I promised Micky I wouldn't, and my word is all I've got these days. He's not making it easy though. I sigh. "You see that guy over there? The one that's built like a Greek god?"

Luka nods. "Yeah, what of him?"

"I'm told he's got the finest goods this side of the bridge," I say. "Don't know if it's true, but it couldn't hurt to try."

Luka smiles, a genuine smile this time. "Thanks, mate," he grins. "Well, I'm off then, going to try my luck with the Greek god."

A half hour later, after extricating myself from a heated political debate, the point of which was kind of lost on me, I scan the room searching for Luka and almost laugh out loud when I finally find him. I've got to give the boy ten out of ten for style but minus twenty for creativity. Luka's now on the lap of the Greek god, Dee, I think he's called, nibbling on the guy's ear. I go off in search of the music discussion from earlier.

Another hour later and I'm ready to leave. I look around for Luka, but he's disappeared. After asking around a bit, I walk upstairs and randomly start opening doors to empty rooms. I'm about to give up and go back downstairs but stop to open the door of a room down at the end of the hallway and suddenly find myself wishing quite fervently I hadn't.

The Greek god waves at me lazily from the couch he's sprawled on, which distracts Luka sufficiently from what he's doing—and I don't want to think too hard about what he's doing—to turn his head slightly. As soon as he sees me he's up like lightning, a picture only slightly marred by the fact that his jeans fall off his hips and drop to the floor.

"Holy shit, I'm sorry, I'll just be outside in the parking lot, whenever you're ready," I sputter and slam the door before he can get a word in edgeways. There are some things you really don't want to catch your brother doing.

I go outside and pace around the lot a bit, smoking a cigarette out of habit more than anything else. A good ten minutes later, Luka appears, dressed and with a huge grin on his face.

"You ready to blow this joint?" he asks.

I pointedly look at his right hand clutched into a fist and ask, "You got what you came for?"

He shrugs. "I got something. It's not what you're thinking, though."

I grab him by the shirt and slam him into a car. "Well, why don't you tell me what I'm thinking then?" I shout. "Because I gotta tell you, from where I was standing it looked a lot like you were sucking that guy off for a free hit."

Oh yeah, nice one there, James, I think. God, I'm such a fucking hypocrite. I've broken damn near every fucking law on the books, just took a little trip to hell and back puking my guts up all over Micky's spare room while trying to clean up, and here I'm standing shouting at Luka for, well, for doing what should come naturally. I can't stop myself though.

"That how you paid your way from Barstow to Portland, Luka?" I shout. "I never asked you how you can get from coast to coast in eight days. That

221

it? That what you do when you find yourself short a few bob?"

Round about then Luka's fist hits me square on the jaw. "Fuck you, James," he shouts. "I am not Her. I am not your wife."

I step back a little and try to calm down. It's no good losing my temper when we've only just achieved a semblance of sanity, and I'd rather not set him off down the road to madness again if I can avoid it somehow. "You tell me what I should think after the way you've been carrying on all night," I say quietly.

Luka's pretty angry now; seems I hit below the belt there. "You wanna know what I got out of this, James?" he shouts. "Do you?"

All I can do is nod. He uncurls his fist and waves a scrap of paper in my face. "There you go, James. This is what I got out of that little encounter: a phone number, just in case, you know, I feel like doing some of that sucking again," he says, voice dripping with sarcasm.

I'm such an idiot. I had better fix this before I do irreparable damage. "Shit Luka, I'm so sorry," I say. "I—"

"I'm gay, James," he interrupts me, his eyes locked with mine.

"Will you still say that when you're sober?" I ask before I can stop myself.

He freezes and pales considerably. "James, I—"

"The truth, Luka, please," I plead.

He slumps against the car, then sets his jaw and says quietly, "I am gay and always have been. I refuse to be scared of myself any longer, because I know who I am now. Is that going to be an issue?"

I shake my head slowly. "No. I'm sorry I assumed—I'll make it up to you. Anything you want. OK? Just forget I ever said anything."

"'S OK," Luka mumbles. "There's one thing you could do though. Do you think it'd be all right, I mean, would you mind if Dee came along to hang out?"

I look at him. Even with the shiner that's starting to come on he's looking quite happy. Happier than he's ever been. "Yeah, OK," I sigh.

He grins and starts running back toward the building, and a few minutes later I'm pulling out of the parking lot with Luka and Dee whispering in the backseat.

We get back to the house, and I pull Luka aside as we walk through the doorway and mumble, "I'll take the couch tonight. You go ahead and take the bedroom. There's... in the drawer of the nightstand."

I'm too much of a realist to believe in fairy tales and happily ever after, but just for a moment, while Luka grins and playfully punches my arm, I see the boys we were. I see my own face—as it was ten years ago and an ocean away, before it all went to hell—reflected in his. And as I lie on the sofa and try not to listen to the harsh pants and soft moans emanating from my bedroom, it comes to me that that too is redemption of a sort.